ATLANTIS
Devil's Sea

book three

BOB MAYER

ATLANTIS DEVIL'S SEA, series book three

COPYRIGHT © 2001 by Bob Mayer, Updated 2011

COOL GUS PUBLISHING
http://coolgus.com

ISBN: 9780984257553

CHAPTER ONE

THE DISTANT PAST
1628 B.C.

The pale blue Mediterranean sky was cut by a thick finger of smoke drifting skyward from the tall volcano in the center of the island. It was just one of the portents of doom for those who called Thera their home. On the western horizon, a low Shadow covered the blue water, a dark wall a mile high and over ten wide. Yesterday, a ship had been sent to investigate the strange cloud. It sailed into the black and never returned. Scouts had been sent up the volcano to look into the caldera to judge conditions and had been overcome with toxic gases, their bodies still visible on the lip of the high mountain.

The priestess who stood on the shoreline, staring at her daughter playing in the warm surf, had told the warriors what the cloud was and what would happen with the volcano, but being men and fighters, they had sent the ship and scouts anyway. A priestess's word had lost much power over the years.

There were dozens of priestesses on Thera who maintained the pyramid in the center of the capital city of Akrotiri, but Pri Lo was the Defender, the dark red trimming on her white robe and the crystal amulet she wore around her neck signifying that unique position. She knew her time was coming. Her people had lived in peace here for many generations, the previous Defenders never being called upon to play their role. Why her time coincided with the appearance of the Shadow, she didn't know, but she didn't feel sorry for herself. She had been raised for the moment that would come soon. All she felt was focused on the seven-year-old girl in the water. Her daughter, Pri

1

Kala, would be the Defender of her generation; if she grew to adulthood and if Pri Lo was successful in her life's task.

A rumble that she could feel through the sand under her feet caused Pri Lo's gaze to shift from the sea to the large volcano. It had begun emitting fumes two days ago, just before the Shadow appeared to the west.

The reason why her ancestors escaping Atlantis had chosen this dangerous island for their new home had been lost over the millennia since the destruction of their mid-Atlantic island, but Pri-Lo accepted that there must have been a valid reason. They were centrally located among the burgeoning civilizations of the Mediterranean. Greece was to the northwest, Persia to the northeast, Crete to the south, and Egypt farther to the southeast. They were a sea away from where their home had been.

Still, the Shadow had found them. It took the dark force over eight thousand years, but the tale of terror that had been handed down through the lineage of priestesses was now a reality.

Another rumble caused her to shift her bare feet nervously in the sand. She turned back to the ocean, staring at the headland that guarded the south edge of the sheltered cove. The boat was late. Pri Lo should be at the pyramid, ready to fulfill her destiny, but there was something she needed to do first.

She didn't want to, but she looked farther out to sea. The Shadow was closer; there was no doubt of that. It was creeping across the water, approaching the island. The blackness was absolute, drawing in the bright sunlight and extinguishing it. If it reached the land, Pri Lo knew that the tales, which were more horrible than the worst nightmares, would come true.

Time was short. The other priestesses would be scouring Akrotiri, searching for her to take her place. Still Pri Lo waited. For she knew the Shadow could be stopped, but the volcano was another issue, one that she could not defend against. It was how Atlantis had been destroyed, and there were many who didn't want to remember when the Earth itself raged.

Her daughter, a slight wisp with blue eyes, fair skin, and red hair cut short, had a shell in her hands and was staring at it intently, as if reading something in the swirls on the surface.

"Kala," she called out as the prow of a sailing ship finally appeared around the headland, entering the cove.

"I do not want to leave you. " Shell in hand, the young girl walked out of the water to her mother.

Pri Lo had known she could not keep her thoughts from her daughter. The connection was too close.

"You must go on this ship. It is your duty, just as I must do mine."

Kala understood duty. Pri Lo had taught her the absolute of that. The ship was closing on the shore, a man in the prow waving for them to wade out to it. There was a loud explosion inland. Pri Lo spun about in time to see the left side of the volcano crumble inward.

"Here." Pri Lo took the Defender crystal off her neck and slipped it over Kala's head. "This is yours now."

Her daughter met her gaze and Pri Lo saw wisdom beyond her age in those young eyes. There was no point in pretending, in telling Kala they would meet again. Whatever thoughts Pri Lo had, her daughter knew. What she felt, her daughter sensed. They hugged briefly, intensely; then Pri Lo took Kala's hand and led her into the water. They waded out until Pri Lo had to hold her daughter's head above the water. She passed her to the captain along with a small purse filled with gold coins. He was from Knossos, to the south, and she had arranged this the previous night in a tavern near the wharves of Akrotiri. She knew he was trustworthy when she had met him and picked up the aura about him.

"You should come, too," the captain said as he lifted Pri Lo into the boat. The purse disappeared somewhere inside his shirt.

"I will stay," Pri Lo said.

The captain wasted no more time, yelling orders to his crew. They strained at the oars, pulling the ship out to sea. Pri Lo stood in the water, feeling the slight sweet lap of the warm Mediterranean at her neck. Kala was next to the railing, staring back.

There was not time to watch the ship until it cleared the headland.

I love you. Pri Lo projected toward the ship. She felt the emotion from her daughter come back, a wave of sadness and love. Then she turned and headed inland. When she reached the stairs that were carved into the rock wall of the cove, she sprinted up them. At the top, she paused to look over her shoulder. The ship's sails were set, and it was racing to the south. It would make it before the Shadow arrived.

She felt the pull of duty, but still she hesitated. Near the bow of the ship she noted several gray forms leaping out of the water and splashing back in. A brief feeling of peace passed through her, and she knew Pri Kala would be safe.

Pri Lo stumbled as the ground spasmed beneath her, cracks forming in the rock. She could see the white towers of Akrotiri a quarter mile ahead and, above them, the top of the pyramid where the priestesses waited for her. She ran, the calluses on the bottom of her bare feet striking the closely set rocks of the path.

The gates were open, the guards staring at the volcano. Several cried out to her as she passed. *Now they believe*, she thought as she sprinted along the main thoroughfare of the city; over ten meters wide, it led to the base of the huge pyramid, the first thing their ancestors had worked on when they arrived

3

from Atlantis thousands of years previously. Three hundred feet high, made of stone blocks, it had a level top twenty feet wide.

A broad set of stairs ran up the face of the pyramid, and Pri Lo took them two at a time. A dozen priestesses waited, along with two warriors, one of whom held a staff. One end of the staff was a spearhead and the other end a seven-headed snake. In the center there was a large slab with the contour of a person etched into its surface.

"Where have you been?" Pri Tak, the head of the order, was an old woman, her face pale with fear. "I sent warriors looking for you."

Pri Lo ignored her. She took a dark red cloth from one of the other women, draping it over her shoulders. There was writing on it, symbols from long ago. Pri Lo looked to the sea. The Shadow was less than a mile from shore and closing.

Pri Lo climbed onto the slab and settled into the stone, her body fitting perfectly into the depression. "I am ready," she announced.

"There are prayers and--" Pri Tak began, but Pri Lo cut her off.

"There is no time for that. And there is no time for you to leave." She laughed. "Don't you see what's coming? You could not run far enough, anyway. Best to have it over with here."

She turned her head to the warrior, a man named Kra Tek, a brave fighter, who had been entrusted with the spear. He was also Kala's father. She gave the slightest of nods and saw relief briefly race across his face. She knew she had chosen wisely in picking him—it was obvious in Kala. "Do it."

He slid the spearhead into a slit next to the slab. His scarred hand rested on the snakeheads. Without hesitation, he turned it.

The pyramid began to vibrate. A blue glow suffused the slab and Pri Lo's body. The priestesses were chanting prayers. The glow centered on Pri Lo's head, the skin rippling as if the bone of the skull was alive.

The skin began peeling off, the eyes turning into two blue glowing orbs. The bone appeared, bleached white, changing, metamorphosing from the inside out. The white became clear, crystallized, suffused with the blue glow. Her mouth was wide open, but no scream issued forth even though she was still alive, the channel for the power that was rising through the structure.

A bolt of blue shot out of Pri Lo's head toward the approaching black wall. When it touched the darkness, there was an explosion.

Again and again, blue lightning seared off the top of the pyramid toward the Shadow, until the black wall stopped moving forward, halting less than a hundred yards from shore. The consistency of the darkness began to change, swirls of blue mixing with the black.

Then the pyramid stopped vibrating, the blue bolts ceased firing, and all was still for a moment. The priestesses and warriors, who had fallen to the stone and covered their heads during the assault, slowly lifted their heads. The

Shadow was fading, breaking apart, rays of sunlight piercing it. They stood, watching the Shadow disappear, jubilation filling their hearts. Except for Kra Tek, who was staring down at Pri Lo's remains. The body was gone, leaving just a pure crystal skull lying on the slab. He reached for the skull.

Then the volcano blew.

The explosion took off the top third of the mountain, sending hundreds of thousands of tons of ash, gas, dirt, and rocks into the air. Toxic gas rode the shock wave downslope, killing every living thing it washed over.

Kra Tek cradled the crystal skull in his arms, turning his broad back to the coming death. The gas killed him instantly, then the blast of heat that followed scorched the flesh from his bones, but his hands still gripped Pri Lo's skull as his remains slammed into the slab.

Several miles to the south, Pri Kala had watched the Shadow dispersed by the blue bolts. She had sensed her mother's power projected from the island, then felt it fade to nothing other than the faint essence of her father's sorrow. But there was an aura of comfort from the dolphins swimming about the prow of the ship, guiding it out to sea and away from the island.

Then the large volcano in the center of the island exploded. Every member of the crew paused as the sound of the blast reached them. They could see the spreading cloud of ash. Rocks, trees, and other debris splashed into the water all around.

"Row, you fools!" the captain yelled as he pushed the tiller, putting the stern of the ship square on toward the island. The tidal wave from the blast was over fifty feet high, bearing down on them at eighty miles an hour.

"Hold on!" the captain cried out. He held on to the tiller with one hand and with the other grabbed Pri Kala. Tears were running down her smooth cheeks, but she gripped his hand. The wave hit, and the ship rode it, the stern going up almost straight, several men sliding over-board, everything that wasn't tied down smashing forward. Then the ship leveled on the top of the wave before slipping down the less steep backslope and settling in the water.

Pri Kala looked back. Less than a third of the island was still above water. The Earth had not known such violence since the destruction of Atlantis over eight thousand years previously. People as far as a thousand miles away would hear the sound the volcano had made and the ash and dirt would circle the globe and drop the world temperature a couple of degrees for years. Once more, the Shadow had been stopped, but the price had been high.

Pri Kala's small hand reached up and felt the Defender amulet around her neck. She knew the Shadow would come again, and she knew her duty.

CHAPTER TWO

THE NEAR PAST
2 July 1937 A.D.

"KHAQQ calling *Itasca*. We must be on you but cannot see you. Gas is running low. Over."

Amelia Earhart knew the sunrise she was watching might well be her last as she let go of the transmit button and there was no reply to her latest attempt to contact the Coast Guard cutter *Itasca*. The very top of the sun was appearing on the eastern horizon, as if directly out of the Pacific Ocean, which stretched in all directions as far as she could see from the cockpit. She was flying at twelve thousand feet, so the range of vision was quite far. But no sign of Howland Island or the *Itasca*, which was supposed to be on station just offshore the unpopulated island. It was waiting for her arrival to refuel the plane.

She and her navigator, Fred Noonan, had already flown twenty-two thousand miles in the past several months in her quest to be the first woman to fly around the world. But this section was the most dangerous: the longest they would be over water. They'd taken off from Lae, New Guinea, the previous day at noon, and they only had about two more hours worth of fuel in the Lockheed Electra's gas tanks. Earhart had had the plane specifically modified for the flight, adding fuel tanks and radio-directionn- finding equipment.

Noonan had been working the direction-finding equipment all through the night, trying to keep them oriented, but reception was intermittent. The *Itasca* was supposed to be transmitting nonstop, giving them a target to fix on, but there had been long periods where they could pick up nothing.

"Give me a fix, Fred." Earhart glanced at her compass. She was on a course slightly north of due east, but Howland was so small that the slightest deviation would cause them to miss it, thus the reliance on the *Itasca's* transmissions. If they didn't make the island, they would run out of fuel and go down in the ocean. There was no other land within range for them to divert to.

"I'm getting a lot of static," Noonan reported.

Earhart reached down and grabbed some smelling salts, taking a deep whiff, her eyes tearing. She didn't drink coffee, and she had learned that she needed the salts on a long flight. She'd been at the controls for eighteen hours, and tired didn't even begin to describe how she felt. She'd recently had dysentery and had still not completely regained her strength. She had made the decision, during one of the long legs of the trip, that this would be her last flight of adventure. From now on, she would only fly for pleasure.

She was a striking woman: tall, with short brown hair. Many in the media had called her Lady Lindbergh, and there was some resemblance between the first woman to fly across the Atlantic and the first man. Of course, Earhart's first trip across the Atlantic had basically been as luggage, a passenger as two men piloted the plane, but that didn't stop the sensation the flight caused in 1928. Ever since, she had been pushing the envelope, to a large degree because of the scorn of the few who pointed out that she hadn't piloted on that first flight, and partly because her husband, George Putnam, the famous publisher, encouraged her, keeping her in the limelight. Throughout the flight, she had filed dispatches from her journal.

She did fly the Atlantic solo in 1932, the second person after Lindbergh to do so, and that was just one of the many long-distance-record flights she accomplished. This was to be her crowning achievement, another first in a long list of firsts. Noonan had been chosen to accompany her because he had served as a navigator on the Pan American Pacific Clipper so he was familiar with the region where they expected the most difficulty.

She had planned on starting from Hawaii and going west, but on takeoff from Luke Field, the tip of one wing of the fuel-laden plane clipped the runway, and the Electra was badly damaged. It was shipped back to the States, and Earhart decided to reverse the direction of the flight and the start point. On 1 June, they took off from Miami, Florida, and flew to Puerto Rico on the first stage. They'd flown along the northern edge of South America to Africa at the narrowest part of the South Atlantic, then across Africa, along the southern tip of Arabia, and across India. That latter stage was another first for Earhart; no one had ever flown nonstop from the Red Sea to India before. They'd then hopped down toward Australia from Karachi to Calcutta, then to Rangoon, Bangkok, Singapore, and Bandoeng. There bad weather delayed them, and she came down with dysentery. Also during that time, Noonan had made repairs on the long-distance receivers and transmitters, which had been giving them trouble all through the long flight. On 27 June, they'd flown from Bandoeng to Darwin, where more repairs on the direction finder were completed, and their parachutes were shipped back to the States. Given that the rest of the trip would be over the Pacific, the parachutes were no longer needed.

They'd reached Lae, New Guinea, on 29 June, over two-thirds of the trip done and seven thousand miles to go. But the last legs were all over the Pacific, the most dangerous part of the journey. At Lae, she had cabled her last article to the *Herald Tribune* and her last journal entry to George.

"I need a fix," Amelia said. "We're getting close, and we're not going to have fuel to turn around if we miss it on the first pass."

"I know that." Noonan's voice was tight. They were both exhausted. "I don't know why I can't pick up the ship. The equipment is working correctly," he added defensively.

There was a smudge on the ocean ahead. Earhart's heart leapt as she though it must be smoke from the *Itasca*. She grabbed the transmitter and keyed it. "K-H-A-Q-Q calling *Itasca*. I see smoke. Are you making smoke? Over."

There was no answer.

Noonan had a set of binoculars, and he put them to his eyes. "I don't think that's a ship's smoke."

"An island?" Earhart asked.

"It's like fog."

"It can't be fog," Earhart said. "It's too small."

"It's getting bigger," Noonan said.

Even without the glasses, Earhart could see that it was growing larger. There was a yellowish tinge to the fog, and it was billowing upward and outward at an unnatural rate.

"I'm getting something," Noonan said. He had his hands over his headset, listening intently.

Amelia's gaze shifted between the compass and the growing cloud on the horizon as she waited.

"I don't know what it is," Noonan finally said. "A lot of static, then what sounds like Morse Code, but I can't--" he fell silent once more as he focused on listening, his eyes closed. "It's clearer now." Noonan opened his eyes and picked up a pencil and began to record the letters in the flight log, speaking them out loud, as he heard the dashes and dots.

"T-U-R-N-O-F-F-R-A-D-I-O-O-R-D-I-E."

"What?" Earhart was so tired her brain couldn't make immediate sense of the letters.

"Turn off radio or die," Noonan succinctly informed her.

"We can't. We won't be able to navigate."

"We haven't' been navigating for hours, " Noonan noted.

"Who's sending?" Earhart was confused. If it wasn't the *Itasca,* who was out here in the middle of nowhere?"

"I have no idea."

The fog was now less than five miles ahead and was huge, blocking their path now at twelve thousand feet and continuing to climb. In all her flights, she had never seen anything like it. She had a feeling they shouldn't fly into it, but if she changed course, she would burn fuel and get off their track to Howland Island. A startling thought crossed her mind: Had she already flown past Howland Island and the *Itasca?* She pushed that negative thinking aside. She knew exactly how fast they had been going and how long they had been in the air. But, she argued with herself, there was the possibility of a strong headwind or tailwind, multiplied by the nineteen hours they'd been in the air, skewing her math.

"I think we should shut the radio off," Noonan suggested, drawing her back to the immediate problem. "I don't like the looks of that."

"Find out who's sending," Earhart ordered.

Noonan had a knee key on his thigh, and he tapped out a quick query in Morse, trying to get the identity of the sender of the message.

A golden beam slashed out of the fog directly for the Electra. Earhart reacted, pushing forward and dropping the nose of the plane. The gold beam missed them by less than ten feet.

"Stop transmitting!" she yelled as she pulled the plane out of the dive and banked hard left. The fog was now less than two miles away, a wall stretching as far as she could see north and south and reaching up at least fifteen thousand feet.

"What was that?" Noonan was flipping switches, cutting power to their transmitter and receivers.

Earhart noted the fuel gauges. Not much left, and she had no idea where they were. Glancing out the window, she noted that even though she was flying a parallel course, the fog was closer, which meant it was still expanding.

"I'm going to ditch," she announced.

Noonan said nothing, knowing there really weren't any other options. They had an inflatable raft on board, and it was best to go down while they still had engine power so she could have some control of the landing.

Earhart turned away from the strange fog and began descending. Fortunately, the water was relatively calm, the swell no more than half a foot. When they were ten feet above the waves, she began throttling back, slowing the plane to just above stall speed.

The Electra hit, bounced, hit once more, and again bounced into the air. Then they were down, both slammed forward against their seat belts as the water slowed the plane. Earhart cut power to the engines, and an eerie silence reigned, strange after so many hours in the air, the sound of the engines their constant companion. Her first thought was that silence was the sound of failure: she had fallen short of her goal. She shook that thought out of her head and knew she had to focus on the immediate problem, which was getting out of the plane. She unbuckled, knowing they had some time before the plane went down, as the empty fuel tanks would keep it afloat for a little while. Earhart got up and began gathering essential equipment.

Noonan opened the door below the right wing, then got the raft. Earhart stuck her head out the door and looked to the rear. The fog was still coming, now less than a quarter mile away. Noonan began to inflate the raft after tying it off to a wing strut, while she piled supplies next to the door. She considered making a distress call, but the memory of what had happened the last time she'd transmitted stopped her. When they didn't arrive, the *Itasca* would come looking for her. And she knew her husband would get the president to launch a search.

"I hope whoever warned us is nearby," she told Noonan.

"That wasn't lightning that almost hit us," he said." It's like someone shot at us."

"With what?"

Noonan had the raft mostly inflated and was still pumping when the fog reached the tail of the plane. Earhart couldn't see more than a couple of feet into it. The plane was beginning to settle deeper, water washing close to the doorway.

"Let's go," she said. "We can finish pumping once we're away." Then she remembered the photos and her journal. "Wait a second."

She dashed back into the plane, ran to the cockpit, and grabbed the box containing the photos she had taken for the Navy and her journal. As she came back, she could barely see Noonan standing in the raft, holding on to the wing. She was just about to step through the door and into the raft when a long tentacle shot out the water and wrapped around Noonan, who gave a surprised yell. She froze in place.

"Help me!" He screamed as he was lifted into the air.

Another tentacle surfaced, searching along the bottom of the wing by feel. Then a half dozen more, like a forest of red, exploded out of the water. Earhart remained still, fear and self-preservation locking her in place inside the aircraft. She could see that there were what appeared to be mouths on the ends of the tentacles, about six inches wide, snapping open, revealing rows of razor-sharp teeth.

As she watched helplessly, one of those mouths struck Noonan in the chest and bore into him, blood spurting out around it. He screamed, his face rigid with pain, his back arching, trying to get away, but being held in place by the first tentacle wrapped around his body. Earhart staggered back in shock as the tip of the second tentacle came out of Noonan's back, teeth covered in his blood, still snapping. Noonan slumped, lifeless.

One of the other tentacles turned toward her, and she finally moved, slamming the door shut. She heard tentacles slithering over the plane's metal skin. Then she noted her feet were wet. There was about a foot of water inside, and the level was getting higher as the plane slowly sank.

She ran forward to the cockpit and looked out. The sea was churning with red arms. Looking back, there was no sign of Noonan or the raft, and the plane was completely inside the fog.

Suddenly, a wide flash of gold came out of the fog slicing neatly through the tentacles in its path. In a second they vanished beneath the surface. A light illuminated the fog, pushing it away—but it was coming from below the plane. Earhart gasped as a curved black wall came out of the water, surrounding the plane in all directions. For several moments, Earhart couldn't comprehend what she was seeing; then she realized, as more of the wall came out of the water and it curved inward, that her plane was in the middle of an opening on the top of what must be a great sphere.

The opening began to iris shut, and something solid touched the plane below, causing Earhart to stagger. When the opening was completely closed, she was in total darkness.

Then a blue glow suffused the plane, and she passed out.

CHAPTER THREE

THE NEAR PAST
26 April 1986 A.D.

Power. That was what had drawn Andrej Shashenka to Chernobyl. The ability to run a nuclear reactor and control power in its basest form, at the atomic level. Reactor Four was Andrej's domain, and he was in the process of overseeing its shutdown for periodic maintenance. His was one of four reactors that made up the Chernobyl complex, each capable of producing one thousand milliwatts of power. Currently, power production from Four was down to two hundred milliwatts, well within the range of the positive void coefficient required for safe operation.

It was 0100 in the morning, the fifty thousand people living in the town of the same name next to the reactor asleep in their beds, including Andrej's wife and three children. He had vacation beginning tomorrow, and he was taking his family to meet his twin brothers, Pytor and Felix, who served in the army. It would be the first time the three of them would be getting together since their mother's funeral. He was anxious to finish the shutdown so he could turn the reactor over to the maintenance people.

Shutdown was a difficult balancing act of reducing power but at the same time drawing enough power from the reactor to keep the cooling system running to prevent the core from overheating. While the reactor was normally self-sufficient, providing the power to run its own cooling system, Andrej was in the process of shifting to generator power.

At exactly 0123, right after the power switch was completed, Andrej noticed the slightest dip in power readings. He scanned the rest of his vast control panel, making sure all was running properly, when Leona Kiril, his senior assistant, gave a startled yell.

"What's the matter?" Andrej went over to her position.

In her shock, all she could do was point at the video monitor that displayed the view of the reactor core. A black triangle, fifteen feet on each side and ten feet high, was floating directly over the core rods.

"What the hell is that?" Andrej had never seen the like.

Gold beams came out of each corner of the triangle, flashing down to the rods. Alarms began going as the power dropped abruptly. At the same time, the lights in the control room went out, and all instruments went dead.

"Emergency backup!" Andrej yelled. His crew was trained to operate in the dark, and he could hear switches being thrown and people moving, but nothing happened.

"All power is down," someone yelled.

If primary and emergency generators were down, that left only one choice. Andrej threw the switch taking the reactor off-line from the generators and back to reactor power. "Power up as quickly as possible," he ordered.

The lights came back on along with instruments as the machines took power from the reactor, but what the gauges told Andrej froze his heart. Whatever the black triangle was, it was drawing power from the core faster than the core could produce it. Andrej knew they had scant seconds before things became critical in an inverse way. The reactor wouldn't be able to provide enough energy to the cooling systems, which meant there would be a point at which the entire system would reverse very quickly. The core, getting hotter, would produce more and more power until it reached critical mass and exploded.

"Emergency shutdown!" Andrej screamed, knowing it was already too late. He slammed his fist down on the emergency reactor trip button.

"Power spike!" someone yelled.

Inside the reactor, power was doubling every second, faster and faster, until it was doubling every millisecond. Within four seconds, it reached critical.

The last thing Andrej saw was the black triangle on the video monitor. The gold beams still sucking from the core, and when the water in the core exploded into steam it destroyed the fuel elements, sending super hot, radioactive gas outward, blasting off the roof of the containment building and blowing through the walls into the control room, killing everyone instantly.

The white-hot graphite in the reactor caught fire, sending a radioactive cloud billowing into the air over a mile high.

The fire burned for days, pouring forty times the radioactivity released by the atomic bombs detonated at Hiroshima and Nagasaki into the atmosphere. Over five thousand tons of lead and stone were dropped by helicopters to both put out the fire and contain the radiation. In the process, many of the crews received fatal doses.

Besides the black triangle, there was another strange aspect to Reactor Four: the lead and stone seemed to hit an invisible, hemispheric wall covering the core and piled up around it. The same with the concrete that was poured next. Still, they dropped the concrete, covering the clear shield completely.

All of Europe was affected by the fallout, particularly in the north.

The world outcry over the accident and the shabby construction of the reactor was intense. Only a handful of people in the highest levels of the Russian government had a copy of the transmission sent out by the monitoring equipment just before the explosion and knew what had really happened.

Even while more cleanup operations were being run, a special unit was formed to monitor Reactor Four and the alien object within.

CHAPTER FOUR

THE PRESENT

The Ring of Fire encircles the Pacific Ocean, stretching over nineteen thousand miles. It is delineated by the volcanoes and fault lines that are the surface evidence of the split in the crust of the planet deep below. From New Zealand to New Guinea, the Philippines, Japan, arching around to the Aleutians, down the west coast of North America to South America.

The Ring is formed by tectonic plates, a theory that is relatively new in scientific circles, first postulated in the mid-1960s. The surface of the Earth, the lithosphere, is divided into nine major plates and a dozen smaller ones. The lithosphere floats on top of the mantle. Generally, each plate delineated a continent; all, that is, except for the Pacific, which encompasses several plates. The boundaries between plates produce one of three types of effects. Where two plates are going away from each other, they produce ridges where material come up through the split. When one plate slides under another, a subduction zone occurs. Where two plates move in opposite parallel directions is a transform fault, a prime example being the San Andreas Fault along the west coast of the United States.

Along the Ring of Fire, all these things had been happening for millennia. It was called the Ring of Fire because volcanoes circled almost the entire Pacific Rim, where plates met and magma boiled up between them. The forces involved in the Ring were staggering in concept, but they played out over eons, rarely noted by man except when an earthquake such as the one that leveled San Francisco in 1906 occurred or a volcano such as Mount St. Helens in Oregon erupted. And those were isolated events, just a fraction of the length of the ring and its potential power.

The Shadow had shown a mastery of manipulating these forces by firing a salvo of nuclear weapons from a captured American submarine at Iceland, hitting along the tectonic line down the middle of the island and literally splitting it in half. It had barely been stopped from continuing the destruction along the Mid-Atlantic Ridge, which would have devastated the east coast of North America and Europe.

Now, out of the Devil's Sea gate, off the coast of Japan new lines of probing were reaching out, noting the composition of the Ring of Fire, the position of volcanoes and their status, fault lines, and critical junctures.

The Shadow was readying a second assault on the planet.

The probing by the Shadow was not unnoticed. Three miles below the planet's surface, in northern Japan, a group of scientists led by Professor Nagoya was gathered around monitors, coordinating the data they were getting from the superkamiokande underneath their feet. They were near the top of the natural cavern, their computers, desks, and chairs set on a steel grate that covered a highly polished stainless steel tank sixty meters wide by sixty deep and filled with water. The walls of the tank were lined with twenty thousand photomultiplier tubes—PMTs. The tubes were very sensitive light sensors that could pick up a single photon as it traveled through the tank's water.

The superkamiokande was a ring-imaging water Cerenkov detector. Cerenkov light was produced when an electrically charged particle traveled through water. The reason the superkamiokande was so far underground was in order to allow the miles of earth and rock above it to block out the photons emitted by man's devices on the surface of the planet.

While Professor Nagoya and his coworkers knew little about the gates and the Shadow, they did know that activity by the Shadow produced muon emissions, which the superkamiokande could trace. Nagoya didn't know yet why the gates produced muons or why the muons emitted did not decay as rapidly as physics said they should.

"The Shadow is checking the fault lines," Ahana, Nagoya's senior assistant, noted. She was a young woman with the sharpest mind Nagoya had ever interacted with. "Also volcanoes. Just like it did with the Mid-Atlantic Ridge," she added, referring to what had happened just before the destruction of Iceland.

Nagoya had been studying the gates for years. Only recently, with the assistance of the superkamiokande, was he beginning to understand them. He tapped the screen displaying the lines of probes. "We have assumed that the Shadow is doing this imagining through the Earth," he said, "but what if it isn't going through the Earth but rather traveling on a different dimension or using wormholes."

Ahana frowned "What do you mean?"

"Most of what we know about physics is traditionally based on the dual foundations of general relativity and quantum mechanics. But, as you know, both cannot be right as they are interpreted by their traditional followers; they cannot coexist as formulated. Some say there is a split: that general relativity is what makes things work on a large scale and quantum mechanics on a small scale but such a concept is ludicrous. Where would such a split occur? Is there a magic point in the size of objects at which the laws of physics change?"

"What about superstring theory?" Ahana asked. "The two theories can coexist in that."

"True," Nagoya agreed. "And string theory requires we rethink our concepts of time, space, and matter. It claims that there are many more dimensions to our universe than what we see."

Ahana held up her hand. "But so far, only at a very small level with Calabi-Yau spaces."

"Which no one has seen and which have only been postulated with mathematical formulas," Nagoya said, "Still, if we stop looking at the Earth as simply a three-dimensional object but accept that there might be much to it that we don't see or understand yet, we might be able to understand these gates better." He tapped the screen once more. "The muon emissions that come out of the gates last longer than our physics say they should. But are they really any different? Or is it our perception that is different?"

"Relativity." Ahana saw what he was getting at. "The muons may well be behaving the same as those in a lab, it's just that we are seeing them act differently. That means that time is variable inside the gates and on the other side, as you noted."

"That would explain the submarine *Scorpion* reappearing after thirty years and the crew not appearing a day older," Nagoya said. "I think they were caught in a wormhole between gates. I think the gates are connected in an inner space where time is very much a variable.

"I remember when Foreman tried high-frequency radio communications through the Angkor gate to the Bermuda Triangle gate back in the early seventies. He was able to make contact when the laws of physics said he shouldn't have been able to. The HF had to travel through the gates as the waves could not have traveled around the planet. If we could get an idea of the constitution of the world beyond the gates, probe from one gate to another, it would give us valuable data."

"We could send a muon emitter into a gate and see what happens," Ahana suggested.

"An emitter and a receiver," Nagoya said. "We have to see how the patterns intersect. Could you rig something like that?"

Ahana nodded. "Yes."

"We would have to use the Devil's Sea gate and the Chernobyl one."

"But--" Ahana began.

"Yes?"

"The Chernobyl gate is hot. Anyone trying to go in there would receive a fatal dose."

"All the gates are dangerous," Nagoya noted. "Sacrifices have to be made in the name of progress."

Ahana's normally calm disposition gave way to an expression of shock, but if Nagoya noticed it, he said nothing.

Eric Dane stood on the platform that ringed the top of the derrick in the center of the ship, looking out past the *Glomar Explorer* below him to the open sea. There was a slight breeze, and the water was calm. The sun was coming up in the east, a glowing orange ball on the horizon foretelling good weather for the day.

The massive ship was idle in the middle of an empty sea. The huge derrick took up the entire center of the ship, towering over it. The *Glomar* had been built by Howard Hughes in 1973 ostensibly to mine the ocean floor for minerals. In reality, as Dane had learned, the ship was built for the CIA to try to recover the remains of a Russian submarine that sank in deep water under the code name Project Jennifer. The classified reason for this recovery was to get the cipher codes the sub used. Even that, though, was a cover story, Dane now knew.

The Russian submarine the *Glomar* went after had gone through the Devil's Sea gate and disappeared for a week. What was on the other side of these gates was something Dane and others were still uncertain about, but there was no doubt there were very unfriendly forces over there in the form of the Shadow. To the consternation of those participating in Project Jennifer, they discovered that some of the nuclear weapons on board the Russian submarine were missing and, even more perplexing, they found bodies on board that were not Russian sailors. One was a Japanese man in his mid thirties, yet he had dental work that dated him to the beginning of the twentieth century. They also discovered that the Russians had sunk their own submarine when it reappeared.

Dane heard someone coming up the metal stairs, but he didn't turn. He had sensed Ariana's approach long before he heard her arrival. A new crew had been flown in by the Navy the previous day and pulled up *Deeplab* and the docked *Deepflight*. There was no sign of the original crew of the *Glomar* except for numerous blood trails, mainly centered around the well pool. More casualties to add to a list that was approaching a half million, Dane thought.

Iceland was now only a dozen or so active volcanoes poking above the surface of the North Atlantic. Puerto Rico was still cleaning up the damage from the tsunami. The sub pens at Groton, Connecticut, were radioactive, and a large evacuation had taken place for miles around after the detonation of the nuclear power plant of the *Scorpion*. The attack submarine *Seawolf* was gone, with no trace of the wreckage, although the Navy was still looking for both it and the remains of the ballistic missile submarine *Wyoming*.

"Foreman wants us back in Washington," Ariana Michelet said. "He says Nagoya has some interesting hypotheses about the nature of the gates he wants us to look at." Ariana was a striking woman, the daughter of one of the richest men in the world. Dane had rescued her out of the Angkor gate after her research plane was brought down by the Shadow inside the gate.

"Can he keep them closed forever?" Dane asked.

"I don't know. From what Foreman said—and he was being very guarded—Nagoya has an idea how the gates work."

Dane didn't turn. "Where are all the people?"

"What people?"

"From the ships and planes we saw in the graveyard? From *Deeplab*? From this ship?"

"On the other side," Ariana said.

"And what does that mean?" Dane asked.

"We'll have to go to Washington to see what Nagoya and Foreman have come up with," Ariana said.

Dane shook his head. "The answer isn't in Washington, and this isn't over. All we did was repeat history. We stopped the gates, but they'll expand again. Next time, I think we need to open the gates and take the war to the other side."

Ariana placed a hand on Dane's shoulder. Her father could be considered a modern-day Howard Hughes, one of the richest men in the world and the current owner of the *Glomar*. His covert relationship with Foreman, the CIA man who had been tracking the gates ever since losing his brother in one during World War II and watching Flight 19 disappear in the Bermuda Triangle gate in 1945, was an example of the devious way Foremen had had to operate for decades before the recent blatant attacks out of the gates had garnered the world's attention.

They stayed like that for a minute before she turned to go. "I'll meet you at the helipad with Chelsea."

Dane heard her go down the stairs. He stared out over the ocean, but what he was really seeing was a tall Viking warrior standing in the prow of his longship, a large ax in his hand. He remembered the message the Viking had etched into the side of the *Scorpion*.

"You will be revenged," Dane whispered before following Ariana.

CHAPTER FIVE

THE PAST
79 A.D.

The Oracle of Delphi had been in the Corycian Cave for six days, refusing food and drinking only the pure water brought to her from the Castilian Spring by her priestesses. She had not spoken a word in that time, and those who had traveled from near and far to Delphi to consult the oracle had been turned away. And there were many who had made the journey, as the portents were dark in many places. Even though Rome ruled the Mediterranean now, the influence of the Greeks and their beliefs was very strong. There were noble men and women from Rome waiting, even those from Persia and Kingdoms beyond the border of the empire. She had listened to the tales many brought before retiring to the cave, knowing that something serious was happening to the world. She isolated herself to listen to her inner voice, which could make contact with the gods.

On the morning of the seventh day, the oracle appeared at the mouth of the cave and spoke only two words to the priestess on duty: "The Defender."

The young woman who climbed the path was covered with a thin sheen of sweat. Her tanned skin glistened, and her short red hair was plastered to the top of her skull. She wore a pair of cloth trousers and a tunic with no sleeves, a dagger stuck in her belt and a pack on her back. She had broad shoulders and was tall, towering over the priestesses escorting her. Her face had broad cheekbones and a sharp nose separating blue eyes. The priestesses paused at the entrance to the cave and indicated for her to go in alone.

She entered and paused just inside, allowing her eyes to adjust to the dimness. She saw the omphalos, the navel stone, deep blue in color, which sat in the center of the cave. On the other side, the oracle was on her stone throne, near the crevice that went to the very center of the Earth according to some.

"Priestess Kaia." The old woman's voice was very low but carried a sense of power.

Kaia knelt on the near side of the omphalos and bowed her head. "Yes, Oracle?"

The oracle tapped the stone of the throne. "I have been listening to the Earth and the gods. All your life you have been preparing and training to take a journey, but I never told you why or where. I know where now, and I will tell you why."

The oracle gestured for Kaia to sit. "I must tell you the truth, and then you must decide. You are a priestess, not like the girls who serve me here, but of the true bloodline. You are a Defender. You sense things others cannot and you have powers they cannot imagine. It is why you have been isolated all your life. You are my granddaughter."

Kaia's head snapped up at the last words. "Why was I never told?"

"It was never time."

"And my mother?"

"She died giving birth to you."

Kaia could sense the truth of what the oracle was saying, and she caught a brief glimpse of a woman—her mother—coming from the oracle's mind. She did not have time to dwell on her sudden sense of loss as the oracle continued.

"Our line stretches back many, many years. And it is always the women that carry the pure blood. The men we choose to mate with are picked by the inner circle of oracles."

"My mother—" Kaia began, but the oracle waved a hand.

"I do not have time to assuage your feelings or explain that which is not important right now. It was the will of the inner circle, and such will is our law. It has been that way since we were forced to separate and pretend to be something that we aren't."

A muscle rippled on Kaia's jaw, but she forced herself to remain under control. "What do I defend?"

"Everything. We are not from here. We came from a place called Thera. The island that is there now is just a fragment of the kingdom we once had. Before Thera, our people lived in Atlantis."

Kaia shook her head, her anger a knotted fist her chest. "Atlantis is a myth. I have read Plato and his writings—as you made me. According to Romans who read him now, it was a device he used to make a point."

"Atlantis is where we came from," the oracle said simply. "I assure you it was most real."

Again, despite her anger, Kaia knew the oracle spoke the truth. "How was it destroyed?"

"It was destroyed by the Shadow."

"What is this Shadow?"

"A darkness upon the Earth and in it. No one knows exactly what it is, but it is deadly to every living thing. At rare times, it appears and tries to expand to cover the world. Now is one of those times."

Kaia's mind brought back the image of her mother she had picked up from the oracle. She heard the oracle's words, but from a distance. All her life she had wondered who her mother was and where she was. To be told she was dead and the oracle was her grandmother overwhelmed her.

"Pay attention!" The oracle's words were accompanied by a sharp mental slap, wiping away the image and bringing Kaia back to the here and now. She was tempted to strike back in the same way, but a lifetime of training held her back.

"The Shadow," the oracle repeated. "It manifests itself in two ways. One is inside the Earth. There is nothing we can do about it in the Earth where it brings forth fire and earthquakes. But the Shadow that comes on the planet's surface in the form of what we call a gate; that we can fight. It appears as a darkness on the surface of the planet. Those who go into it don't come back out.

"We have not seen a gate since Thera was destroyed. From Thera we went to Troy. The Helen of whom stories are told was of our line. After Troy was destroyed, we scattered once more, seeking sanctuary as oracles and priestesses. Always waiting, listening, and watching. And now the Shadow is coming once more. A gate has appeared."

"Where?"

"To the north, beyond the borders of even the Romans. But the Earth is troubled in many places, and all will be affected."

"What do you want me to do?"

"You were told to be prepared for a mission, and now that time is here. But you have no idea of the scope and importance of what you must do. There is a shield that can stop the Shadow and close the gate. You are one part of the Shield."

"How?"

"I cannot tell you that. The knowledge has been lost, but I know that you will find someone on your journey who can tell you. I also know that you need more than you have." The oracle closed her eyes, and her voice changed. Kaia knew she was hearing the voice of one who had had a vision. She had had many herself, some while sleeping, some while awake.

"I see a staff with a blade on one end and a seven-headed snake on the other. Such a snake is called a Naga. You must find the Naga staff, as it is part of the Shield and it is also the only weapon useful against the emissaries of the Shadow. They are creatures who I have seen in visions passed down to me. With hard white skin and red eyes. They are called Valkyries. They can travel out of the gate for a limited amount of time.

"I have seen a man. A killer. He was a soldier but is no longer. You will need his help and military force to get to the gate and enter it.

"Some of the visions are from now, some are from the past through the bloodline." The oracle paused, then continued, "But some are from times to come.

"You must go to Rome. Tell the emperor of the threat." The oracle reached into her robe and pulled out a ring. "Given to my grandmother long ago. It will gain you an audience with the Emperor. Convincing him of the danger, that is another matter. You must keep your eyes open for signs. You have more power than you know. You would have taken my place if the Shadow had not come."

"My mother--"Kaia began.

"Yes?"

"Where is she buried?"

"In the sacred grove."

"I wish to see her grave before I leave."

Steel on steel, the sound of mortal combat echoed off the stonewalls of the arena, rising above the screams of the bloodthirsty crowd. Forty thousand people lined the stands of Rome's amphitheater, and they were on their feet, as the highlight of the first day of the games was under way, a fight to the death between local favorite Falco and four *retiarii*.

Falco was a *mymillo*, the most heavily armed type of gladiator, the name coming from the fish symbol on his helmet. He had a breastplate, metal rings guarding his sword arm, a heavy shield in his right hand, and a sword in his left to complete his armament. The *retiarius*, or net men, were more lightly armed, each having just a net, trident, and dagger. They were also the only class of gladiator that did not wear a helmet. All four had light skin, prisoners from the northern territories, perhaps Britain.

A net flew, and Falco sidestepped, shoving it away with his shield, careful not to get the edge of the shield caught on it. The four men were working in pairs, two approaching, two waiting, trying to wear him down, waiting for him to make a fatal mistake.

Falco was a large man, as befitted a *mymillo*, towering over the net men. His body was solidly muscled and covered with scars from former engagements. His skin was burned dark from the hours he spent training outdoors. His hair was clipped close to his skull and prematurely gray, a normal thing among those in his occupation. His most intriguing feature were his eyes, deep blue, which spoke of foreign blood.

As the man who had cast scuttled to recover his net, Falco bellowed and charged forward toward his partner. That man took a step backward, and Falco whirled toward the first man, slashing with his sword. He caught the first *retiarius* as he was gathering up the net. The man was good, blocking the blow with his trident and trying to rip the sword from Falco's grip by twisting the haft, pinning the blade with forks. He might as well have been trying to move the arm of the statue of the emperor that gazed down from above the imperial box.

Falco's arm not only didn't move, he slid the sword down until the guard rested on the base of the trident, then thrust upward with his shield, the metal edge catching the *retiarius* under the chin, smashing into his jaw and lifting the smaller man off his feet. Falco was still going with the flow of the blow, turning, knowing what was coming even before he saw it, that the second *retiarius* was casting, trying to catch from behind. He still had the first man hanging on the edge of his shield, and as he completed the turn, he heaved with all his strength, tossing the body at the net. The man went down in a tumble, wrapped in the net.

The other two *retiarii* had used the opportunity to fan out, one fighter on each flank of Falco as he faced the third survivor. Falco forced himself to relax, to focus on the three men who were trying to kill him. They were going to double cast; he knew it a second before either on the flank moved. Falco charged the one he sensed was the better fighter of the two, his shield now over his head, his sword held forward. The caster behind him missed, but the man he was charging, settled his net perfectly over Falco, or at least his shield, which Falco let go of a split second before the net completed its drop and caught him. The net fell to the ground, the shield it's only captive. Falco dove to the ground at the feet of the *retiarius*, his sword point now extending forward and up, slicing into the man's upper thigh as he tried to dance away, severing the artery.

Falco rolled twice to the right, feeling the sand against his exposed skin. The dying *retiarius* was brave as he stuck with his trident, narrowly missing pinning Falco's neck to the ground. Falco was on his feet, giving ground, letting the wounded man bleed out as he struggled to approach. Falco could feel the wounded man's pain, the faintness as his blood pulsed out with each beat of his heart. The other two *retiarii* were behind, recovering their nets.

The wounded man raised his trident and screamed something in his native tongue, charging forward. Falco stood his ground and met the trident with his blade, stopping the man's charge as if he had run into a wall. With his free hand, Falco grabbed the man's throat. He squeezed, massive muscles in his forearm rippling, and the man's trachea gave way. Still Falco kept the pressure, breaking through the skin, his fingers reaching the carotid arteries, popping into both as if into grapes, blood flowing over his hand. The *retiarius* went limp, and Falco threw the body from him.

The last two *retiarii* were approaching very slowly, trying to maneuver him to have their backs to the late afternoon sun. Falco risked a glimpse toward the imperial box. A large awning shaded the box, but Falco knew she was there: he could feel her evil presence. His hatred grew.

Falco turned his attention to the approaching gladiators. He could pick up fear from them now. Their numbers were halved, and he wasn't even scratched. They had recovered their nets, and he was without his shield, which gave them a slight advantage.

One said something to the other in their tongue. The second replied. Falco didn't understand the language, but he picked up their intent. He had always been able to do that, a trait he possessed that he had only told one other person about in his entire life, his wife Drusilla. He had known since he was a small child that he was different, and he had instinctively known that showing off that difference would not endear him to others. The difference, though, had saved his life many times in the army and the arena and made him the crown at the gladiator school in Rome for the past two years.

They were going to attack him full on, at the same time. Nothing fancy. Casting simultaneously, side by side, and then charging, hoping to get in an incapacitating strike with their tridents and then finish him with daggers.

Falco smiled. He spread his arms wide apart, bloodstained sword glinting.

The crowd roared its approval and began to chant his name.

He turned his back to the two *retiarii*, which surprised them. It was his trademark to turn his back on his enemies, to acknowledge the crowd all around. It was as if he sought death, but it never quite found him.

He knew they would be charging a split second before they moved. Still he kept his back to them, sensing their approach, feeling their anger and fear bearing down on him. He even knew when they threw their nets, fifteen feet out as they had been trained. Time had slowed down for Falco, each second passing as if a minute. He could see details in the crowd, the crazed faces of the men and women who came here to see others die and then go home and make wild love, their lust provoked by the sight of the blood. Their roars were a faint sound in his ears, the sound of his own heart beating much louder to him. The dark seed in his heart wanted him to remain still, to let the nets settle over his head and body, to allow the barbed trident points to do their job and release him from the pain of life.

26

Falco whirled, sword slashing, getting caught in one net, and he let go of the pommel, the weight of the heavy weapon taking the net with it to one side. The other net fell to his left harmlessly. He could pick up the thrill from the two men charging, tridents leveled, as they saw that although they had not captured him with their nets, he was now unarmed.

Falco anticipated the first thrust, coming from the *retiarius* to his right. The three prongs of the trident narrowly missed, and Falco jumped toward the weapon, putting the shaft against his side, looping his right arm over it and clamping down, even as he turned to face the charge of the second man. As the second man thrust, Falco bobbed left, still holding the shaft of the first trident, catching the *retiarius* who held the haft by surprise and pulling him forward, right into the path of the second trident. The *retiarius* screamed as the three prongs pierced his skin, spitting him.

The *retiarius* desperately tried to pull his weapon out of his comrade's body, but the barb on the end of each prong refused to release from muscle and bone. Falco let go of the other trident and raised his empty hands toward the last surviving *retiarius*. The man stepped back, whipping his dagger out of its sheath. He retreated as Falco came forward.

The crowd was in a frenzy, screaming Falco's name. The *retiarius* turned toward the emperor's box and cried out, begging for mercy, tossing his dagger away to make the point obvious and getting to his knees. Falco paused, peering into the shadow, out of which the new emperor Titus stepped. The games were in honor of him, as he had just taken office two months ago after the death of Vespasian, his father. Titus scanned the crowd.

Falco suddenly felt tired. When he had begun fighting, more often than not, mercy was shown, and a man who fought well would be spared. But each year the crowd's thirst for blood could not be sated so easily. They could not see beyond the immediate moment and the fact that every gladiator who died was very difficult to replace. Life was cheap in the arena and growing cheaper with each new set of games.

The thumbs were almost all down. Titus then gave Falco the same sign. He picked up the *retiarius's* dagger and walked up to the man whose head was now bowed, his lips moving in some prayer to his gods.

Falco didn't waste any time in showmanship now, slicing the blade across the man's neck and stepping back out of the way of the flow of blood. The body slumped forward onto the sand, the blood soaking into it.

Falco turned and raised the blade to the emperor, then slowly spun about, showing it to the stands. The crowd roared its approval. When he completed the turn, he saw that the emperor was in his seat, another man leaning over, talking to him.

Gaius Marcus was the *Ianista* or head of the emperor's gladiatorial school at Rome. When men had first been pitted against each other in such contest, the *Ianista* worked for private factions, and it had been a business. But the revolt at Capua in 73 B.C. led by Spartacus had forced the emperor to put all such schools under his own control. It was a move that went beyond security, though, as considerable sums of money flowed from such schools.

Now gladiators were a mixture. Many were slaves, sold into the life. Some were ex-soldiers who entered the arena for their own reason, most to make money, but some with a darkness inside that only found solace in combat. Falco was both, having been born a slave and sold to the *Ianista* while still young. Then he'd been drawn into the army during the desperate civil war of '69. When his service was up, he returned to the arena.

Falco saw the darkness not only in his own heart but also in most men's souls, and nothing could quiet the voices in his head. He knew, in a way, his lack of normal fear of dying gave him a large advantage over those who entered the arena with debilitating fear. And every time he was in a situation, as today, where he could have allowed death to over take him, something had burst forth and caused him to fight, to survive, but he didn't know what that was.

A legionnaire ran out with a red-hot poker in his hand and laid it against the skin of each of the *retiarii* to insure none was faking. Occasionally, gladiators used bladders of pig's blood inside their armor to simulate wounds. Certain they were dead, slaves ran out and began removing the bodies and raking the sand, covering the blood, preparing for the next contest.

In the shadow of the imperial box, he saw her. Smiling as she always did, leaning forward, scented scarf covering her mouth. He had been freed years earlier, but she owned him as securely as any of his former masters.

Falco slowly walked toward the entrance that led to the tunnels below. Today was only the first day of the games, which were to last a month. There would be much more death.

He paused just before going into the tunnel, and his head turned toward the south. Unbidden, a vision came to him. A mountain, looming above a city, a cloud at the peak of the mountain. He'd seen that peak before, that city, but it would not come to him at first; then he recognized it. The city was Pompeii, where he had fought on occasion. And the mountain, Vesuvius.

It was as if he could see into the Earth itself, and he saw a darkness, like a disease, boiling up below Vesuvius, clawing its way toward the surface. An overwhelming sense of dread blanketed him.

Then a gladiator entering the arena bumped into him, the man's eyes glazed with fear, knocking the vision from Falco's head.

Falco entered the tunnel.

Kaia had both hands on the grass that covered her mother's grave. A small piece of marble marked the spot. She was surrounded by the trees of the sacred grove, where only the priestesses of Delphi were allowed to enter. She turned as she sensed someone behind her. The oracle stood there, wrapped in her fine robes. The old woman's face was lined and pale.

"Why did you never tell me who I was?" Kaia asked as she stood.

"Your thoughts must be pure," the oracle said. "There is so much that I do not know, that I thought it best not to influence you one way or the other. It is the way it has been for a long time."

That made little sense to Kaia, but she said nothing.

The oracle held out a crystal. "This is yours. As it was your mother's once, and mine before her." As Kaia took the crystal, the oracle crooked a finger. "Come."

Kaia followed her out of the grove and into the temple. Going to the altar, the oracle pointed. "Lift the top stone."

Carefully, Kaia lifted the heavy marble. Underneath was a black slab with writing etched on it.

"This is the list of oracles, dating back to the first to come from Thera, Priestess Kala." The oracle ran her old fingers over the markings. "Here is your mother's name, the last to be etched. I will have yours added."

"And if I don't return?" Kaia asked. "Does the line end with me?"

"The things I see," the oracle said, "are uncertain. The visions come from the gods, but who are the gods?"

"The gods are the gods," Kaia said simply.

The oracle smiled. "So you have been taught. Let me tell you what I do know. I have spoken of the Shadow, but there are those on the other side, where the shadow comes from, who oppose the Shadow. They are called the Ones Before. They might be gods, I do not know, but they have helped us. Long ago they gave us the power to stop the Shadow.

"You need to talk to the Akrotirian Oracle at Thera. She knows more of this than I do. It was where our ancestors fought the Shadow last." The oracle placed a hand on Kaia's shoulder. "I suggest forgetting everything you have been taught. You must trust the visions you have. They are the gods speaking to you." Her finger slid over the long list of names to the very first. "Priestess Kala was the first. She escaped the destruction of Thera. Let us hope you are not the last. It is time for you to go."

Gaius Marcus slapped Falco on the back. "An excellent fight, old friend."

Falco barely acknowledged the praise, his eyes moving along the rows of tables in the banquet hall. He could feel her presence, a malignant tumor obvious even on the cancer that was Rome.

"On the last day of the games, I want you to do an exhibition with Corlius," Marcus continued. "Wooden swords in between some of the fights."

Falco nodded. "All right." He had done many such exhibitions where neither man was injured. Gladiators of his skill level were rare and could not always be risked in mortal combat.

Falco saw her. "Excuse me."

Marcus followed Falco's gaze. "Careful."

"I am always careful," Falco said.

"In the arena, yes," Marcus agreed. "You have something very special there. But this" –he waved, taking in the elite of Rome dining on their couches—"is a very different arena."

"What would you have me do?" Falco asked. "Ignore her? Her brother is commander of the Praetorian Guard. Her family has links everywhere."

"With the new emperor, things are liable to change," Marcus noted.

"She has promised to tell me where my children are after the games," Falco said.

"Why?"

"She says because of her love for me."

Marcus laughed. "She loves only herself. She is playing a game with your mind, with your heart."

"Does that make her worse than you?" Falco asked. "You only play with my life."

"I do it as a job," Marcus said. He looked at the woman. "She does it for sport."

"You are the one who sent me to her in the first place," Falco said.

"You know I had no choice. Servicing women like her is part of your life. Everyone knows it."

"But she is different than the other women," Falco said.

"She wanted you," Marcus said simple. "Be careful."

"I will take care of myself. " Falco walked around the edge of a table, greeting various noble men and women, nodding at their praises for the day's fight.

"Ah, Centurion Falco," General Cassius raised a hand as Falco reached the head table. "Come here and join us."

Falco settled down on a cushioned couch. A slave ran up and poured him some wine and setting a plate of food. He was rarely called centurion now, the rank he had held in the army, but he had served with Cassius in Palestine, where they had been members of the famous X Legion and present for the fall of Jerusalem. Cassius was a tall, thin man with a large nose, sunken, sad eyes and thinning white hair. His right arm was crooked at an unnatural angle at the elbow, where a javelin had pierced it many years ago in battle and the surgeon's efforts at repair had not taken well.

"Greeting, General," Falco said as soon as the slave had moved away. He knew Cassius had retired from the army, disgusted after what had happened at Jerusalem, and gone to live on his country estate. He had not had much of a future in Rome given that he had brought a Jewish woman back with him to live on his estate. Even among the debauchery of Rome such a union was considered ill advised. "How is Lupina?"

A shadow crossed the old man's face. "She passed away last winter."

"I am most sorry, General. She was most special." Falco had been with the general on the return trip from Palestine and gotten to know Lupina quite well. A slight woman, not pretty, but full of humor and intelligence. He had seen the love between Cassius and Lupina, even with the strain of what had happened to her people in Jerusalem casting a shadow over it.

"Thank you," Cassius said.

Falco could tell that Cassius did not want to talk about Lupina, that the wound of her death was still too strong. He understood that feeling. "I did not know you were in Rome," he said.

Cassius grimaced. "The new emperor is, how shall I say, counting heads. Deciding which ones he can count on and which ones it might be best to lop off."

"General—" Falco was surprised. He had always appreciated Cassius's forthright attitude in the field, but here, in the emperor's own palace, even Falco knew the words were inappropriate.

Cassius smiled. "Still guarding my sword side, Falco?" The reference was to the man who stood to the right in a shield wall, where one's shield actually only covered half of one's own body and half of the man to his left. It required all in the line to stand fast in order to be protected and to rely on each other. If one man broke, he exposed the man to his side, and the entire line could collapse.

"You can always count on me," Falco said as he glanced down the table at the woman who had just taken the couch to the general's other side.

The general caught the look. "Let me introduce the Lady Epione, wife of Senator Domidicus, nephew of the emperor," Cassius indicated the woman on his left.

"Lady," Falco bowed his head. In this matter at last, Cassius was being diplomatic, as he knew well the situation between Falco and the lady. The General had even tried intervening a year ago, another reason for his exile to the country and removal from affairs for the army and the state.

"Noble gladiator." Epione was lying on her side, her blue robe flowing over her body. She picked up a grape and laid it on her tongue, slowly drawing it in before speaking again. "You fought well and bravely."

"The gods were with me, lady," Falco answered.

"Which gods might that be?" Epione asked.

Falco knew she worshiped in the cult of Isis, a very powerful group of women. "Whichever ones watch over the arena," he answered.

Epione laughed. "Well phrased. Much better than that religion of the Jews where there is only one god. How can one keep track of all that needs looking after?" She had turned to Cassius as she said this, and Falco knew it was a barb at him for bringing Lupina back and putting her in his estate. The general did not rise to the bait.

She turned back to Falco. "I would like to talk with you later about the arena."

Falco could see the general's eyes shifting back and forth between the two of them, but Cassius said nothing.

"Your likes are my commands," Falco answered.

"Yes, they are, aren't they?" Epione said.

"The emperor," Cassius nodded his head toward the door, where people were hurriedly getting to their feet, acknowledging the entrance of Titus.

Falco scrambled off the cushions and stood, head bowed, as Titus made his way around the tables. An aide to the emperor was introducing each person that Titus didn't know.

"The gladiator—"" the aide began, but Titus interrupted him.

'Falco. I remember. Centurion of the most noble X Legion. We served in Palestine together. A most miserable place with a most miserable people. I was quite surprised to see you today. I understand you have been fighting in the arena for a few years now."

"Emperor," Falco bowed his head even lower, then looked up, meeting the emperor's level gaze. Titus had only recently been called back to Rome as Vespasian's condition worsened and had just assumed the title upon his father's death.

"And Cassius," Titus turned and faced the old general. "It has been a while since I saw you, General. In fact, the last time, Falco was also at your side, was he not?"

"Yes, Emperor," Cassius said.

"Curious," Titus muttered, looking between the two of them. "Most curious." He slapped Cassius on the shoulder. "We will talk later. There are strange reports from the borders, and I know how much you like strange things." Then the emperor moved on.

"What did he mean?" Falco asked Cassius as soon as the emperor was out of earshot.

"He fears all," Cassius said, watching Titus. "He has to. Very few emperors die naturally. He has two fears. One is for the health of the empire. And one is for his own health. The problem for Rome is that, no matter what the emperor thinks, the two are rarely the same."

"And if he has to choose between the two?" Falco asked.

"What would you choose in his place?" Cassius asked in return.

* * *

Kaia stood on the high mountain pass, looking back toward Delphi. She could sense the oracle standing in the sacred grove, looking up at her in the darkness, miles away. Reluctantly, she turned back on Delphi and strode off into the darkness toward the shoreline and transport to Rome.

As she walked, she searched for the third eye she had always had, an ability to see things distant in time or place. She had seen the man the oracle had told her of. The killer. Not his face, but his essence. She had no doubt she would know him when she saw him. Then she turned her inner gaze toward Rome. She could feel the power of the empire all around her, but there was a dark cancer in it, under it.

She saw a mountain with a cloud at the top. Then she heard the oracle's voice echoing in her mind. *The month of Augustus. The twenty-fourth day. Remember.*

CHAPTER SIX

THE PRESENT

Dane was more concerned with rubbing his dog Chelsea's ears than what the Secretary of Defense was saying. He'd missed Chelsea, an old golden retriever, whom he'd been forced to leave behind when traveling to the Caribbean. Her tail thumped against his chair as he scratched, to the annoyance of the chairman of the Joint Chiefs to Staff, who was seated to his right. Ariana Michelet was seated to his left.

They were deep under the Pentagon in the War Room, and the mood was grim. Dane didn't need his special ability to pick that up. Situation displays along the wall of the conference room showed the devastation in Iceland, Puerto Rico, and Connecticut wreaked by the Shadow. And they were no closer to knowing what the Shadow was.

Dane shifted his attention from Chelsea to the podium when Foreman took the Secretary of Defense's place. He had first met Foreman over forty years ago at a secret CIA base camp in Cambodia, just before he had unknowingly gone with his team into the Angkor gate. He hadn't trusted Foreman then, and didn't' trust him now, but he did acknowledge that the CIA man was the foremost expert on the planet on what little was known about the gates. Despite being well over 80, Foreman was in surprisingly good health, as if his personal war against the Shadow gave him some special energy.

"We stopped this assault through the Bermuda Triangle gate." Foreman didn't waste time on preliminaries. "And we stopped the first attack before that, through the Angkor gate. I don't think we're going to be able to stop a third attack."

"Hell," the chairman of the Joint Chiefs said, "let's just throw some nukes through one of these things."

"And most likely get them thrown back at us," Foreman said. "Gentlemen, let us remember that the Shadow has shown itself to be quite adept at using our own weapons against us."

Dane stirred. "The Shadow will come at us in a new way. We were lucky the first two times. They used our satellites against us the first time and our own nuclear weapons off the *Wyoming* the second. I think it's obvious the Shadow learns from its mistakes."

Ariana Michelet leaned forward. "The Shadow knows how to cause mass destruction. The loss of Iceland proves that. It used the juncture of two tectonic plates in the Mid-Atlantic Ridge and gave the forces there a nudge, and look what happened.

"I just checked, and Professor Nagoya in Japan has picked up muonic transmissions indicating the Shadow is probing out the Devil's Sea gate off the coast of his country and measuring the Ring of Fire that surrounds the Pacific Rim. If they can do there what they did in Iceland, then half the world could be destroyed. I think Iceland was just a test."

"The Shadow destroyed Atlantis over ten thousand years ago," Dane said, "So we know they have the capability to do more than they did in Iceland."

"We don't even know what these gates are," Ariana noted.

Foreman answered, "They could be a door to another dimension in our own world; one that we have not been able to access yet but coexists with the world we know. Or they could be a gateway to an alternate universe. Or they could be an attempt by an alien culture to open an interstellar gateway from their planet to ours.

"The Russians had a theory," Foreman continued. "In 1964 three of their scientist with backgrounds in electronic, history, and engineering published a paper in *Khimiyai Zhizn;* the journal of the old Soviet Academy of Sciences, titled 'Is the Earth a Large Crystal?' Their theory was that a matrix of cosmic energy was built into our planet when it was formed, and these gates are at key junctures of this matrix. They divided the world into twelve pentagonal slabs. On top of those slabs they drew twenty equilateral triangles. Using this overlay, they pointed out that these lines along the edges of the triangles have had a great influence on the world in many ways: fault lines for earthquakes lie along them: magnetic anomalies exist; ancient civilizations tended to be clustered along some of them.

"The places where the triangles met they labeled Vile Vortices, which also happen to be where most of our gates are located, so they were onto something, even if some of their logic was off. They put together a mathematical formula to explain the fluctuation of the Vile Vortices based on a crystalline structure.

"I initially dismissed that theory," Ariana said, "because the lithosphere, the upper level of our planet, has been moving for millions of years. Thus a crystal formation would not be consistent in location, but perhaps this formation is deeper than the lithosphere.

"Perhaps they weren't so far off," Ariana continued. She turned to Dane. "When Sin Fen transformed, her head changed into a crystal to channel the energy of the pyramid?"

Dane nodded. The memory of what happened to Sin Fen on top of the underwater pyramid near the Bermuda Triangle gate was something he would never forget.

"I also did some research and found out that this isn't the first time crystal skulls have been seen. Apparently it is quite a popular subject among New Age enthusiasts and several skulls have been found in different places."

"Where?" Dane asked.

"South America, Russia, other places. It's hard to pin down because most of the skulls are in private hands, and there is also quite a variety of skulls out there."

Dane considered that. "Were they found near pyramids?"

"I don't know," Ariana said.

"The only thing that has worked against the gates is this ancient weapon, combining a person like Sin Fen with the pyramid and Naga staff," Dane said. " I think we need to track down these crystal skulls. Try to find where they came from."

"That's a good idea," Ariana agreed.

"The ancient people had help fighting the Shadow," Dane said. "We saw that by what just happened in the Bermuda Triangle gate. Whatever that temple was, I don't think it was human technology that designed it. We should send someone to check the pyramid where Sin Fen and I were. And we need to get in contact with these Ones Before. I believe that the enemy of our enemy is our friend. My teammate Sergeant Flaherty told me that also."

"Your teammate who disappeared over forty years ago," the chairman of the Joint Chiefs noted, "and who reappeared to you not looking any older in Cambodia. Right."

"I can't explain it," Dane said. "All I can do is tell you what happened. You saw the *Scorpion* and its crew. The same thing. Disappeared for decades and reappeared with everyone looking exactly the same as the day they were lost."

"And then destroying the sub pens at Croton," the Chairman noted. "So why should we believe your friend Flaherty?"

Dane spread his hands. "Then believe what you want. It doesn't get us any closer to solving our problem."

"How do we get in contact with the Ones Before?" the Secretary of Defense asked.

"We go into a gate," Dane said.

"That hasn't been very healthy," Ariana noted.

"That's because we only entered gates when the Shadow opened them," Foreman noted. "And we've only been able to go to the part of the gate that's on our planet, where the Shadow has extended its influence. What we have to do is go through the gate into the Shadow's world."

"How do you propose to do that?" Dane asked.

"Professor Nagoya is working on that," Foreman said. "It appears that there are two phases to a gate. The fog and blackness that comes into our planet is sort of the foyer they project into our world. But somewhere inside that gate is a smaller area, which is the actual doorway to the Shadow's side, which Nagoya calls a portal." Foreman checked his watch. "In fact, the first phase of Nagoya's operation is about to commence. Dr. Nagoya has discovered some muonic traces that indicate there may be another 'graveyard' like one you found in the Caribbean. He's detected a larger chamber in the deepest part of the ocean—the Challenger Deep. We've sent a specially rigged submersible to check it out."

"What's that got to do with the next phase?" Dane asked.

"We want to see if there is any reaction to the submersible from the Devil's Sea gate, which isn't far from there," Foreman said. "If we get activity, Nagoya can use the data he picks up to check this theory and try to pin-point the Devil's Sea gate.

Mount Everest could be dropped in the Challenger Deep with six thousand feet of water still between its peak and the surface. It was the deepest point on the surface of the planet, the lowest spot in the Marianas Trench, which swept in a fifteen-hundred-mile arc from just below Iwo Jima to south of Guam. It was due south of the Devil's Sea gate, an area off the coast of Japan where mysterious disappearances of planes and boats had been recorded throughout history.

For the two members of the crew of *Deepflight III*, the opportunity to dive into the Challenger Deep was the equivalent of a climber given the opportunity to go up Everest. The major difference was the somber tone to the preparations as the craft was lowered over the side of its tender ship the USS *Roger Reveille*.

Deepflight III was a radical departure from previous submersibles. It looked more like an airplane than a submarine. The crew compartment was a titanium sphere in the center. Wings with controllable flaps extended from each side. Forward of the sphere a specially designed beak that reduced drag when the submersible was moving forward. In the rear were two vertical fins right behind the dual propeller system.

The sphere was solid with just two holes in it; one a section that screwed out to allow ingress, egress, and the second, smaller one that accessed control and command cables. To see outside, the crew used various cameras and radar. Powerful spotlights were bolted all around the craft, allowing the crew to illuminate the area immediately around it. It was forty feet long, and the wingspan was fifteen feet. The submersible had been hastily rigged with a pod, the purpose of which had not been explained to the crew.

Inside *Deepflight*, Captain Gann insured that all checklists for the dive were completed, and then turned to his partner, Lieutenant Murphy. "Ready, Murphy?"

"Ready."

"Release umbilicals."

"Released."

"We're going down."

"The submersible is at ten thousand meters' depth," Ahana reported. "The pod is working." She looked up from her computer monitor. "Sir, do those men in *Deepflight* know what exactly their mission is?"

"Reconnaissance," Nagoya replied shortly.

"Their *real* mission," Ahana amended.

"That is Foreman's responsibility," Nagoya said.

"Sir . . ." she began, but stopped.

"It is dangerous," Nagoya agreed. "But the pod is designed to be jettisoned. We don't know what the reaction from the Shadow will be or if there will even be a reaction."

"And if there isn't?"

"Then we send the submersible into the gate itself. We're hoping by just approaching the graveyard and using the pod to send out the frequency we've determined that we will draw some sort of reaction, but the crew will have a chance to escape. The odds are much lower if they have to go into the gate."

"And Russia?"

"Kolkov says he is working on a plan to insert their pod. That is phase two."

Deepflight III passed through nine thousand meters. It was descending into the center of the Marianas Trench, radar making sure they were clear of walls on either side. Gann and Murphy were focused on navigation, insuring that everything was functioning correctly. With the outside pressure at seven tons per square inch, the slightest malfunction could be fatal.

"Depth to bottom?" Gann asked.

"Two thousand, one hundred thirty-three meters," Murphy replied.

"Right on target."

"There," Ahana was pointing at her computer screen. The solid black triangle marking the Devil's Triangle gate was changing shape, the southernmost side stretching as if giving birth.

"Everyone ready!" Nagoya yelled. His assistants bustled; making sure their gear was tracking correctly. They all watch as a circle separated from the triangle and began moving southward picking up speed.

"Just like the sphere from the Bermuda gate." Ahana finally said.

In the War Room, Dane looked up as Foreman activated a screen that relayed what was being picked up by Nagoya's people in Japan.

"We have activity from the Devil's Sea gate," The CIA man announced.

They could all clearly see the sphere of muonic activity moving southward.

"What's it going for?" Dane asked.

"Our probe," Foreman said.

The Secretary of Defense and chairman of the Joint Chiefs rushed out to the main operations center, leaving Foreman alone in the conference room.

"Does the crew know they're bait?" Dane asked.

"They know enough to do the mission," Foreman said.

On *Deepflight*, Gann and Murphy were completely unaware of the sphere coming toward them. The bottom of the Challenger Deep was thirteen hundred meters below when Murphy noticed an anomaly on the radar screen.

"Captain, check the side-looking radar."

Gann looked at the screen and saw what had grabbed his partner's attention. The bounce back from the north wall had suddenly become totally smooth. Gann immediately stopped their descent.

"Distance to bottom?" Gann asked.

"Twelve hundred meters."

"Let's take a look." Gann goosed the propellers, guiding them toward the north face. "External lights on."

Murphy flipped on the switch activating the powerful searchlights mounted on the top and bottom of the submersible.

"Cameras on," Gann ordered.

The video monitors flickered, and then came alive, showing the glow of lights but nothing else.

"Range to the north wall?" Gann asked.

"Four hundred meters."

"What do you think it is?"

"Either the most perfect underwater geological formation that ever occurred or somebody built something down here," Murphy answered.

"At eleven thousand meters?"

'I'm just telling you what the data indicates."

"Range to wall?"

"Three hundred meters."

The largest man-made underwater craft is the Russian Typhoon class submarine, which is one hundred seventy-one meters long, just shy of two football fields in length, and displaces twenty-six thousand, five hundred tons. The black sphere that was heading toward the Challenger Deep dwarfed even a Typhoon, being almost seven hundred meters in diameter. It was not only larger than any man-made moving object; it was larger than most man-made stationary objects, including the Great Pyramid.

It also moved faster than any man-made submersible, punching through the ocean at eighty knots.

"Fifty meters," Murphy warned, and Gann slowed *Deepflight* to a crawl.

As Murphy watched the radar screens, Gann shifted his attention to the video monitors.

"Forty. Thirty. Twenty."

Gann bought them to a dead halt. "Look," he said to Murphy.

Directly in front of them the rock wall on the North Side of the Deep gave way to a smooth, gray surface. The edge of the gray curved slightly downward.

"Do a down scan along the wall," Gann ordered.

Murphy did so and whistled. "We've got a perfectly round, flat wall in front of us, over a half mile in diameter."

"So what is it?"

In the War Room, Dane saw the image relayed from *Deepflight's* camera and could have answered Captain Gann's question. What was on screen was exactly like the doorway they had discovered in the Milwaukee Deep off the coast of Puerto Rico, which led to a large chamber where all the craft lost in the Bermuda Triangle had been stored. His gaze shifted from the image to the display showing the large sphere that had left the Devil's Sea gate, closing on the Challenger Deep. He got up and walked up to Foreman.

"Are you going to warn them?" Dane asked him.

"What good would it do?" Foreman replied.

"You sent them there deliberately."

"It's war. Even you must accept that now."

'It's easy to send other men to their deaths, isn't it?"

Foreman turned. "No, it isn't easy, and I'm getting sick of you trying to take the moral high ground. I'm worried about the survival of our species, and you give me grief over every single individual involved."

"Our species is made up of individuals," Dane said. "Why didn't you let the *Deepflight* crew know what their mission was?"

"Would it have made a difference?"

"What exactly is their mission? Did you send them to find the door or draw something out of the gate?"

"Both."

Dane picked up something from Foreman's guarded mind. "What were they transmitting?"

"The pod they took with them was transmitting muons on a frequency that Dr. Nagoya felt would draw attention from the Shadow."

"Mission accomplished," Dane said. "Now get them out of there."

"There isn't enough time for them to get to the surface," Foreman said. "And even if they did, what makes you think the surface is going to be safe? Remember what happened to the crew of the *Glomar*. It's called sunk cost, and there's no way around. We knew there was a good chance that anything we set there was going to draw a reaction and that if it did, there was nothing we could do about it."

"They can hide inside the graveyard," Dane said. "We went through a smaller door in the center of the door we found in the Atlantic. Have them search for it."

'How do you think those craft in the graveyard you visited got there?" Foreman asked.

"Most likely the sphere," Dane said, "but it's worth a chance." He looked at the display. "They don't have much time. They might be safe in there."

"All right," Foreman agreed. He picked up a handset and called to the submersible via the *Reveille*.

Gann and Murphy were mesmerized by the massive door they had uncovered when Foreman's voice came over the radio.

"*Deepflight*, this is Angel Six. Over."

Gann picked up the mike. "This is *Deepflight*. Over."

"Do exactly what I tell you to," Foreman said. "Go to the center of the circle. Look for a smaller black circle there. Go into it. Jettison the attached pod before you go in."

"What is this?" Gann demanded.

"You don't have time to argue or ask questions," Foreman said. "You've got an enemy bogey heading your way."

"Enemy bogey?" Gann repeated glancing at Murphy.

A new voice cut in. "This is *Reveille*. Roger that, *Deepflight*! Roger that! Something very big is coming this way. Range ten kilometers and closing at eighty knots. It's freaking huge, and it is not responding to hails!"

Gann shoved the controls, turning the nose of *Deepflight* toward the ocean bottom. He increased the throttle, and they headed down.

"*Reveille*, this is Angel Six. Recommend you head away at flank speed."

"Roger that."

Dane watched the sphere closing on the Challenger Deep as relayed from Nagoya's computers and integrated with the Department of Defense positioning information on both *Deepflight* and the *Reveille*. It was going to be very close. He felt impotent, unable to influence what was about to happen.

* * *

"Geez, look at that," Murphy whispered. "Whatever's coming is filling the entire screen in the north."

Gann didn't have time to look at the radar. He was navigating visually, staying oriented on the gray wall.

"There," Gann said as the gray changed to black. He had the submersible do a roll, and then the nose was pointing at a small black circle.

"Looks solid to me," Murphy said.

Gann finally spared a glance at the radar. He saw what had shocked Murphy. A curved edge had filled the entire top half of the screen, and it was coming closer. The only thing he'd ever seen that big moving was an iceberg, but this thing was coming under its own power.

"I'm going in," Gann said as he edged forward on the controls.

"Don't forget we need to jettison the pod," Gann said. "Do it."

On board the *Reveille*, the engines were maxed out as the ship made to the south. On the bridge, the captain was watching the approaching sphere on radar also. Unfortunately, the ship was built for research, not speed or combat, so even at full throttle they could only make eighteen knots. And they had no weapons on board, although the captain doubted that any weapons they might have would be effective against whatever was coming.

Deepflight blinked out of existence on the status board, the image of the sphere completely filling the canyon deep inside the Challenger Deep, the video feed from the submersible going blank.

Dane sat down at the conference table and shook his head. "How many on board?"

"Two," Foreman said. His attention still on the board. "Damn," Foreman muttered.

Dane looked up. The sphere was moving, ascending. "It's going after the *Reveille*."

Foreman picked up the microphone. "*Reveille*, this is Angel Six. Over."

"We've got it on radar, range five thousand meters horizontal, nine thousand meters vertical and closing. Any suggestion would be helpful. Over."

Foreman looked at Dane, who simply shook his head.

"Five us a video feed," Foreman ordered.

A screen on the wall flickered, and then they could see the Pacific Ocean from the bridge of the *Reveille*. The water was perfectly calm, the sun shining. The only thing marring the tranquility of the scene were the increasingly anxious reports from the *Reveille*'s radar man coming out of the speakers.

"Range four thousand meters horizontal, seven thousand meters vertical, and closing at high speed."

"We're still waiting on any suggestions," the captain of the *Reveille* said. "Over."

"It might be bluffing," Foreman suggested.

"What the hell is it?" the captain demanded.

"We don't know," Foreman admitted.

"Great."

"Range three thousand meters horizontal, five thousand meters vertical, and closing at high speed."

Gann felt the air around him changing, the pressure increasing. His head pounded, and the video screen was dark.

"What is going on?" Murphy demanded.

The nose of the submersible had hit the dark circle just moments ago, and then slowly they'd gone into it, as if being absorbed. Alarms began going off. Gann ran through emergency procedures but could find nothing seriously wrong until he glanced at the outside pressure-reading gauge.

"That can't be," he murmured.

"What?"

"Outside pressure is one atmosphere."

"The gauge is broken," was Murphy's immediate assessment.

Both men blinked as the light inside increased dramatically as the three screens showing the outside view suddenly brightened far beyond what the searchlights could do.

"Where are we?" Murphy whispered. His training took hold, and he checked his instruments. He didn't believe what he was seeing, but he reported it anyway. "I've got a reading of the surface ten meters above us."

"That would explain the atmospheric reading," Gann observed. He checked the radio, trying to reach the *Reveille* and Angel Six, but only static came back. "Let's see where we are," he finally said.

* * *

The sphere was solid black and perfectly round. There was no external sign of a form of propulsion; nevertheless, it was pushing through the water at high speed, closing on the *Reveille*.

It was also picking up anything in its path via a hole that had irised open on the very front, about fifty meters wide. It had swallowed the transmitting pod before halting in front of the large door, then reversing direction and heading for the surface.

"Range zero meters horizontal, one thousand meters vertical, and rising at high speed. Closing on us, sir," the radar man added, a quaver in his voice.

The captain of the *Reveille* nodded. He opened the door that led to the bridge wing on the right side and stepped out onto it, a crewman following him with a video camera that was connected by satellite to the War Room. The captain leaned over and looked down at the smooth ocean, waiting.

On the top portion of the sphere, the opening grew as the metal irises moved back. As the sphere got closer to the surface and the *Reveille*, the opening grew larger until it encompassed a quarter of the surface.

"Oh God," those in the War Room heard the captain of the *Reveille* exclaim. Then they saw what had caused the reaction as the video camera was pointed downward.

Rising out of the water all around the *Reveille* was the edge of the opening in the sphere, water pouring down the side of the massive object until the edge was a hundred meters above the mast of the ship. Then the opening began to iris shut, daylight disappearing rapidly as it closed.

The screen went blank.

* * *

Captain Gann threw the hatch open and blinked in the bright light, trying to get his bearings. The air was stale, with a texture to it that Gann couldn't identify. He was in a huge, semicircular space. The submersible was floating in the center of a body of water that extended a mile and half in all directions. Above, a bright, glowing orb illuminated everything. Beyond the water, a black beach two miles in width ran up to the wall that curved around overhead to the light.

What caught Gann's attention, though, were the planes and boats that littered the black beach. Thousands of them. He saw an ancient Polynesian raft beached next to a modern oil tanker; a jet fighter with Russian markings next to a biplane. It was overwhelming, a veritable mechanical graveyard of the ages.

"It's moving again," Dane noted. He watched the progress of the sphere on the screen for several seconds, then realized what he was seeing. "It's heading back to the Deep."

There was no sign of the *Reveille* in the live spy satellite feed they had of the area. The ship had disappeared, swallowed up by the sphere.

"Look at that!" Murphy exclaimed, pointing.

Gann shifted the binoculars in that direction. A silver-skinned plane with two engines, one on each wing, was on the black beach. Among all the other craft here, he found nothing particularly spectacular about that particular plane.

"A Lockheed Electra," Murphy said. He twisted the knob on his binoculars. "A Lockheed Electra 10E!"

"And?" Gann was trying to absorb the variety of ships and planes he was seeing. Some he didn't' recognize at all.

"Do you know what the *E* in the 10E stands for?" Murphy didn't wait for an answer. "Earhart. That's Amelia Earhart's plane!"

Both men staggered as a large bubble of air broke the surface just in front of the submersible, rocking the craft. Gann felt a spike of pain in both ears and realized there had been a sudden change of pressure. He leaned over and looked down, just in time to see the top edge of the opening in the sphere break the surface all around the submersible.

* * *

"The sphere is heading back for the gate," Ahana reported, even though Nagoya could clearly see that on the screen.

"What about the probe?" he asked.

Ahana flipped a switch, and a red dot appeared inside the sphere.

"Working."

"Excellent."

They watched as the dot entered the black triangle marking the boundaries of the Devil's Sea gate."

"Do you have a lock on that position?" Nagoya asked anxiously.

"Locked and all data recorded," Ahana confirmed.

In the War Room, Dane saw the red dot appear. "What's that?"

"The sphere must have sucked in the pod," Foreman said.

"What about *Deepflight*?" Ariana asked.

"No sign," Foreman said.

"How does this probe open the gate?" Dane asked.

"You'll have to ask Nagoya that," Foreman said. "We aren't even certain it will work. But it's a good sign that we can track it. Pack your gear; we're heading to Japan. By the time we get there Nagoya should have been able to analyze the data the probe is sending."

Ariana had been on her laptop while all this was occurring. "I've located someone who claims to be an expert on crystal skulls in New York City. Also, the Museum of Natural History has one in its collection. I've arranged to meet with a museum representative and the expert this evening."

Dane stood. "Keep in touch."

"I will." She paused. "We're missing something."

Dane paused. "What do you mean?" Foreman was already out of the room, heading for the elevator.

"Nagoya is coming up with theories, Foreman has been studying these gates almost all of his life, and yet we still know almost nothing about them or the Shadow, or the Ones Before." She spread her long fingers, covering several of the gates marked on the globe. "I don't know what it is, but we're missing something very important."

"I know we are," Dane agreed. He smiled. "If you find out what it is, let me know, OK?"

"Be careful," Ariana warned.

"I will."

"Don't trust Foreman."

"That's a given."

CHAPTER SEVEN

THE PAST
79 A.D.

Emperor Vespasian had been dead for one day short of two months. There had been the obligatory month of mourning. Then the month-long games celebrating the new emperor, Titus, had begun. They would end on the next day. The games had been such a success that Titus had already begun plans for a bigger arena, to be called the Coliseum, which would be built so that larger and more elaborate games could be held with more spectators than the current arena could hold. It had long been said that as long as the emperor provided bread and games, he would stay in power.

In the Imperial Palace on the Palatine hill, Titus walked through empty rooms that had been cleared of his father Vespasian's things and awaited his. He had watched his father's ascent to power from the son of a tax collector to emperor, and he had learned much in the process. One key lesson was to look for plots everywhere and stop them before they had a chance to gain momentum. It is with this in mind that Titus went down a long corridor where two Praetorian Guards waited. As he approached, they saluted and opened the tall doors.

Titus entered his audience chamber and went directly to the chair set on a dais. His senior advisers were all in place, waiting. Titus leaned back, head against the high back of the chair. Only two months and already he felt the weight of the empire on his shoulders. He raised a finger to Thyestes, the Greek who had also been Vespasian's adviser. Thyestes had the pulse of Rome, it was said, and thus knew the health of the empire and, more importantly, the health of the emperor.

Thyestes bowed, then stepped onto the dais, leaning close so only Titus could hear. "Yes, Emperor."

"Tell me about General Cassius."

Thyestes was a tall, thin man. He had thick, white hair and the long, bushy beard that so many of the Greeks favored. His face was pinched, and he always looked like he was experiencing a bad bowel movement. He had a long staff in his right hand, a symbol of power as the emperor's voice. His old fingers curled over the end of the staff as he composed his answer.

"Cassius retired to his country estate with his Jewess. She died last year of the fever, and he did not take it well. Since then, he has been occupying himself taking long walks and planting a garden."

"Cassius a gardener?" Titus was surprised. He couldn't envision the old warrior as such. "And his loyalty?"

"Is to Rome and to the Army."

Titus knew what that short answer meant. Cassius, despite his retirement, held great sway with the legions. And the legions were the seat of power.

"And the gladiator Falco? He served with Cassius, and I saw today that he is very popular with the crowd in the arena." The crowd was a dangerous thing in the city. Let the grain stop flowing for a day or two, and they might storm the Palatine.

"Falco is an odd man," Thyestes said. "He is involved with Domidicus' wife, Epione. She plays with him, something that might come back to harm her in more ways than she can imagine."

Titus knew Epione. She was a powerful and dangerous woman. "What do you mean?"

"She bought Falco's children while he was in the legion and secreted them away. With this power, she makes him fight, even though he was granted his freedom from his service in the X Legion. Now, he is under the *lanista* Gaius Marcus, but he really fights for her. She holds out to him the promise she will free his children one day. That day has never come."

Women. Titus knew they were like vipers. Domidicus was an ally, a powerful member of the Senate. A threat to Domidicus was a threat to the emperor. If Epione was undermining her husband's position... Titus filed that thought away for the moment. There was also the issue that Gaius Marcus worked for him, not Epione.

"Does she take any of Falco's purse?"

"No. She likes the power of controlling such a man. He has a reputation of being as good in the bedroom as he is in the arena."

"Is there a link between Falco and Cassius?"

"Other than their service together? None that I know of."

Titus relaxed slightly. The thought of a general popular with the army and a gladiator popular with the people conspiring together had him worried. But hearing that Cassius was gardening and Falco was in a woman's thrall reduced that fear. "What do you have?" he asked, indicating the doors beyond which those who wanted to see the emperor waited.

"There is a most strange envoy from Delphi I believe you should see first."

Titus frowned. He knew the waiting hall must be packed with supplicants and envoys.

Thyestes held out his hand and uncurled his fingers. A ring lay on the Greek palm. "It is Caesar's."

There had been many Caesars, Titus knew, including himself now, but he knew from Thyestes's tone who he was referring to. The first emperor, Julius himself. The ring was gold with a jewel set in the center.

"The envoy had it. It is not well known, but Caesar did stop at Delphi on his way to Egypt to consult the oracle."

"The oracle did not warn him of Cleopatra," Titus noted with a laugh.

"Actually, I believe she *did* warn him of Cleopatra," Thyestes said.

Titus scowled. "What does this envoy want?"

"She would not tell me."

"She?"

"A priestess of the oracle."

Titus rubbed a finger along his bottom lip. Priestesses and oracles. He had learned they either lied to give false good news or were honest and thus delivered bad news.

"Clear the chamber, then admit her," Titus ordered.

Thyestes emptied the room, then went to the double doors that were directly opposite Titus. The room between was lined with larger than life statues of all the previous Caesars looking down on those who came forward to see the present emperor. Thyestes rapped on the door, and they swung open, admitting a woman dressed in trousers and a short-sleeved tunic under a long, black, unadorned cloak. As the doors shut behind her, Titus studied her. She was tall, impressive looking, almost what he would consider Amazonian, and her red hair was quite striking, most unlike a Greek. He had seen some of the women of the Germans who fought next to their men, and she would fit in quite well with those maddened shrews who threw themselves onto Roman swords so their men could strike.

"Most noble emperor," the woman bowed at the waist but did not kneel as proper protocol directed.

Titus let it pass. If she was one who delivered false good news, he would have her head on a stake on the walls of the palace. If she delivered bad news, he might also do the same, he mused.

"What do you know that is so important you could not tell Thyestes?" he demanded.

"My name is Kaia. I come from the oracle with grave news."

Not a sycophant, then, Titus knew. He was disappointed. He might have had some fun with her before having her head lopped off. He held up the ring. "Thyestes tells me this was Julius Caesar's."

"The oracle gave it to me as a way to gain admittance with my message."

"It must be an important message," Titus noted.

"There is a threat to not only your empire but the entire world." Kaia said simply.

A half smile curled the left side of Titus's mouth. "A most dire pronouncement. What is this threat?"

"A Shadow grows in the land north of your province in Regnum Bosporus," Kaia said.

Titus waited. Bospora was on the north side of Ponus Euxius, the sea north of Persia. It was a poor region that he didn't even really control other than on paper, a place of barbarians and little profit.

"The Shadow is in the form of a gate to a terrible place. It opens every so often, and when it does, death and destruction spew forth into our world."

"Why should I be concerned about a shadow outside of my kingdom." Titus asked.

"Because its reach is far. It has already sent its power in the land under your feet. And it will grow stronger the longer this gate remains open."

"Where does this gate lead to?" Thyestes asked.

"I do not know," Kaia admitted.

"How does it send power under our feet?" Titus demanded. "It there a god on the other side of this gate?"

"Something with the power of gods is there," Kaia said.

"Do you have proof of this?" Titus asked.

"The oracle has foreseen it. And it has happened before. My homeland in Thera was destroyed long ago by this Shadow."

Titus knew of Thera. He had sailed by there on his way to Palestine. It was obvious to anyone that the island had been smashed by some terrible force long ago.

"I do not doubt the word of the oracle," Titus said, "but I have learned that such words can have many meanings. Isn't that the way you can keep all your supplicants happy?"

"I am not here to make you happy." Kaia's eyes met his. "Tomorrow you will see the power of the Shadow not far from here."

Titus straightened. "What do you mean?"

"You will see the power of the Shadow come out of the Earth itself. Then we will speak again. I mean no disrespect, Emperor, and I understand your reluctance to believe me, but tomorrow I think there will be no questions."

Titus glanced at Thyestes, then back at the priestess. "You speak very boldly in the presence of the emperor of the known world. You will stay in the palace tonight and tomorrow attend the games under the guard of my

Praetorians. If I happen to miss this display of power tomorrow, I will have you placed in the arena for my amusement, and your head will adorn the wall of my palace tomorrow evening.

"You will not miss it," Kaia assured him.

"I will let you visit your children after the games are over," Epione said. "I've even been thinking of freeing them."

"You lie," Falco said.

Epione indicated for him to start rubbing her other foot. Falco was on his knees, his scarred hands working the tender flesh of her feet. They were in her quarters, adjacent to the Imperial Palace. Falco had come here after dark, and he knew he would be leaving before dawn, after he had performed for her.

Epione laughed. "That is what makes you such a darling. All these other men, they are so afraid of being blunt, especially with me, but not my gladiator Falco. He says what he thinks, no matter what the consequences might be."

"Things cannot be worse for me," Falco observed.

"Things can always get worse," Epione said. "You need more wine, I do, too." She signaled for him to get the jug.

Falco was already light-headed from the potent fine wine, nothing at all like the slop served at the gladiator school. As he poured, he considered the noblewoman lounging in front of him. She was older than he, in her mid-forties. Why she had chosen him to be her toy, he didn't know, and he regretted that she had ever laid eyes on him.

He had been with her once, before he went into the army, and she had been waiting when he came back. That one time, as a slave, he could not refuse her, and he had never told Drusilla about it, although he knew that she knew something had happened. But they had both spent their lives in captivity and accepted, in the way those with no choice did, the things their lowly fate bound them to. The mistake he had made was using his special power of sense to please the lady, hoping that by doing so he might earn a powerful ally, which every slave could use. He had performed too well, he knew in retrospect.

He had certainly never expected Epione to do what she had done after Drusilla died while he was in Palestine. Phaedra and Fabron were the only things he had to come back to, and she had taken them away.

"Actually, my gladiator, I do not totally lie," Epione said as he handed her a full chalice of wine.

Falco sat and waited.

'I will not free them. I am not done with you yet."

"When will you be?"

She laughed and took a drink. "I don't know. When it strikes me to. They have not earned their freedom like you did."

"What was not a lie then?"

"I may let you see them. I think you think I lie about them. That maybe they died also with the fever as did your dear Drusilla, who you constantly mope over."

Falco had indeed considered that possibility, but he had not dared take the gamble that she did lie. Plus, sometimes he had visions of them, but he was never certain if he could trust those visions. "Where are they?"

"Pompeii. With a trusted friend of mine."

Falco felt a fist thud into his heart.

"I will allow you to travel there the day after tomorrow when you are done with the games. You will meet your spawn. And then you will come back here and continue to serve me."

Two days. Falco remembered the vision he had had. Of Vesuvius. If there were gods who determined such things, would they control the fury of the mountain for two more days?

Epione lay back on her couch. "Now, more wine, my gladiator."

CHAPTER EIGHT

THE PRESENT

Pytor and Felix Shashenka saw the cooling towers first as the helicopter approached the Chernobyl Reactor. Three were intact, one was covered in a sarcophagus of concrete. This was not their first trip here. They had come many times before to pay their respects to their brother's tomb, the mass of concrete enclosing Reactor Four.

Today was different in one important aspect. They were here to conduct a mission. The twins were both officers in the Russian Army, both serving in the elite Spetsnatz commandos, and both had volunteered for this mission. But it was Pytor who had the cancer, and thus it was Pytor who would go.

The helicopter landed next to Reactor Three, which was still in operation along with the other two. Pytor and Felix got off, each carrying a heavy backpack. Several soldiers were waiting for them, also Spetsnatz and heavily armed.

"This way," the major in charge of the security detail indicated. They followed as he approached the massive edifice of concrete that covered Reactor Four. Two soldiers flanked a steel door, which the major opened with great effort. They were in a tunnel that had been bored into the concrete. The corridor went ten meters, then ended in a room protected with lead shielding. Numerous video monitors lined one wall. Pytor and Felix put the packs down and went to the monitors. This monitoring station was highly classified and had never been shown to the foreigners who came to the area to check levels of radioactivity.

"That's the core," the major said. "We had to send in a remote-controlled robot to put the camera in place."

But both brothers were looking at a different monitor, the one featuring the remains of the control room. There were several skeletons littering the floor.

"They died instantly, the gas burning the flesh from their bones," the major said. "A better fate than the ones who got a fatal dose and died the slow death."

Pytor and Felix knew one of those skeletons was Andrej. And they knew everything the major was telling them as Pytor had been the commander of the first group to watch the reactor. There was little doubt in both their minds that is when the cancer started. Even though the control room was heavily shielded, the entire area was still a dangerous place.

"The orders I received--" the major began.

"Yes?' Pytor asked. He was now looking at the core. The black triangle was still there, as it had been since that fateful day in 1986.

"Well, they said one of you was going in. Of course that must be wrong, is that not so?" The major was stumbling over his words.

'No, the orders are quite correct," Pytor said. He went over to one of the packs and opened it. He began pulling out pieces of a radiation suit.

"But it's hot in there. Even with that on, you'll get a fatal dose inside of a minute. No one's been in there since the explosion."

"I know that," Pytor said as he began pulling on the suit, Felix helping. "Have you picked up anything new in the monitoring?"

"There were some scientists here from the Academy of Sciences," the major said. "They picked up indications of time fluxes coming out of the triangle."

"Time fluxes?" For the first time Pytor was surprised. "How do they know that?"

"The time indicator on the video cameras shifts about. Sometimes running backward, sometimes making jumps." The major pointed at the monitor. "Whatever you have to do in there, why not use a robot?"

"There is not time to rig such a thing for what we want to do," Pytor said. "Perhaps I should take my anti-radiation pill?" he added, referring to the placebo tablets that used to be issued to all Russians soldiers with the instructions that if taken, they would protect them from radiation. He pulled out the helmet and set it on his head.

Felix picked up the second backpack and put it on Pytor's shoulders.

"Where is the new access point?" Felix asked.

The major pointed to a steel door on the side of the chamber. "You go through there. Down a corridor fifty meters, then it turns left to another door. That door leads to the air chamber. You hit the red button. When it turns green, you go in. Then you reverse the process to come out, but--" the major fell silent. They all knew that once someone went inside, they could never come out. Even the remote robots that had been used over the years had to be left inside.

Felix gave his brother a hand as they went to the indicated door.

"Good luck," the major offered.

Pytor could hear his breathing inside the enclosed helmet. Sweat was already running down his back, and he knew it would get hotter. He almost laughed aloud at that thought: hotter. Soon he was going to be very hot indeed. The pack was heavy, and he had lost much strength in the last several months from the chemotherapy treatments. The doctors had given him two months at best, and they promised to be a very painful two months. Because of that, Pytor was actually grateful to be able to do this mission, to die doing something positive rather than wasting away in a hospital bed.

They reached the airlock, and Felix hit the button. A steel door slid up. Before Pytor stepped in, Felix wrapped his arms around his brother as well as he could, considering the pod his brother carried in addition to his air tank. They exchanged no words; everything that had needed to be said had already been discussed. Felix turned the valve on the oxygen tank, sending oxygen to his brother, then he stepped back. Pytor went into the lock, and Felix hit the bottom, closing the steel door.

Felix turned and walked toward the control to watch his brother conduct the mission.

Pytor flinched as the inner door opened. He knew with that simple opening he was now the walking dead. He laughed once more. He had been the walking dead before he entered here. He stepped through. It was strange; there was dirt under his feet, the former outside of Reactor Four. He walked across the small open space toward the entrance to the control room. The world thought that the entire core and building had been buried under the concrete poured from the helicopters in the weeks after the explosion. But the black triangle had hollowed out a space, refusing to allow the concrete to pass, and when the concrete dried, the entire reactor was in the midst of an open space that made up the Chernobyl gate. Whatever field the triangle had propagated had subsequently disappeared, as the robots had been able to go in.

Pytor knew the rest of the world wanted the other three reactors shut down, the entire place abandoned, but there were two reasons Chernobyl was still in business: one was the desperate need for the power, and the second was the need to monitor this space and the black triangle inside.

Pytor felt his skin tingle, and he wasn't sure whether that was real or a product of his imagination. Could it be the radiation, slowly seeping through the suit, or could it be the barrier of the gate? If he was indeed inside the gate already. This gate was different from the others for some reason. Pytor had met with Professor Kolkov, the Russian expert on the gates, and the scientist had expressed his own uncertainty about why it was different.

Pytor didn't care that it was different. He didn't care about the science, Andrej had been the scientist amount the three brothers, and this thing had killed him. It was a matter of honor, an oath the three had sworn when Andrej had been the first to leave home, they would always be there for each other, and if anything happened to one, the others would revenge. Pytor had had to wait many years, but now he was taking the first step in that revenge. It would be up to Felix to complete it.

Pytor opened the door leading to the control center and stepped in. The skeletons littering the floor were the first things he noticed. He knelt in the center of the room and pulled a bunch of daisies from the top of the pack and placed them there. They had been given to him by Andrej's widow.

Then he went to the heavy door that led to the reactor core. Slowly he unbolted it and swung it open. He was drenched in sweat, and the inside of the mask was beginning to fog up. Even the oxygen coming from the tank tasted strange.

He stepped into the core and saw the black triangle. Each side was fifteen feet long, and the entire thing was about ten feet high. Its composition was hard to make out, not appearing solid, but the sides were perfectly straight. It was almost as if the triangle was made of a thick, black liquid. Pytor approached and stopped just a few feet short of the side. He knew Felix was watching on the video monitor, so he turned and waved. He reached out with his hand. As the glove touched the black, it felt as if it were going into molasses. He pulled his hand back out and looked at it. No apparent change. With no hesitation, he stepped into the black and was swallowed up.

"The second probe is transmitting," Ahana announced.

"Linkage?" Nagoya asked as he looked over her shoulder.

"The transmission is propagating," Ahana said as a red line on the screen began extending slowly toward the dot that represented the probe that had been taken into the Devil's Sea gate. "Contact," she said as the line met the dot.

The probes were preprogrammed to run through a variety of tests in contact with each other, and Nagoya stepped back to allow his people to accumulate the data.

Major Pytor Shashenka was kneeling over the probe. He smiled as he saw the readout scroll through various programs, indicating it was working. Then he looked around once more. He was in the center of the triangle, the floor beneath him perfectly smooth, the air full of that thick yellowish gray fog, just as Kilkov had told him areas inside the gates on Earth appeared. He realized this was an anteroom to the real portal. The fog was so thick he couldn't see the edge of the black triangle across from him.

He could feel the effects of the radiation now. His stomach was churning, his head pounding in pain. He was soaked in sweat. He vomited into his mask, fouling it. Bowing to the inevitable, he removed the mask. He knew he was shortening what little time he had left, but he saw no reason not to.

As the probe continued to work, he got up and walked around. His foot hit something, and he paused. Reaching down, he picked up the object. A bronze helmet with a chinstrap, the metal highly polished, he leather on the chinstrap oiled. A spasm passed through his body, and he collapsed to the floor next to the probe, the leather in his lap.

The air was foul almost oily. Pytor ran a hand across his forehead, wiping the sweat away. He placed the helmet on top of the probe. There were Lain numbers imprinted in the bronzed in the front. He squinted. XXV.

Most strange, he thought before he passed out.

In front of him, a circle of black appeared, eclipsing down to the floor until it was six feet high and three feet wide.

"We've got the Chernobyl probe!" Ahana announced. "Through the Devil's Sea gate," she added. "So there is a definite connection between the two on the other side."

"Excellent," Nagoya said. "Phase two is successful. Now it is time for phase three."

"Which is?" Ahana wanted to know.

"Going into the gate itself and opening a portal."

'How do you propose to do that?" Ahana asked.

Instead of answering, Nagoya asked a question in turn. "What do you think of the physics of the gates now that you have this data?"

"I think the muon emissions are important," Ahana said, "to understanding the gates." She had the data gathered from the probes spread out on a large table and was checking it as she spoke.

Nagoya nodded. "Muons are part of the second family of fundamental particles. Most of what we are used to in our world is in the first family, consisting of electrons, up-quarks, and down-quarks. The second family consists of muons, charm quarks, and strange quarks. And all these things are not single points, according to string theory, but rather a tiny one-dimensional loop hat that is vibrating. That gives it several characteristics that allow us to merge relativity and quantum mechanics."

Ahana considered that. "I understand what you are saying, but we cannot even see particles at that level. We only know they exist because of their effect, as evidence by the tank we are on top of."

Nagoya nodded. "I know, but you don't need to see something to manipulate it. Reverse what you just said. We know these basic particles exist because we can study their effect. Then why can't we use an effect to manipulate the particles?"

He continued, "I think this is what the Shadow is doing and why the muons we detect are not decaying as quickly as we believe they should. Because the Shadow is using the muons and the quarks." He held up a finger. "Power. That is the key. We know the Shadow likes to draw power from this side, whether it be in the form of radioactivity as it did at Chernobyl, or from the planet itself along the tectonic plates, one of the greatest, if slowest, powers on the planet. I think it uses the fault lines not just before attacking us but to draw power. That is what this is all about. And how many base forms of power are there?" he asked Ahana.

"There are four base forces in nature: gravity, electromagnetic, strong, and weak."

"Correct."

Ahana gave a slight smile. She viewed Nagoya as a father, and when he got in this mode, she felt a strong affection for him. It was how they had worked out many problems in the past, going to the elementary level and examining things from scratch.

"And the force particles for each?" Nagoya asked.

'For electromagnetic it is the photon. Gravity…well, it's postulated that there is a particle called the graviton but again, only because of effect, not that we've ever seen one. For strong, the particle is the gluon. And for weak, you have weak gauge bosons."

"I think the Shadow can manipulate the strong and weak forces," Nagoya said. "We can do so, but only crudely. A nuclear weapon explodes when we split atoms, and the strong forces are released. When uranium decays in a reactor, we are using weak forces. But what if you could manipulate strong and weak forces like we use electricity?"

"The power would be tremendous." Ahana was beginning to get excited. "Also, consider gravity. Very powerful, but we cannot manipulate it at all."

"Correct," Nagoya said. He held his hand up and let it drop to his side. "We fight it constantly. Think of the energy required to put a rocket into space. Something that weighs relatively little requires a tremendous expense of energy. Turn it around. Imagine the energy that is going the other way, all the time. But I do not think the Shadow can manipulate gravity. If so, there would be an inexhaustible supply anywhere in the universe. No." he shook his head. "It is the strong and weak forces at the smallest level that the Shadow controls.

"Imagine then," Nagoya continued, "if one could manipulate those forces at the smallest levels, then apply the right focus to bring it to the visible universe! I think that is what the gates are. Now, the issue is, how do we use that?'

Ahana's mind was racing. "The Shadow comes to our side and extends its environment to a certain extent into our world to tap power here. Would it not make sense that we could do the same to it? Go into their world and tap their power?"

"With what?" Nagoya asked.

Ahana pointed down at the superkamiokande. "We've only used this to receive, never to transmit. The first probe proved that we can make contact with the other side through the portals. The Russian probe proved that the gates are connected on the other side. What if we develop a portable superkamiokande and take it to a gate and transmit using the data we've just picked up?"

Nagoya considered that. "That might work, but I doubt if we could focus enough power to open the gate."

"We do what the Shadow does," Ahana said.

"What do you mean?"

"We take power from the Shadow's side like it's taking power from our side and bring it to bear at the portal."

"How?"

"We run an extension cord and plug in," Ahana said.

Pytor's eyes hurt to open. It was as if his eyelids were crusted shut. With great effort, he opened them and blinked, trying to clear his vision. His entire body throbbed with pain.

The first thing he saw was a smooth, white face with no mouth or nose, just two red eyes staring at him. He looked down. The body of the creature in front of him was also encased in white, something that looked like plastic, but he could tell it wasn't. A cloak covered its shoulders. He was startled to note the thing was floating a few inches off the ground.

His arms were locked to his sides, and straps ran over his chest and legs, holding him in place on a vertical table. He struggled to move, but there was no give to the straps. The air was strange, even thicker than where he had just been. Beyond the creature was a cavern hewn out of black stone.

Looking to his right. Pytor saw a row of tables similar to the one he was strapped to. He cried out as he saw the condition of the poor souls on them.

Many had been flayed, their skin gone, replaced by some sort of clear wrapping that glistened obscenely, revealing the muscles and internal organs beneath. Various leads went into the bodies, particularly the heads. Most of those he could see had had the top of the skulls neatly sliced off, and needles went into the exposed brains. The tops of the needles were small, glowing bulbs of various colors, the entire spectrum of the rainbow.

Piles of clothes lay near some of the bodies, and he could tell that some were the uniforms of American sailors. It was impossible, given the condition of the bodies, to tell nationalities. And they were alive. That was the worst part, as he watched the slow rise and fall of the chests of those nearest him.

He shifted his gaze back to the creature in front of him as it finally moved. Its left arm ending in a shining blade. The tip came forward to Pytor's sternum. He looked own and could see ugly red splotches on his skin, blisters breaking though as the radiation ran its course.

Another creature appeared, floating smoothly, a group of needles in one claw, a small red tube with a glowing tip in the other. The tube was raised, and despite his high level of pain, Pytor screamed as a beam cut into the top of his head, neatly cutting through flesh and bone, stopping a millimeter from his brain. With dazed eyes, he saw the top of this skull tossed to the ground in front of him. He distantly felt pokes as the second creature inserted needles into his brain.

He cursed at the creature in Russian as the first one slid the blade into his chest, smoothly parting the skin. The radiation was taking too long, he realized. And the cancer... The creature stopped the blade as if reading his mind. It turned and faced the other. They stayed like that for several moments as if exchanging information, then the second disappeared behind him. It reappeared a moment later with a pair of inverted forceps.

Pytor screamed as the tips went in between his ribs and split them open, shattering bone, exposing one of his diseased lungs. They seemed to find the cancer most interesting as both hovered there, probing and poking. Blood was flowing out of his chest, he could feel it seeping down over his legs, but one of the tubes that they had put in him was replacing it as quickly as it left.

Then they both disappeared. One—which one he had no idea— reappeared, with a tube. It jabbed it into his chest, right into his heart. Pytor finally passed out.

How long he was unconscious he didn't know, but when he awoke, one of the creatures was still in front of him. Pytor forced himself to look down. The creature with the blade was cutting, slicing his lung out of this chest. The other lung was already gone. Through his pain, Pytor was amazed. How was he alive? Or was this hell, he suddenly thought, and these were demons tormenting him?

And why was he able to tolerate the pain? It was bad but not what he would have imagined for the damage that had been done to his body. The tube that went into his chest pulsed, and he had to assume that it was supplying his blood with oxygen, although how, he had no idea.

The second creature floated into view, something lumpy and grayish red in its claws. A lung. Pytor had to look away as he felt them working on his chest. He passed out once more.

When he woke once more, the creature was simply there in front of him, not moving, unblinking red eyes staring at him. Pytor looked down. The same transparent wrap was over his chest, covering the muscle and bones. The tube was still stuck in his chest, and he realized he wasn't breathing: although not painful, this was the most disconcerting experience so far.

Seeing he was awake, the creature reached forward and ripped the tube from his chest with one abrupt jerk. Pytor gasped, air streaming into his mouth, down his throat and to the new lungs. He screamed, the sound echoing through the cavern.

Dane stood on the beach, staring out at Chelsea playing in the Pacific Ocean. The golden retriever would dash out with the surf, then retreat as each wave approached, then repeat it each time as if it were a new experience and she was surprised at the water coming in.

"You're not very bright," Dane said.

Chelsea turned and gave him a disapproving look, only to get soaked as the next wave hit her in the side. Dane was also startled as a voice suddenly caught his attention to his left.

"My brother disappeared out there in 1945." Foreman nodded toward the ocean off the coast of Japan. They were waiting for a helicopter to meet them and fly them north to meet with Nagoya. The runway was adjacent to the beach, and Dane had taken the opportunity to walk Chelsea. He had been surprised when Foreman accompanied him.

"You believe he went into the Devil's Sea gate?" Dane asked.

"The entire flight, minus my plane, simply disappeared," Foreman said. "I was spared because I had engine trouble and had to ditch. The weather was fine, visibility to the horizon. They were all experienced pilots on their way back to the carrier. We had the Japanese licked to the point where there was practically no opposition in the air. What else could have caused all those planes to vanish?"

Dane saw no reason to argue with Foreman's reasoning. The old man had his own crosses to bear with regard to the gates. "You recruited Sin Fen, didn't you?" Dane asked.

Foreman nodded. "She was living on the streets of Phnom Penh. Barely surviving. I sensed something about her, that she had some connection with the gates. Just as I sensed it about you."

"Are you sure you recruited her," Dane said, "and it wasn't the other way around?"

"What do you mean?"

"What she did to stop the Bermuda Triangle gate," Dane said, "was not normal, to say the least. She was special. It seems strange that you would be so lucky to simply find her on the streets of Phnom Penh. It seems more logical that she sought you out."

"What difference does it make?" Foreman asked.

"The difference," Dane said, "is that if she sought you out, then you're not running things like you want to believe." He let the silence after that statement last for several seconds before he spoke again. "You had no idea she was part of the pyramid system or the role she was to play. The problem, as I see it, is that Sin Fen is gone now, and we're on our own."

"And?" Foreman finally asked.

"And," Dane said, "I suggest you start being honest with me. Stop making plans behind my back and informing me of them after the fact. We might have been able to get that information about the gate without losing the *Reveille* or the *Deepflight* and all those people."

"I do what I have to do," Foreman said.

"One of these days *you're* going to be the point man," Dane said.

"And if I am, I'll do my duty," Foreman said.

Dane realized that Foreman meant what he said. He was willing to give up his life if it meant defeating the Shadow.

"There's another problem," Dane said.

"Which is?"

"We don't have another Sin Fen handy," Dane said.

"And?"

"And that means we don't have an important piece that's needed to shut a gate," Dane said. "She came from a long line of priestesses. Do you have any information on that?"

"No."

"Don't lie to me," Dane said.

"There've been many cults that promoted priestesses," Foreman said. "And, yes, I've looked into them. I'll have a copy of the file forwarded for you. But I don't have a line on a *current* group."

"Sin Fen was current," Dane noted.

"I'm not an idiot," Foreman said. "I checked Sin Fen out as much as I could. She was an orphan on the streets of Phnom Penh. I think she was descended from the priestesses of Angkor, but the line has been scattered, and it was the power of the gate and my investigating it that drew her to me, not a deliberate plan on her part."

"How did she know her role in the pyramid?" Dane asked.

"That I don't know. I would assume some sort of genetic memory. Or the voices of the gods you two were babbling about."

Dane wasn't sure how much he agreed with Foreman. It could have been genetic memory, or it could have been the voices of the gods that he himself heard: where that came from or what exactly it was, he didn't know, but he was learning to trust that inner voice more and more.

"How would—" Foreman began, but Dane held up a hand, hushing him.

Chelsea was absolutely still in knee-deep water, her head cocked, ears erect, looking out to sea. Dane almost mimicked her pose, intense, still, except his eyes were closed as he tried to see with his special sense.

There was a strong presence in the water not far away. Dane didn't feel any danger, but the presence was something he had never experienced before, very foreign and alien. He picked up thoughts but could make no sense of them. Correction. There were several presences, highly intelligent, very close by, studying Foreman, Chelsea, and him on the beach from the security of the water.

"What is it?" Foreman finally asked.

Dane held his hand up once more. Foreman's voice an irritating insect's buzz in his ear. He took a step into the water toward Chelsea. The fact that the dog showed no sign of fear was reassuring. He knelt in the surf next to Chelsea, putting a hand on her neck. For some strange reason, he knew that the dog was actually picking up the strange presence better than he was.

Dane scanned the surface of the water. He saw a spray of water in the air, then a dorsal fin cutting the blue surface, curving around, coming toward him and Chelsea. He stood.

"Dane!" Foreman's voice was alarmed.

But Dane could see the fin change course once more and head to his right. He turned, then was startled as Chelsea leapt through the surf in the same direction. Dane splashed after her.

Fifty meters down the beach, something was caught on the beach in the area between water and land, struggling in the outgoing tide. It was about two feet long and bluish gray and also sported a small dorsal fin. Dane relaxed when he realized he was looking at a baby dolphin. Chelsea ran right up to it and pushed it with her nose, helping it out toward the ocean.

In a few seconds, the small dolphin was in deep enough water to swim. It shot away from Chelsea, who gave a triumphant bark, then galloped back to Dane.

"Good girl," Dane said, as he turned back toward Foreman, but then he picked up something from Chelsea. Together, they looked out to sea. A row of dolphins, at least a dozen, were coming toward them, fins cutting the surface. Then they all stopped about twenty meters away and rose up on their tails, half out of the water, dark eyes staring at Dane and Chelsea.

One of them, a magnificent specimen almost fifteen feet long, moved slightly forward. Chelsea barked. Dane knew that the dolphin was communicating in some way with his dog, but he couldn't pick up anything directly. Then he saw it, relayed from Chelsea: a darkness in the ocean, danger.

Just as quickly as they had come, the dolphins turned and disappeared beneath the waves. Dane was startled as the sound of helicopter blades slicing through air cut into his conscious mind. A Japanese military chopper came in low over the water, circled, and set down. The side door slid open, and a crew member waved for them to get on board.

"What was that all about?" Foreman demanded as Dane helped Chelsea on board.

"We're not in this alone," Dane said.

Ariana Michelet got out of the Lincoln Town Car on Central Park West and stared up at the large sphere enclosed in a glass cube: the Frederick Phineas & Sandra Priest Rose Center for the Earth and Space. The glass cube was ninety-five feet on each side, and the sphere inside housed the Hayden Planetarium. Lit by colored searchlights, the sphere, inside the glass, was a magnificent sight.

She stood still for a few moments looking at it. The sphere, the interior upper half of which was the most sophisticated virtual reality machine in the world, had always seemed large to her. It was eighty-seven feet in diameter and weighed over two thousand tons. Impressive as it was, she knew that it was dwarfed by the sphere that had come out of the gate.

Shrugging off the disturbing image, she turned and headed for the front steps of the American Museum of Natural History. Since her father was one of the largest contributors to the building of the new planetarium, her phone call to the museum's curator asking for assistance had been greeted with quick acquiescence.

The person waiting at the top of the stairs, Jaka Van Liten, had agreed to meet Ariana here because of the nature of the subject matter of the meeting: crystal skulls. As Ariana got closer, she could see that Van Liten was a small, wizened old woman, clutching a leather briefcase in her gnarled hands. Ariana had found the woman's name on the Internet, constantly mentioned as the number one expert in the world on crystal skulls and purported to own quite a few in her personal collection. Ariana's invitation to join her at the museum to see its crystal skull had been greeted with enthusiasm by Van Liten, who lived in Manhattan and was only a short cab ride from the museum.

"Good evening, Ms. Van Liten," Ariana greeted her as she arrived at the top of the stairs. "I'm Ariana Michelet. Thank you for coming on such short notice."

"Michelet," Van Liten said. "I knew your father many years ago."

Ariana had not known that. "Where did you meet him?"

"My family is like yours. The same circles. I've been a recluse for the past ten years, but before that, I was quite… how shall we say… a party girl."

Ariana smiled at the thought of this little old lady partying. The smiled disappeared though when Van Liten asked a question.

"Are the skulls connected to these gates that are causing so much trouble?"

"We're checking into that," Ariana hedged. She noted that a guard was waiting for them, holding a door to the now-closed museum open for them. "Shall we go inside?"

She escorted the old woman through the door. The click of their heels echoed in the massive Theodore Roosevelt Memorial Hall. A middle-aged man in a white coat and sporting a most serious manner was waiting for them in the center of the hall.

"Good evening," Ariana said as they approached.

"I'm *Dr.* Fleidman," he said, emphasizing his title.

Ariana introduced herself and Van Liten, picking up the doctor's disdain for both her and the old woman. Ariana held back telling him of her own two PhDs, having run into this type of person before.

"This way," Fleidman said and began walking away, causing them to hurry to keep up. As they passed through the hall, Ariana Michelet remembered her first visit to the museum as a child and her predominant memories were of the model of the huge squid that hung in one hallway and the squid fighting a large blue whale in another. She had found that place wondrous and returned many times over the years. The museum was located right across from Central Park, where Central Park West and West Seventy-ninth Street intersected, taking up an entire city block.

They exited the Roosevelt entrance hall and turned left, going into the Hall of Biodiversity, where the arms of the squid cast strange shadows on the walls. As they passed under the squid, Fleidman caught Ariana looking up at it.

"It's the oldest model on display in the museum," he said. "Purchased in 1895. Made of papier-mâché and forty-two feet long. We actually have a real giant squid body, twenty-five feet long, that was brought here in 1998."

Ariana nodded. They'd recovered videos from the *Glomar* of the attack by the strange, squid like creatures—krakens, Dane had called them—with tentacles that ended in mouths. She knew there would be no model of that bizarre creature, because it wasn't part of this world's natural history.

They reached the Hall of Gems and Minerals, Fleidman's domain. He stopped at a box just outside the entrance and punched in a code. "The hall is secure. Laser detectors, pressure sensors, and constant live video feed." He waved up at an unseen camera. "There is, of course, ample need for such security. We have over one-hundred-fourteen-thousand specimens. Ninety thousand minerals, twenty thousand rocks and four thousand gems. Of note, we have the Star of India, which is the world's largest blue star sapphire." He pointed to his right as they passed a glass case, and Ariana could see the sapphire, highlighted by a single light above it.

"And how many crystal skulls?" Ariana asked.

Fleidman pulled a ring of keys out of one of his deep pockets and unlocked a metal door that had *No Admittance to Public* prominently stenciled on it. He ushered her and Van Liten through, into a long, dimly lit room, the center of which was filled with rows of tables holding crates and boxes.

"One," Fleidman said as he hit the overhead lights. The skull rested in the center of one of the tables. It was human-sized and pure, the eye sockets empty.

Ariana walked over and peered at it. It was quite beautiful, the surface translucent. She reached, then paused. "May I touch it?"

Fleidman nodded. Ariana ran her fingers lightly over it. The surface was perfectly smooth and cool. She felt a tingle of power, so subtle she wasn't sure if it was real or not. Fleidman walked around to the other side of the table.

"Quartz is mostly composed of silicon dioxide and is found in almost every rock. It can also form huge crystals that can weigh up to several tons. However, it is extremely rare to find pure quartz like this, which is colorless. Even the slightest influence of other material can greatly tinge quartz. Onyx and agate are two types of quartz that are streaked with bands of color from mother elements. Amethyst is violet quartz.

"Quartz is also very difficult to work with," Fleidman continued. "If you work against the grain of the stone, the crystal will shatter. There are three common denominations to crystal skulls. Those considered ancient, those called old, and those manufactured now."

"Why would someone manufacture one now?" Ariana asked.

Fleidman glanced at Van Liten, then answered. "There are those who believe such forms hold tremendous power. Nothing proven, of course. It's like those who believe pyramids focus power, which has also never been proven."

"What about the ancient ones?" Ariana asked.

"The numbers vary, as most are held in private collections"—again the hard look at Van Liten—"but some say there are as many as forty-nine."

"No," Van Liten spoke for the first time. "Many of those are copies. There are only nine ancient skulls of the pure form that have been found that I know of."

"Pure form?" Ariana asked.

"Many that people claim to be ancient are made of the wrong material. They come in amethyst, sapphire, smoky quartz, topaz, moonstone, etcetera. The pure form are those that are composed of perfect, unflawed, quartz crystal. As Dr. Fleidman noted, quartz is very easily corrupted. Also, they are human-sized. There are others made of pure quartz, but they are smaller."

"This one"—Fleidman seemed bothered that Ariana was asking questions of Van Liten in his museum—"was found in an ancient Mayan Pyramid in Central America."

Ariana stared at it, sensing something, the empty eye sockets looking back at her. "Why isn't it on display?" she asked.

"Well…" Fleidman seemed at a loss, and Van Liten answered.

"Because they can't explain it. Correct, young man?"

"It's simply an artifact," Fleidman said.

"It is not simply an artifact," Van Liten said. "Can't you sense the power in it?"

"There are some strange aspects to this," Fleidman allowed. "We've analyzed it, and the carving is perfect, which is difficult to explain, given the dating of the pyramid it was found in. You see, to carve quartz, which has a hardness of seven on a scale of ten, with diamond being a ten, you need something harder than seven. No ancient society we know of had such tools. Also, the carving, what little we can tell of it, seems to go against the natural axis, although that is very difficult to determine. As I mentioned, if you carve against the grain, the quartz should shatter. Obviously, in this case, it didn't."

"That's because there is no carving." Van Liten said.

"They don't occur naturally, growing on trees," Fleidman snapped. "Where do you think they come from?"

"That I am not sure of," Van Liten said. "At least I am willing to admit my ignorance."

"Quartz has interesting properties," Fleidman said, trying to get back to an area where he was an expert. As he went on, Ariana had to almost bite her tongue to keep from speaking.

"Quartz is the second most common of all minerals," Fleidman said. "It's composed of silicon dioxide. It's the primary constituent of sand. It crystallizes in the rhombohedra system. It exhibits interesting properties, one of which is the piezoelectric effect, which means it produces electric voltage when subjected to pressure along certain lines of axis. Therefore it has important applications in the electronics industry for controlling the frequency of radio waves." He reached out and turned the skull on its stand under the light. "In addition, it has the optical property of rotating the plane of polarized light."

"It also goes through structural transformation when heated," Ariana said. "Low quartz, when heated to one thousand sixty-three point four degrees Fahrenheit becomes high quartz, which has a different crystal structure and physical properties. When cooled, high quartz reverts back to low quartz." She pointed at the skull. "It would be interesting to see what properties these skulls have as high quartz."

Fleidman seemed disconcerted by her detailed knowledge of geology. Ariana had spent most of her adult life working for her father, searching the world for valuable minerals. She had been drawn into the entire gate phenomenon because of a search for a diamond field in northwest Cambodia, where her plane had been downed inside the Angkor gate.

"How many skulls do you have?" Ariana asked Van Liten, deciding now was not the time to tell what Dane had seen happen to Sin Fen.

Van Liten reached into her leather briefcase and drew out five photographs, which she spread across the table in front of the skull. "Five pure ancients."

"From where?" Ariana pressed as she checked the pictures. All five were almost exactly the same, with some slight differences in size. All were very realistic, exact approximations of the human skull.

"One from Central America. One from Russia. One from Mongolia. One from Canada. And one from under the Atlantic."

"All found near pyramids?"

"The origin of some I have no idea about other than general vicinity," Van Liten said. "I bought two on the black market, where naturally, the sellers were loath to say where they obtained them. I own Shui Ting Er, which was found in Mongolia inside a large burial mound. I also own what is called the Jesuit Skull, which purportedly has an association with the Jesuits and Saint Francis of Assisi; and a skull found in a burial mound in Russia that contained artifacts from the Scythalians.

"You have to understand, though, that just as I have purchased these skulls, I believe they have traveled far from their original sites. A crystal skull is rumored to give great power to whoever possesses it, so it is impossible to determine where each one originated or how many people have possessed each one over the course of the ages."

Ariana turned back to Fleidman. "Anything else you've discovered about the skulls?"

"I've told you all that we've learned."

Ariana was frustrated. She knew that Dane had sent her here instead of accompanying him to Japan to get her out of the way. *Why does it matter about the skulls now?* She wondered. *They are an end product, worthless.* She checked that thought. As they were now, they were worthless, but that didn't rule out other possibilities.

"Have you ever checked the skull for muon emissions?" she asked Fleidman.

"Muon emissions? No."

Ariana doubted he even knew what muons were. She turned to Van Liten. "What else do you know about the skulls?"

"There are several theories," Van Liten said. She glanced at Fleidman. "Most are considered rubbish by the scientific community, but there are events occurring now around the world that scientists are having a very difficult time explaining, are there not?"

Ariana nodded. "Go ahead."

"There are those who believe the skulls are a form of – for lack of a better word – a computer, or a critical part of a larger computer, perhaps a hard drive, so to speak. These people believe that the skulls record everything that occurs around them and perhaps, even draws in the memories of those who touch them, thus making them a recorder of history."

Fleidman snorted, but Van Liten ignored him as she continued.

"Other people claim the skulls were brought to our planet by extraterrestrials. Others suggest that they were made by people who live inside the Earth. They propose that there are twelve pure skulls, each representing one of the twelve tribes of people who dwell there."

Ariana fought to keep her reaction to herself, while Fleidman had no such compunction.

"A hollow Earth theory?"

"I'm just relating various theories," Van Liten said, "not saying whether they are valid or not."

Ariana considered that. It wasn't as far-fetched as she would have thought a month ago. It would definitely seem to ancient people that the gates were doorways into the Earth itself.

Van Liten continued, "In many of the theories, though, the numbers twelve and thirteen do crop up. There seems to be some acceptance, even among radically different theories, that there are twelve pure ancients, along with a thirteenth master skull, and that if they are brought together, something momentous will happen."

"Are there any—" Ariana began, but then she paused.

"Yes?" Van Liten pressed her.

"Are there any rumors that these skulls are someone's real skull transformed in some matter?"

This time Fleidman's snort of disgust was loud. Ariana spun toward him. "*Doctor*, we have a very reliable eyewitness who saw this transformation."

"You're joking, right?"

"You've seen what happened in Iceland, right?" Ariana didn't wait for an answer. "These skulls are related to the gates, so I am definitely not joking."

"Most interesting." Van Liten seemed to get taller as she straightened. "Yes, there have been similar stories. When did this occur?"

"During the last outbreak of the Bermuda Triangle gate," said Ariana. She quickly related what Dane had seen happen to Sin Fen on top of the sunken pyramid. When she was done, Van Liten turned to the skull on the table. She reached out with her wrinkled hands and ran her fingers lightly over the cheeks. "So this *was* indeed a person. A priestess. Who died to stop the Shadow."

"It appears so," Ariana confirmed.

"Amazing," was Van Liten's summary.

"You said there was a spear with the figure of a seven headed snake on the end," Fleidman said. "How come none of those have turned up?"

"I don't know," Ariana said.

"And the master skull—if there is one—" Van Liten said, "What about that?"

"Maybe," Ariana said, "that's still in someone's head and hasn't been transformed yet. I do think, though, that we need to start gathering up the pure ancient skulls. Just in case."

"You can have mine," Van Liten immediately offered.

CHAPTER NINE

THE PAST
25 AUGUST 79 A.D.

The blast of war trumpets echoed down the stone tunnel to the ears of the waiting gladiators, indicating that the next contest was about to begin. Falco lay on a bench, the fancy armor he'd worn during the *pompa*, or procession into the arena, to one side, his battered fighting gear on the other. A slave carefully oiled his body, paying particular attention to the numerous scars, kneading them to loosen the knotted muscle beneath the skin. It was the last day of the games. He was underneath the arena floor, the place dimly lit by smoky torches. The bellow of animals deliberately starved so they would perform—if eating poorly armed or even unarmed people were performing— adding to the din of the crowd above. The entire place stank of fear and death.

Tomorrow. It was all he could think of. He would travel to Pompeii. And he would see Phaedra and Fabron. His son would almost be a man now and his daughter approaching womanhood. He had last seen them when they were barely able to walk.

Falco heard the shuffling of feet and turned his head slightly to watch those going by, heading for the arena: a quartet of criminals, their eyes dull from the drugged wine they'd been given. He could tell from the inexperienced way they held their swords that none of them had any combat training. Execution in the form of entertainment. They had been condemned to the sword by the state court and sold to the *Ianista* under the provision that they enter the arena within one hundred days.

Falco lay his head back down on the scented pillow and relaxed his muscles, allowing the slave to do his job. Falco had never known his parents or even his country of origin. He'd been a slave from birth, his large size, apparent even as a baby, saving him from being exposed, placed on a hillside and allowed to die. His earliest memories were of working in the fields in Sicily at four. At seven, he was sold to the *lanista* of the emperor's gladiatorial school outside Rome. The first three years were spent doing menial work around the stables. Then he was chosen to train for the arena. Every day of the year. From before dawn until after dusk. When the issue at stake was one's own life, such training was taken seriously. His muscles grew as he matured, but more importantly, became attuned to instinctual moves with the various weapons he handled until they were an extension of his body.

He'd been pressed into the army during the civil war of '69 and spent eight years serving in the X Legion, most of that time under the command of General Lucius Cassius. It was in Palestine that he had come to the general's notice. He had been part of a cohort chosen to accompany the general on an inspection tour of the relay forts that allowed messengers to move speedily about the territory, exchanging horses at each small post.

Encamped at a post near the Sea of Galilee, the centurion in command had failed to properly encamp, feeling that the small enclosure of the post was sufficient for the general and himself, deploying his troops around the wall. It was standard procedure for any element of a legion to erect a barricade around any camp and for sufficient sentries to be posted. But the Jewish rebels had been smashed, only a few hands left, and the campaign was winding down.

Falco had noted the lack of preparations, but he was only a soldier, so he'd pulled his cloak over his body and immediately fallen asleep, always amazed how cold it could get at night after the boiling temperatures of the desert day.

He'd awakened to the screams of men dying. Grabbing his sword, he leapt into the fray, not even knowing who he was fighting, simply swinging at anyone he didn't recognize as a legionnaire. All was chaos, the camp thoroughly infiltrated, many men having been slain in their sleep.

In the starlight, Falco made out a group of men, Jewish rebels, no doubt, in a tight formation, cutting their way toward the small post. And on the low wall, General Cassius sword in hand, yelling orders, trying to rally the soldiers.

Falco made his way toward Cassius, where five rebels were also headed. He reached them just before they got to the general. He killed two before they even knew he was upon them. Two others came at him, the one in the center continuing toward the general.

Trained for the arena, Falco's skill and speed were no match for the rebels. He feinted at the one on the right, and when that man jumped back from the blade, he slashed left, severing the other man's sword arm from his body, blood spurting from the stump as the man screamed and went to his knees, staring in disbelief at his arm lying on the ground. Falco went at the other man with a flurry of jabs and slashes, penetrating his defenses on the fifth strike, the edge of his *gladius* splitting the man's head like an overripe melon.

Then he turned to the general, whose withered sword arm forced him to fight with his left hand. He was doing a credible job, off the wall now, giving ground slowly to his attacker, until he tripped over a rock and fell on his back. Cassius blocked the first blow aimed at his face. There was no second blow. Falco took the rebel leader from behind without warning, severing his head from his body in one vicious swipe of his blade.

Falco reached down and picked up the head, eyes still blinking as the blood drained out of it. Falco held it over his head, screaming loudly. The other attacking rebels, seeing their dead leader, scattered, disappearing into the dark.

Cassius slowly got to his feet and called for the centurion. When the officer arrived, Cassius had him remove his armor and strip naked. Then the general banished him to the desert on the spot for failing to camp properly. Falco knew that was a death sentence for the centurion. Either the desert would get him or the rebels; either would be slow and cruel. Then Cassius turned to Falco and offered him a commission as the cohort's centurion.

"On one condition, General," Falco replied.

"A condition?" Cassius slapped dust from his cloak. "I would say you were impertinent and not very grateful if it were not for the fact that you saved my life. What condition?"

"You buy my wife and children when we return to Rome and free them, General."

Cassius had stuck out his hand. "My word as a Roman, Centurion."

But it was not to be. While he was away, his wife Drusilla died of the plague, hurriedly buried in a mass grave. And Epione had swooped in, buying the children, sending him a copy of the bill of sale and a promise to take care of them if he returned to the arena. If he did not... the threat was obvious.

Offered a discharged from the army when the campaign was over, he did as she demanded and went back to the arena, the only life he knew, to ply the only skill he knew.

"Water," Falco ordered, and another slave brought him a goblet. He went up on one elbow and drank deeply. His head throbbed; too much wine at the banquet opening the games the night before. He usually never drank before a contest, but his match today was an exhibition of skill with wooden swords, not a fight to the death. It was taking more and more wine for him to be able to spend time with Epione, to drown the rage in his heart at the woman who used him and was master to his children with the power of life and death over them.

"Gladiator."

Falco lifted his head in surprise both at the choice of words and the tone. Gaius Marcus stood in front of the table, dressed in his fine tunic.

"Yes?"

"Prepare yourself for battle," Marcus said.

Falco frowned. "I do not enter until this afternoon."

"You enter when I tell you to. And that is now."

Falco swung his feet to the ground and stood, oil glistening on his naked skin. "What is happening?"

"Your opponents await you in the arena," Marcus' eyes shifted, not meeting Falco's harsh gaze.

"And they are?"

"You will enforce the emperor's laws against the criminals who have been sentenced to the sword. You will carry steel in your hand, not wood."

Falco felt the bottom of this stomach fall. Not all the thought of having to fight but at the realization that someone was pulling strings. He had only fought like that in his early days, fighting both criminals and animals, honing his deadly trade. It had been years since the last time he had done so. This was an insult of the highest magnitude and he knew it didn't come from Marcus.

Falco stepped closer to his owner. "Marcus. Tell me."

"A distinguished senator has returned to Rome. He has made a special request." Marcus said the words flatly.

"For me?"

"For you."

"Who is the senator?"

"Domidicus. He arrived late last night."

Epione's husband. He was supposed to be in the Province of Gaul for another three months, but he had returned while his wife was still in Falco's arms. Marcus met Falco's eyes, and they both knew why Domidicus was back and why he had made these arrangements.

"I cannot refuse Domidicus's request," Marcus continued. "He is the nephew of the emperor, and the emperor concurs."

Falco struggled to understand. Why make him fight the criminals? Even four against one, Falco felt confident he would be the only one left standing. There was more to this than Marcus was telling him.

"You should have kept that"—Marcus gestured at Falco's groin—"under control."

"I should have refused her?" Falco was angry now. "You were the one who first sent me to her."

"Get your gear on," Marcus ordered. He turned and walked out before Falco could say anything further.

*****

The Emperor Titus had a headache. He'd spent the morning in his audience chamber, listening to the petty squabbling of those who came to him for decisions. And now he had to sit here in the heat, sweltering even in the shade, and watch criminals die in pathetic and usually brief encounters.

Then there was Domidicus and his demand that a certain gladiator be put to death for cuckolding him. Titus knew if he did that in all such instances, there would be no gladiators left. Still, he had allowed Domidicus to bribe the *lanista* and arrange a match according to his own desires. After all, the senator was a very powerful man and his nephew. And the gladiator was Falco, Cassius's friend. Killing two birds with one battle in the arena.

And there was still the issue of the Delphic priestess. So far, there had been no sign as she had indicated there would be. He had her seated in the back corner of the imperial box. If there were no sign by dusk, he would have her killed in the arena. It alleviated his headache somewhat to envision various ways he would have the woman dispatched.

Titus turned to Thyestes. "Where is Cassius?"

"In the Praetorian box."

"Summon him."

Titus looked over at Domidicus and Epione, who were below him and to the left. It would be interesting to see their reaction when her gladiator died.

"Emperor." Cassius was in front of him wearing a plain white toga.

"Cassius." Titus nodded a greeting. "There is a woman there." Titus waved his imperial staff toward the priestess. "Go to her and listen to her story. I think you will find it interesting."

"Yes, Emperor."

Behind the emperor, Kaia was struggling to keep from being sick. The black emotion of the arena was overwhelming. She understood now why the oracle had kept her isolated for so many years. It was difficult to block out the array of feelings that bombarded her from the outside. She could feel the crowd's blood lust, the fear of those in the arena itself, even the hunger of the animals. Under it all, though, there was something else. A presence, as if under the Earth itself. She pulled her focus on that by the appearance of a man.

"I am Lucius Cassius," the man said.

Kaia could see the wounds, the leathery skin, and the look in his eyes. He was a killer, but not the one. "I am Kaia, priestess of the Oracle at Delphi."

"The emperor has sent me to hear what you have to say."

Vesuvius had never been a quiet mountain. In 5960 B.C. and 3580 B.C. it had erupted with a force to rival the largest known in Europe. In 62 A.D., an earthquake, centered on the volcano, had rocked the entire area, causing great damage.

But the land was fertile with the volcanic soil, and the sea was close, making the area prime real estate, so cities grew under the smoldering brow of the mountain. The largest of these was Pompeii to the southeast, and not far from it the port town of Herculaneum, to the west, on the Bay of Naples. Twenty thousand people made Pompeii their home, while five thousand lived in Herculaneum.

On the slope of the volcano, facing the southern sun, was the smaller town of Oplontis, which catered to the rich villas that dotted the slope, with excellent views of the countryside in all directions. At one of these villas, Porta Vintus, lived Epione's brother, the distinguished Flavius Lucella, although what exactly he was distinguished for other than inheriting the villa and great wealth from his father, no one was quite sure. There were twelve family members living at his estate, including his wife, six children and various cousins. There were also over two hundred slaves, including Phaedra and Fabron, Falco's daughter and son.

Lucella had at first protested when Epione had pressed the two small children on him. Not that he was adverse to slaves, but they were too young to work. But as the years had gone by, he had changed his mind. They both worked hard, never complained as slaves were wont to do, and were both growing into quite handsome creatures. In fact Lucella was planning, the next time his fat wife was out of town on one of her insufferable trips to Rome where she spent uncounted amounts of his money, of having first one, then the other, summoned to his quarters. It would be an enjoyable experience, a dip in both waters, hot and cold, so to speak, and the thought of both of them virgins, and siblings, truly excited him.

At the moment that Falco was putting his armor on, Lucella was behind his main house in the shade of an olive tree, seeking relief from the terrible heat that had plagued the summer so far. The two slaves were on his mind because one was on either side of him, waving their fans in unison, back and forth, moving the humid air over his corpulent body.

"Faster," Lucella ordered.

He felt his stomach rumble. *Damn that new cook*, he thought, before he realized it was not his stomach that was rumbling. He looked up. Thousands of feet above, the ever-present cloud hat tipped Vesuvius seemed darker than usual.

"The Earth mother stretches," He muttered. He tried to remember the various gods his wife paid homage to. Which one was responsible for the underground again?

"Phaedra."

"Yes, master."

"Who is the god of the underworld?"

"That would be the goddess Proserpine, my lord."

"You are very bright."

Lucella smiled at her. She was thirteen and just coming into her womanhood. Her brother, a year younger, had already reached puberty, and he would be a large man, much like his father. Lucella had determined that Fabron would have to be sold before he became large enough to be a threat. He thought that game his sister played with the gladiator most dangerous, but that was her way. While his only interest was money, hers was power. He knew she hated men, particularly her husband, but she loved power more than she hated the male species. So she played all the men who crossed paths with her.

The ground shook, and Lucella reached out and grabbed the side of the couch he was on. He stared hard at Vesuvius, as if by sight alone, he could see the inside of the mountain. He waited. A minute. All was still.

"Ah." Lucella put his head back on the pillow. "Faster," he ordered.

*****

Falco entered the arena to the accompaniment of a blare of trumpets. He saw the criminals who had just passed but now there were six, not four. And the two additions, even though they were armed as the others and as poorly dressed, Falco could immediately tell by their stance and demeanor that they were trained gladiators.

He turned toward the imperial box, raising his sword in the obligatory salute. "We who are about to die, salute you!" his voice echoed across the stones and the murmur of the crowd. The six did not give the salute, as they were not entitled, although he imagined the two impostors had been forced to resist their urge to raise their swords.

He saw the emperor, and below, Epione and Domidicus. He saw the surprise on her face, the satisfaction on her husband's. He was about to turn back to the ring when he felt as if he had been hit by a bolt of lightning, searing through his very being. At the very back of the imperial box was Cassius, huddled next to a strange woman. It was her eyes that had transfixed him, straight to his soul. He had not experienced such a thing since seeing Drusilla the first time, but this was different; this wasn't man and woman but a kindred soul, one that saw into the darkness.

He had no more time to ponder this as the trumpet signaling the beginning of battle sounded.

Kaia had felt a sense of confidence in the old man the emperor had sent to talk to her. He had listened carefully to her story of the Shadow and the threat it posed. He had questioned her only once, when she told him that she had promised the emperor there would be a sign of the Shadow's power this very day.

"In what form?" he had asked.

"Out of the Earth."

He had simply nodded and asked her to continue, but when the trumpets blew, signaling another bout of butchery, she had fallen silent, her heart missing a beat. A man had walked into the sunlight and raised his sword to the emperor.

She knew immediately. This was the man she had seen in dreams and the man the oracle had told her to look for. The killer. With the heart of darkness.

And she saw what he had seen: the same mountain she had seen in a vision. Now she knew what was to come, what form the sign was to take.

With great difficulty, Falco forced his attention back to the arena. The six men were spreading out. The two gladiators, neither of whom Falco had ever seen before, fanned to each wing, leaving the four criminals in the middle. One of the gladiators was tall, with a shaved head. The other was short and powerful, with muscle layered on muscle. While they were the real threat, Falco knew he could not ignore the four armed criminals, because while he was engaged with one of the gladiators, one of them could slip the blade into his back as easily as the best trained man. Falco always let opponents come to him. He had found the reactions were harder to anticipate than actions.

The Delphic priestess was the most intriguing woman Cassius had ever met. He found that reaction strange, considering he'd been talking to her for only ten minutes. But there was something about her, an aura, which had drawn him, as had her story of a Shadow and a gate to another place. Her abrupt shift of attention from him to the arena had been as shocking as a splash of cold water in the face. He turned and followed her gaze and was surprised to see Falco facing six criminals. This was not on the program for the day's events.

Cassius's eyes narrowed. The two criminals on the flanks were anything but. He could tell by the way they held their weapons, the movement of their feet, that they were trained killers.

"Something is wrong," Cassius told Kaia.

She turned to him. "What do you mean?"

"He's being set up. The two men on the ends are not what they appear to be."

Her gaze shifted back to the arena. "No, they aren't," she said after a second. She closed her eyes. "He is to die. It is what the emperor wants, but most particularly what that man there" – she pointed at Senator Domidicus – "wants."

"How do you know that?"

"It is my gift."

The two gladiators were moving forward, a pair of pincers, circling to drive him forward against the four, who held fast, uncertain what they should do. Falco decided it was time to change tactics. Shield held tight against his off side, he charged the four silently, knowing silence was more disconcerting than screaming. They brought their swords up awkwardly, then, as he had hoped, they scattered.

Falco ran one down, spitting him on the point of his sword and pulling it out in one quick jab; then he went after a second criminal who was running for the wall. The man threw his sword down and jumped, his hands scrambling for a hold, but the rim of the wall surrounding the arena was topped with two-foot-wide rollers to prevent this very thing. His hands spun off the roller, and he slid back into the arena. Falco cut through the man's hamstring, sending him screaming to the sand. Falco turned, breathing hard, feeling the sweat run under his armor.

The two gladiators had accepted that their original plan wasn't going to work. They were shoulder to shoulder now, edging in. The remaining two criminals were hanging back.

"You did not give the salute," Falco said to the gladiators as they approached.

"We don't plan on dying," the tall one said.

They were opposite-handed, another advantage they held, the tall one holding the sword in his left, the short one in this right. Falco blinked. For a second, their images had wavered. Then it happened again.

You've been drugged.

It wasn't as if the words were spoken but the thought sent to him. And he knew from who. The woman in the back of the imperial box with Cassius.

Falco blinked once more, trying to clear his vision, but he knew she was right. The glass of water the slave had given him just before Marcus had ordered him to the ring. He could see the smiles on the faces of the two gladiators as they saw him take an uncertain step backward. They knew, too. He had heard of all types of different drugs; ones that slowed a fighter's reactions, ones that dulled pain, but this one seemed to be specific to his eyes, causing his vision to waver and dance.

The two were coming closer now.

Close your eyes. I will see for you.

Falco yelled and swung his sword back and forth like a madman. The two gladiators retreated slightly, letting him waste energy on ghosts. Time was on their side as his vision grew worse.

Trust me.

Falco felt the emotion, more that he heard words inside his head. He had trusted no one in his life other than Drusilla. He closed his eyes. He saw the arena inside his head as if from above. He could see the two closing on him, edging in, swords at the ready.

They both charged. Falco saw it, and he also could sense it as he had always been able, the two views complementing each other. He turned, shield out, and took the tall one's blade on the shield, while he caught the short one's blade with his own steel, sliding along until they locked guards. He shoved, pushing both men back, and they disengaged, retreating to ponder the strange fact that they were fighting a man who had his eyes closed, the easy kill they had anticipated turning out to be not so easy.

In Pompeii everyone could see the tall cloud that rose out of the top of Vesuvius. It was higher than anyone could recall, reaching into the heavens. The tremors in the Earth had also been felt. But what were they to do? Leave everything they had and run away every time the Earth moved and smoke came out of the volcano? They all knew they were living on borrowed time, but the hope was that the note would not be called in during their lifetime.

At Porta Vintus, Flavius Lucella was finally asleep, decadent dreams floating inside his head. Phaedra and Fabron waited nearby for his summons, seated together underneath an olive tree. They knew their life was not difficult, especially when compared with the slaves who worked the fields. But they had seen what Lucella did to the other household slaves when they reached a certain level of physical development. Both had seen his eyes going over their bodies as they fanned, and they knew the time was getting close.

"I will not allow him to take me." Phaedra had been saying that every day for months now.

"Father will come for us," was Fabron's stock reply.

"He cannot come," Phaedra replies, picking up a twig and snapping it. "He is bound to the arena as tightly as we are bound here."

Fabron looked at the fat man sleeping on the hammock. "If he does not come and Lucella tries to force either of us, I will kill him."

"Then we will be killed."

Fabron shrugged. "I would prefer death."

"Why don't we escape?" Phaedra asked.

Fabron smiled at his sister. "And go where?"

"Anywhere."

"The Romans put to death anyone who helps a slave escape. All around us is the sea. We would need to get on a ship. And north are the mountains. I have talked to men who have seen them. They say you cannot get across them unescorted."

"It is not fair!" Phaedra threw a stick down.

"It is the life we have been given," Fabron said.

"Why?" She pointed at Lucella. "Why does he have the power and money he has, and we are slaves? He didn't choose that, as we didn't choose this. He didn't work for this wealth or freedom."

"I don't —" Fabron began, but he halted as the Earth trembled. They looked up the slope and were the first to see the initial eruption. Directly above them, a thousand feet higher, a hole was blasted outward in the side of the mountain with a loud sound like the crack of thunder. They started, staring as the jet of black smoke raced out laterally from the side of the mountain, going over their heads and extending outward for several kilometers.

"What is it?" Phaedra asked as her brother wrapped an arm around her frail shoulders.

Fabron didn't have a chance to reply, as a wave of searing gas came down the slope, burning everything in its path. He saw the trees above them bursting into flames, pulled Phaedra to his chest, and turned his back to the coming wave.

The two gladiators were closing again, this time more carefully. Falco hefted his shield and sword in preparation when a shaft of pain blanked out the vision being sent to him and even his own sense of the arena. He fell to his knees, crying out in anguish, dropping his shield and sword.

He had not been certain Phaedra and Fabron were alive, but now he was certain they had just died.

Kaia jumped to her feet. "Emperor!" she called out.

Titus turned, irritated. "Priestess, you —"

"It comes, Emperor," Kaia pointed to the south. "Stop the fight."

Titus raised a hand, which surprised even him. Trumpets sounded, and the two gladiators froze, just scant feet from finishing off Falco.

Silence fell over the stadium. Titus stared at his hand as if it wasn't his. He felt as if he had been a puppet for that brief moment, the strings pulled by someone else. But he didn't signal the action to begin.

The first explosion on the side of Vesuvius was minor compared to what happened next. It gave enough warning to the people of Pompeii for most of them to get out of their houses and into the streets. Then the top of the volcano blew. The sound washed across the town first.

Just behind it, a wall of black, containing superheated gases and choking ash, raced over the countryside. Thousands died as the wall swept over the town, killing every living thing it touched, either by heat or suffocation, depending if they were indoors or out.

"Kill me." Falco could no longer see the gladiators, but he knew they were close by. "Kill me," he begged.

The stadium had been unnaturally silent for almost a minute. Now there was a murmur as the crowd wondered why the emperor had signaled all to stop. And he had yet to indicate what should happen to Falco, on his knees, head bowed in the arena.

In the imperial box, Kaia had made her way past all the flunkies surrounding the emperor. She stood in front of him.

"I see nothing," Titus said. "I hear nothing. What is this thing you say has happened?" He was angry now, himself unsure why he had stopped everything.

Kaia reached up and touched her neck. "You may strike here with your sharpest blade if I am wrong. It has already happened." She pointed to the arena. "He knows."

The emperor signaled for Falco to be brought forward. Two soldiers ran out and grabbed his arms, dragging him to his feet and across the sand. He hung limply in their arms. The crowd noticed and began signaling, thumbs up or down, what they desired. The majority were in the down position, the years of entertainment Falco had provided forgotten in the desire to see more blood.

"Gladiator, why did you stop fighting?" Titus demanded.

Falco's head came up, his eyes filled with tears. "Pompeii is gone. Vesuvius has erupted. They are all dead. All dead.

The murmuring in the crowd grew louder, as those who heard spread the word around the stands.

"How do you know this?" Titus was on his feet.

"My children were there. I felt them die."

Titus laughed, but there was a nervous edge to it. "I am growing tired of seers and those who see what has happened far away. He raised his hand, and his thumb was extended downward.

At that moment, a deep rumble cause the entire arena to quake. Titus had to grab the arm of his chair for a second to steady himself. On the north side of the stands, people were pointing. Looking in that direction, they could all see the plume of smoke on the far horizon.

Titus turned for the tunnel that led out of the imperial box. "Bring her," he jabbed a finger at Kaia.

"We need him also," Kaia was pointing toward the arena, where one of the soldiers had drawn his sword in preparation for killing Falco.

"Immediately," Titus ordered Thyestes.

Falco had washed his eyes with water, and he could see, but his vision was still blurry. It was good enough, though, for him to note that he was in the reception hall of the emperor's Imperial Palace. The strange woman was in front of the emperor's throne, and the escort shoved Falco to the front to join them. As he went forward, he noted Cassius, Epione, and Senator Domidicus along with other notables off to the side, among the various statues of the Caesars. In the arena, Thyestes had stopped the soldier just as the steel was ready to slice across his neck. Falco had felt the coldness of the blade, and he even had a scratch where the razor-sharp edge had rested. He'd wanted the relief of nothingness, of not feeling pain, but it was not yet to be.

"We have received no messenger from Pompeii yet," Titus said.

"You will receive none, Emperor," the woman said. "The city is destroyed. Everyone is dead."

"How do you know?" Titus demanded.

"I could feel them die," the woman said, which made Falco blink several times to try to get a better view of her.

"And you say this is caused by a Shadow outside the borders of the empire?" Titus asked.

"Yes, Emperor," she replied. "And it will get worse. This was only the beginning."

And you, Falco?" the emperor asked. "What did you feel?"

"My children die," Falco said. He did not address the emperor properly and could care less.

The emperor looked past him. "Epione. Were his children in Pompeii?"

Epione stepped forward, for once looking small. "Yes, Emperor. At my brother's estate, Porta Vintus, on the slopes of the mountain itself."

The emperor waved a hand. "Everyone out except these three."

There was the shuffling of feet on tile, then the large doors swung shut. Titus sat down and placed his elbow on his knee, his chin on his fist as he regarded Kaia.

"How can this Shadow do this?"

"I do not know."

Titus frowned. "What can I do about it?"

"You can aid me. I will travel to the Shadow."

"You can defeat it?" Titus asked.

"Yes. It is my destiny."

Falco heard her confident words, but he could sense the uncertainty inside her.

"How?" Titus asked.

"That is not clear yet. The gods will show me when it is time."

"The gods." Titus tapped his staff on the arm of this throne for several moments. "What do you need from me?"

She turned and pointed at Falco. "Him. And soldiers to help me on my journey to the Shadow."

Titus stood once more. He looked down at the woman. "Let me discuss with my advisor."

They were escorted out of the room.

"Who are you?" Falco asked the woman once they were in the antechamber.

"My name is Kaia."

"You helped me in the arena."

"I helped you help yourself," she said. "You have the same power I do."

"And what is that power?" Falco asked.

"To see into the hearts and minds of others. And to hear the voices of the gods."

"There are no gods."

"Not as worshipped here in Rome, there aren't," she agreed. "But you have heard their voices, haven't you?"

"If there are gods," Falco argued, instead of answering, "why do we suffer so?"

Kaia didn't respond right away. When she did, her voice was very low, so that only he could hear. "You wish to die. We all will die, gladiator. Your time is not now. To die like an animal led to slaughter in the arena is no fitting death of a soldier."

"Death is death," Falco said. "You cheated me of mine."

"Then I owe you your death," Kaia said. "Trust me, I will repay you."

Titus grabbed a goblet and downed the wine in one long swallow. Then he faced Thyestes as his senior advisor came in.

"An imperial galley landed at Ostia, and a messenger just arrived from there," Thyestes said. "They report seeing smoke and flame on Vesuvius."

"So it's true?"

"I would say so, Emperor."

"Recommendations on how to deal with this problem?"

"Every problem is an opportunity if looked at correctly," Thyestes said.

"Speak clearly," Titus snapped, tired of the Greek's way with words.

"She wants Falco. Let her have him. This will placate Domidicus. She wants troops. Give her the XXV Legion."

Titus smiled. The XXV was a legion formed by the rebel Vitellius, who had briefly held the emperorship before Vespasian established the Flavian line. Vespasian had sent the legion to the Regnum Dacae, at the very northeast part of the empire, to face the barbarians out of Asia and to keep it as far away from Rome as possible. Despite Vitellius's assassination, the XXV Legion was a potential source of trouble.

"And," Thyestes continued, "give command of the legion to one of your best officers: Lucius Cassius."

"Very good," Titus acknowledged. Killing three birds with one stone: the XXV, Cassius, and Falco. "Order them to come in."

He took another drink of wine as Falco, Cassius, and Kaia were brought in and lined up in front of his throne.

"General Lucius Cassius, your emperor has need of your services."

Cassius nodded. "Whatever my emperor commands is my duty."

Titus shifted his gaze to Falco. "Gladiator, you are ordered returned to the army at your former rank of Centurion. You will accompany General Cassius."

There was no response from Falco, but Titus didn't care as he turned back to Cassius.

"General, you are hereby directed to use imperial transport to travel to Regnum Dacae and take command of the XXV Legion. You will lead the legion northeast, into Regnum Bospous in search of this Shadow. You will then destroy the Shadow."

"And then, Emperor?" Cassius asked.

"You are to depart immediately via imperial dispatch to Brundisium. I will give you orders to be opened once you complete your journey."

CHAPTER TEN

THE PRESENT

"This is Colonel Felix Shashenka, of the Russian Army," Foreman introduced one of the men waiting for them outside the elevator entrance. "And Colonel Loomis from our Special Operations Command."

Dane shook each man's hand as the elevator's doors slid open, revealing a short Japanese man and a taller woman. "Professor Nagoya and his senior assistant, Professor Ahana," Foreman continued the introductions.

When that was done, they got on the elevator and began descending. Chelsea pressed herself against Dane's leg, nervous about the strange feeling of going into the Earth. Dane had worked search and rescue with Chelsea before being recruited by Paul Michelet to rescue his daughter, Ariana, from the Angkor gate in Cambodia, and neither liked being underground.

"Any updates on the Devil's Sea gate?" Foreman asked.

"Both probes are on-line, and we are still receiving and analyzing data," Nagoya said.

"How will these probes allow us access into the gate?" Dane asked the question that Foreman had been unable to answer.

'Well, it is only a theory," Nagoya said, "but we —"

Dane cut him off. "We're going to be living this theory, Professor. How good a theory is it?"

It was Ahana who answered. "I will be living it also, as I will be accompanying you on this reconnaissance. The theory is as good as we can make it with the information we have. Somewhere inside those gates is the true gate, the access point to the other side, which we are calling the portal."

"The black hole that Flaherty came through," Dane said. The elevator was still going down, rock walls sliding by. "That was a portal."

"As was the black hole you went through, traveling from Cambodia to the *Scorpion*," Ahana said. "That along with Foreman's high-frequency experiments years ago, indicated the gates are connected in some way. The connection between the Chernobyl and Devil's Sea's probes again proves that; we've been able to gather considerable data."

"How come the Shadow hasn't shut down the probes?" Dane asked.

Nagoya shrugged. "We don't know. But I suspect that they haven't even really noticed them. Think about it. The Shadow has been attacking our world for millennia. We've barely been able to defeat it with help from the Ones Before. I would imagine there is a degree of arrogance on the part of the Shadow that may blind it to the possibility of us crossing to its side."

"You're giving it human qualities," Dane noted.

"You're correct," Nagoya noted. "And that may be denigrating the intelligence that is over there. Bringing it down to our level."

"You sound like you admire it," Dane said.

"I can admire its capabilities, not its goals," Nagoya said.

"Back to gates," Foreman cut off the discussion. "The connections between them?" he prompted Ahana.

"You might consider these connections wormholes," she said. "Whether the other side is a separate dimension or another planet, we don't know, but what the probes allowed us to do is have a direction and a destination. We tracked the path the Devil's Sea probe took as it went into the gate, and once you go into the gate, you should be able to pick up the path between portals, which will give a destination or at least an idea where one of these wormholes are. More importantly, the probes gave us the data we need to make a device that we believe can open a portal if we can tap into sufficient power. An interesting aspect is that there is time variance on the data."

"Which means?" Dane asked.

"That time is a variable on the other side," Ahana said. "We've even had some of our data time-reversed, as if time was going backward at certain points."

"That would explain Flaherty and the *Scorpion*," Dane noted.

The American officer, Loomis spoke up. "We'll be using a specially modified prototype attack craft designed for the SEALS for the reconnaissance. Waterproof, airtight. Able to go on land or water. Heavily armed. It's called the Crab for Combat Reconnaissance Assault Boat."

Dane remembered some of the creatures that had attacked his team in the Angkor gate over forty years ago. He wondered how well this Crab would stand up against them. Before anyone could say anything else, the elevator came to a halt.

"This way," Nagoya pointed. "We have to transfer to another elevator."

"How deep is this place?" Colonel Shashenka asked.

"Three miles down," Nagoya said as they followed him.

"We're also going to use biotechnology," Loomis continued.

"What does that mean?" Dane asked.

"Project Rachel," Loomis said.

Dane waited, letting the military man feel superior by giving out information in pieces.

"Rachel is something the Navy has been working on for a long time. She's a Pacific dolphin, specially trained to follow commands and make a modicum of contact with humans. She will expand our reconnaissance abilities. Since there seems to be a problem using electromagnetic equipment around the gates, Rachel will give you an organic capability that shouldn't draw unwanted attention."

Dane remembered the beach and the dolphins. He glanced at Foreman, but the CIA man didn't seem to make any connection.

"And once we complete the recon?" Dane asked. "Let's say we find the portal. You said you had the means to open it if you could tap into enough power."

Nagoya nodded. "Yes. We mean to draw power out of the gate to allow us to turn it around to open the portal."

"And how do you plan to draw that power out?" Dane asked.

"With an extension cord," Ahana said.

"What's the plug?" Dane asked.

"We are," she answered.

"This is getting smarter and smarter," Dane said. "Then what happens?"

"Then we go through," Loomis said. "We have forces assembling; as do the Russians," he acknowledged his Russian comrade in arms.

"What kind of forces?" Dane asked.

"Whatever we can get through," Loomis said. "That's another reason why we're running a recon first."

Dane could sense the confidence of the military men. They believed in the power of their weapons, but he wasn't as sure they would be successful. Their weapons were designed for human enemies. The elevator came to a halt, and they followed Nagoya to his lab.

He pointed to a monitor that showed a solid black triangle. "This is Devil's Sea gate. It has assumed this size, approximately four miles on each side, and visual reports indicate the perimeter is delineated by solid black."

He nodded to Ahana, who sat down in front of the keyboard and typed in some commands. A small red dot appeared near the bottom of the triangle. "That is the pod," he said. "It's transmitting muons, but a slightly different pattern than the gates are transmitting. It's the first time we have successfully sent anything into a gate and been able to receive a report."

"Other than the few people who've come back out," Dane said.

"Ah…" Nagoya was obviously embarrassed. "Yes, that is true. My apologies. What is curious is that Chernobyl seems to be providing the power that is coming out of the Devil's Sea gate."

"So the Shadow is once more using something we invented against us," Dane said.

"It appears so."

"How soon will your recon craft be ready by the gate?" Foreman asked Loomis.

"Six hours."

Ahana changed the display, and he could see another black triangle with another red dot inside, not far from the Dnieper River.

"How did you get your probe in?" Dane asked the Russian.

"A brave volunteer," Shashenka said.

"Right." Dane glared at Foreman who ignored him. "Did the gate there cause the problems at Chernobyl?"

"Yes," Shashenka said. "We have kept it tightly classified, but the gate tapped into the core of Reactor Four. When we tried to shut it down, it was too late, and the reactor went critical. And the volunteer was my brother," he added giving Dane a hard look.

"I'm sorry," Dane said.

"He was dying of cancer," Shashenka said. "My brother, Andrej, was an engineer at the reactor and was killed when it went critical. My brother, Pytor, felt it was his duty to give his life in a meaningful way to avenge Andrej's death rather than dying by wasting away."

"Then he was indeed a brave volunteer," Dane said. "My apologies."

"Your apologies are accepted," Shashenka said.

"Why is the gate at Chernobyl different?" Dane asked.

"A good question," Shashenka said. "Our Professor Kolkov believes one of the major purposes, perhaps *the* major purpose, is to gather energy from our world. The Chernobyl gate might be smaller because the small size sitting over the core of Reactor Four is sufficient to get the power needed. The other gates might have to be larger in order to accomplish the same thing.

"Kolkov analyzed data taken during the construction of the Chernobyl Reactor, and found some anomalies. He believes that the gate was there but not active during construction. The data were quite strange. There were signs of radioactivity at the site prior to the first tree being cut down."

Ahana spoke up. "Since we are considering time to be a variable inside the gates, it is possible that radiation that comes from the gate is moving backward and forward in time from the point of the tap into the core."

"What are you talking about?" Dane demanded.

Ahana pointed to her right. 'Our time is going this way. But what if the Shadow's time inside the Chernobyl gate is going that way also," she pointed in the opposite direction.

"So the energy tap could be for energy the Shadow has already used?" Dane asked, trying to understand.

"We know some of the energy is being sent to the Devil's Sea gate in our present," Ahana said. "But there is also the possibility that the energy is being spread through not only space but time."

Dane considered that. "That means Chernobyl could be a very critical node to the Shadow."

Ahana nodded. "If we could get a better understanding of the entire gate and portal system, it would help."

Dane thought they were focusing too much on the scientific aspects of all of this. "What purposes do you think the gates have other than gathering energy?" he asked.

"Besides trying to destroy our world?" Foreman asked. "Obviously they gather humans and our vessels as the graveyard in the Bermuda Triangle showed."

"We saw the vessels, and some of them had been cannibalized. But what do they do with the people they take?" Dane wondered.

There was no response to that.

A scream woke Pytor Shashenka from a nightmare into an even worse reality. Why was he still alive? Why hadn't the radiation taken him? How could he be alive after what had been done to him?

The scream echoed in the cavern. Out of the corner of his eye he could see one of the strange creatures moving about. He had no energy to turn and look, and he didn't want to see what it was doing to whoever was screaming.

He was glad Andrej had died in the explosion and not been brought here.

One of the creatures paused in front of him. It had something metallic in its claw. It jabbed forward, and Pytor felt something go into the middle of his chest, then be withdrawn.

He passed out once more.

In the southeast Pacific, a quarter-mile-thick-crust of solid igneous rock had covered a mile-wide chasm between the Pacific and Nazca tectonic plates for millennia. An empty chasm extended two miles down below the cap to red- hot lava coming out of the Earth's mantle. Even though the gap was growing bigger year by year, the rate had been slow enough to allow discreet adjustments.

The muonic probing from the Devil's Sea gate changed that in an instant. As the power moved through the covering rock, a section gave way, causing a cascading effect along a forty-mile stretch.

That far under the ocean, the effect was hardly noticeable, even though the power that was expended was tremendous. However, as the power reached the surface, a wave began to form, very long in length and low in height heading for the westward side of South America at seven hundred miles an hour.

"What's the limit on weaponry?" Dane asked.

"What do you mean?"

"Are you authorized to use nuclear weapons through the gates?" Dane clarified his question.

"The Shadow has used nuclear weapons," Foreman said.

"I take that as a yes," Dane said. He turned to Nagoya. "Since you don't know exactly what's over there or how the gates are connected, you have no clue what the use of a nuclear weapon will do inside of a gate or portal, do you?"

"No, I don't," Nagoya admitted.

"It's war," Foreman said simply. "You don't use a hammer when you can use a battering ram."

"At what point will you decide to use nukes?" Dane asked.

"When we have determined they're needed," Foreman said.

"I hope that doesn't occur while we're still in the gate," Dane said.

"Of course not," Foreman replied. "This is a reconnaissance mission."

"What else do you have?" Dane asked Nagoya, knowing it was a waste to extract promises from Foreman.

"The Shadow has been probing constantly," the Japanese scientist answered. "We've been analyzing the pattern of the probes, and while it is covering the entire Ring of fire, there are two key points that the Shadow seems to be paying particular attention to." He nodded at Ahana, who once more changed the display on the monitor.

"Here," she pointed. "Mount Wrangell in Alaska. The northernmost volcano on the Ring of Fire. And here." She changed the view. "Mount Erebus, in Antarctica. The southernmost volcano."

"I think you need to clue Ariana in on this," Dane suggested to Foreman.

"We have our experts," Foreman said.

"Ariana has been inside a gate," Dane pointed out. "That gives her an insight your experts don't have. She also has a degree in geology and a lot of practical experience."

"I've already forwarded the data to her."

"Back to opening the portal," Dane said. "What's the plan?"

Ahana pulled a folder out and opened it. "We have our people specially modifying this craft."

A long, thin craft, almost looking like a pencil, was next to a dock in the picture. The front end of it was bulbous.

"What is it?"

"It's called a FLIP," Ahana said. "Floating Instrument Panel. The government began working on it, adding a superkamiokande to the bow" – she tapped the bulb—"about six months ago. There was concern that this site might be targeted by the Shadow, and it was felt it might be good to have a mobile detector.

"It's over two hundred meters long and has no engines. It gets towed to wherever we want to set up. Then ballast is shifted to the bow, and it goes underwater. The bow sinks, while the stern remains above water until it's vertical, like this," she turned the picture, bow facing down. "About twenty meters of the stern, where our control center is located, remains dry. The floor rotates as the entire ship does."

"And what will having a detector on scene do for us?" Dane asked.

"We're not going to detect," Professor Nagoya said. "We're going to transmit. This is the other end of the extension cord. We're going to lock on the Devil's Sea probe coming out of the portal and transmit a beam of muons into the gate, into the probe, toward the Chernobyl probe. What we're hoping to do is tap into the forces at work inside the gate; the weak and strong forces, and then draw them out to us and use them to open the gate and portal."

Dane had little idea what Nagoya was talking about, and he could tell the military men didn't either.

"We've got support from a carrier task force," Colonel Loomis trilled in. "The Crab will be launched off the deck of the *Grayback*, our special operations submarine. The *Grayback* will remain on station for recovery, five kilometers outside the perimeter of the gate."

"When do we go?" Dane asked.

"Everything will be ready tomorrow night," Foreman said. "Tonight, we deploy to the task force."

"Why don't we check out the graveyard tomorrow then?" Dane suggested. "As long as we aren't sending out a signal like *Deepflight* did, we should be safe doing that."

"Why do you want to check that?" Foreman asked.

"We found that Atlantean ship in the Bermuda Triangle graveyard," Dave said. "And the Viking ship. Who knows what might be in there? Perhaps your brother's plane." He could see that last thought hit home.

"All right," Foreman agreed. "I'll arrange a submersible to be ready."

"How long do we have on the Ring of Fire?" Dane asked Ahana.

"It's hard to tell," she said. "So far, it just probing. We're not even sure if the probing will lead to anything."

"Ours will," Dane noted. "I would assume theirs will, too."

Ariana Michelet felt like a ghoul, carrying a satchel containing six crystal skulls into her father's Learjet. She had Van Liten's five plus the one from the museum. She put the bag in the seat across from her, then instructed the pilot to take off. She was going from New York to London, were Van Liten had told her another skull was being held by the museum there.

The fax machine on the other side of the plane began spitting out pieces of paper, and Ariana went over to check them, ignoring the Fasten Seat Belt sign, and staggering slightly as the plane accelerated down the runway at JFK International.

She recognized what was on the papers as she scanned: muonic imagery from Nagoya's superkamiokande. She sat back down and traced the lines. She immediately noted the probing around the Ring of Fire and the focus on Mounts Erebus and Wrangell.

She accessed her geological database and looked at Erebus first. It was the second-highest peak in Antarctica, surpassed only by the Vinson Massif. It was also an active volcano, overlooking the largest base on the continent at McMurdo Station. There was an observatory on the side of the volcano at the three-hundred-meter mark that transmitted telemetry and was the jump-off point for visual inspections once a year, during the brief two month of relatively decent weather.

The volcano was wired, which was a good thing, Ariana thought. Six vertical geophones listened to it; gas emissions were checked by a COSPEC V; and seismic stations at McMurdo and around the world were tuned in to any disturbance that might occur. She went to the Department of Geosciences of New Mexico Tech's web site, where all this data was collected. She accessed the latest reading and was disturbed by what she saw. The volcano was acting up, and a stage-two alert had been issued. A stage three required evacuation of all those who might be affected.

But why Erebus? Ariana wondered. There were only a couple hundred people at McMurdo, certainly not a significant target for the Shadow. She went back to the map and checked the location. Erebus was located in the Ross Dependency of Antarctica, almost an island, connected to the mainland on one side. It was also adjacent to the Rose Ice shelf, the largest ice shelf on the planet. She saw part of the reason then. If Erebus had a major eruption, the ice shelf would be shattered all along its eastern edge, causing massive blocks to float out to sea. Also, the heat from the volcano would have devastating effects on the ice cap.

And what about Wrangell? She cleared her screen and searched for information on the mountain. It was located in Alaska at the west end of the Wrangell Mountains. It too, was an active volcano. It was also being monitored, and she checked the data. Activity, but not as much as Erebus.

Ariana then looked up the Ring of Fire and immediately saw the significance of Wrangell. It was like the top of a zipper of volcanoes along the west coast of the Americas. If it went, and the Shadow moved south, it could set off a chain reaction that would tear down the coast of North America, into South America all the way to Erebus in the south; or Ariana reflected, the effect could go the other way from Erebus to Wrangell. She remembered the devastation when Mount St. Helens in Oregon had erupted. She had been on one of the first geological survey teams to go in.

She shuddered to think what effect dozens of simultaneous eruptions all around the Pacific Rim would have.

As the water grew shallower, the water power from crustal displacement had nowhere else to go but up. A tidal wave grew until it towered sixty feet high, carrying millions of tons of water at high speed toward the Chilean coast.

There was no warning, no chance of escape for the thousands who lived in the region where the wave hit. The death toll was low compared to the devastation that had been wreaked in Puerto Rico, Iceland, and Connecticut, but that was little consolation to those who died.

CHAPTER ELEVEN

THE PAST
79 A.D.

"We must stop by Thera," Kaia announced as the ship slipped its moors in the port of Brundisium.

"Why?" General Cassius asked.

This was their first chance to really talk since leaving Rome. They had traveled the Via Brusdisii by horse, switching at every stage to new horses, escorted by a troop of Praetorian Guard. The smoothly set stones that made up the way were flanked by a deeply rutted dirt track on which the horses ran. The road, an example of spectacular engineering, was designed for marching troops and carts, not speedy horses.

The road passed thirty miles to the east of Pompeii, and they had ridden at night, the way lit by the red glow on the top of Vesuvius. They'd encountered columns of dazed refugees, and what they heard confirmed what Falco and Kaia had seen: Pompeii had been completely destroyed. The tales of horror were so bad that Falco had forced himself to stop listening. The only solace he had was that he knew his children had died quickly; at least that was the sense he had had in the arena. He had been quiet the entire ride, his mind turned inward, dwelling on the fact that his special talent always seemed linked to death and mourning.

"There is someone at Thera I must talk to," Kaia replied.

Captain Fabatus was the commander of the ship, a forty-foot-long galley, part of the imperial fleet. It was designed for speed rather than cargo, with sleek lines and two rows of oars poking out of the side, manned by sixty slaves. There was a small contingent of soldiers, one *contuberium* of eight men.

They were there more to keep control over the slaves than for defense, as the Mediterranean and Aegean were Roman seas.

Fabatus was as short, fat man, with a face weathered by the sea. He had outlined the route the ship would take. Southeast around the tip of Greece, passing between there and Crete, then through the Hellespont and into the Pontus Euxinus to make landfall and link up with the XXV Legion.

"My orders are to take you where you wish," Fabatus said, "but Thera is a little off our route."

"Who is it you must see?" Falco asked.

"The oracle of Akrotiri."

Cassius nodded as if that made perfect sense. "How far out of the way is Thera?" he asked Fabatus.

"A half a day, but it is a bad place."

"A bad place?" Falco repeated. He was wearing the uniform of a centurion, and the armor felt strange, not the same as that which he had worn in the arena. He had brought his gladiator armor with him, but it was tucked away in his campaign bag.

"There is a harbor inside the island," Fabatus said. "Two ways in with high land all around. It would be an excellent anchorage, superb indeed. But no one uses it."

"Why?" Falco pressed.

"Bad spirits," Fabatus said. "Neptune does not favor it. A man would be a fool to go there unless it was absolutely necessary."

Falco knew that seamen were an extremely superstitious lot, almost as bad as gladiators, but both groups had reason to be. Their lives and livelihood were very dependent on forces beyond their control.

"Is there a harbor on the outside of the island?" Cassius asked.

"A small dock at the base of the cliff," Fabatus said.

"You will make for that," Cassius ordered.

Fabatus waddled off into the dark, muttering under his breath about landlubbers and whims of the gods.

"I am tired," Cassius said. "I must get some rest."

"I will take watch," Falco said.

"We are in the bosom of the empire," Cassius said. "Do you think a watch is needed?"

"Even more so because we are in the bosom of the empire," Falco said.

Cassius's teeth flashed in the dark as he smiled. "Very good, Centurion. The right answer as always. I will relieve you in four hours."

Cassius headed toward the rear of the galley. Falco and Kaia could hear the slap of oars in the water and the low steady beat of the drum as the master kept the rhythm for the slaves who handled the rowing. Falco felt the cool breeze of the Mediterranean on his skin and knew that here was no such comfort below decks.

"Who are you?" Falco asked, a question that had bothered him since the arena and her assistance in his fight.

"You know my name."

Falco waited.

Finally she turned to him. "Why don't you tell me who *you* are first?"

Falco shrugged. "I was a slave. A gladiator. Then a soldier. Then a gladiator again. And now it appears I am a soldier once more."

"Where did you come from?"

Falco nodded toward the center of the boat and down. "You might as well go there and ask those chained to the oars where they come from. Most don't know. My earliest memories are of chains and the fields and the darkness of the mines. I even rowed on a ship like this for six months, chained to my seat, fearing and yet praying at the same time that we would go down in a storm or pirates would take the ship. Sicily was the first clear place I remember, but I don't think I was born there."

"And you've always been different from those around you?"

"Yes."

"But you loved someone," she noted.

"How do you know that?"

"I felt your pain when your children died, and I saw a woman through that pain. An even greater pain."

"Drusilla."

"A pretty name," Kaia said.

"She was the only nice person I've ever met," Falco said simply. "I could always feel what others felt. Slaves." – he indicated the inside of the ship once more—"are either dulled into nothingness or seething with rage. The latter don't last long. Drusilla, even though she was a slave also, was different. She saw beauty in the smallest things. I don't know why. But I could sense that in her."

"And because you appreciated the best part of her, she loved you," Kaia said.

Falco had never examined the why of his love for Drusilla or hers from him, so he didn't reply. This was not something he felt comfortable talking about.

"You were lucky," Kaia said.

Falco was surprised. "Lucky? She's dead. My children are dead."

"But you had her for the time you had her," Kaia said simply. "It is more than most have. To experience joy you have to risk pain."

"Easily said."

"No so easily," she said without elaborating. "Why did you choose killing?" Kaia asked.

"It is what I am good at."

"No, it's something you became good at," she said. "You used your gift to kill."

"My gift?"

"Your sense of others."

"And what did you use it for?"

"Nothing yet," she said with a slight smile. "I was isolated throughout my childhood, meeting only with those the oracle sent to me. Various teachers and instructors. I am beginning to see why she kept me so alone. I might have ended up like you."

Falco shifted, and she hurriedly continued.

"I do not mean to be disrespectful. Just realistic."

Falco felt uncomfortable both with the conversation and wearing the armor of a centurion. The deference paid to him by the crew of the ship and the slaves was also disconcerting. He had become so used to the arena and the strange life one led there, he had forgotten about this world he had once been a part of. In the arena, the blade and sharp point ruled. Outside the arena, there was the *lanista*, the nobles, the servants, and the other gladiators. In the arena, all were equal, at least for the moment. Even outside the arena, a gladiator was judged by what he had done inside it. But here, one was treated differently by rank, whether earned or not. In the arena, rank was earned.

"Why have you chosen me?" Falco demanded, tired of her questions. He noted that she had never answered his question that started the conversation.

"I saw you in a vision."

"You believe your visions?"

"Yes. Some have come true. Others will come true."

Falco reluctantly nodded. "Some things I have seen in dreams, they came true."

"What about things you have dreamed that haven't happened yet?" she asked.

Falco spat over the railing at the water going by. "Many I can't remember. Some are very strange."

"I recommend that for the rest of this journey, you focus on your dreams," Kaia said. "And tell me what you see. I need you for more than your sword arm."

The Oracle of Delphi was standing in the entrance to the Corycian Cave, peering into the darkness, her hands pulling her heaviest cloak tight around her bony shoulders. Still she shivered. She had sent all the priestesses away to the town. They had protested, but in the end, their discipline had held. A fog was seeping through the sacred grove, swirling about the trunks and branches of the trees.

They were out there in the darkness. Searching. Coming closer with each passing moment. She could sense their coldness, but no thoughts, no emotions. The closest thing she had ever sensed like this was when a group of travelers from the east had passed through, bringing with them a large black cat they called a panther to present to the emperor in Rome for the games. The creature had given off the same coldness. But the panther had been driven by hunger and rage. She had no clue of the driving force behind what was coming.

Her eyes shifted back and forth, but her sight had been failing for years, and she saw nothing. She knew they were very close. Looking over her shoulder, she could see the omphalos was glowing, giving off a blue light that illuminated the walls of the cave.

Since being moved here to Delphi, the stone had never glowed. Hours earlier, the faint glow had been the first sign to alert her that danger was coming. Where the omphalos came from, she didn't know. What it warned of, she wasn't exactly sure, but from what she was sensing, she knew her time was coming to a close.

Something flitted in the dark. She peered. A white figure moved through the trees. Then another. Valkyries. They were coming toward her. As they got closer, she could see the smooth white skin, the lack of nose or mouth, just red eyes glaring at her. They floated, not touching the ground, a half foot of darkness separating them from the grass below.

The oracle stepped forward, raising her wooden staff. "You can not come here!" She cried out, her voice sounding old and weak even to her, she who had advised kings and emperors and had thousands wait upon her slightest utterance.

The strange beings took no notice. One came right up to her, halting four feet in front. The other headed past her into the cave. She stuck her staff out, but it didn't' even notice the obstruction, pushing through. After searching the cave, it was back with its partner. The two Valkyries hovered in front of her.

The oracle stood tall, staring at the red eyes.

Something flickered out from under the cloak of the creature on the left, a very thin spear moving faster than the oracle could follow. It hit her right above and between her eyes, piercing through skin, bone, and into her brain. She staggered backward from the impact.

She would have fallen, but one of the Valkyries was behind her, claws on her shoulders, holding her up. There was a line from the spear to a small box held by the first Valkyrie.

The oracle, through the pain, could feel the invasion of her mind, the search, and she knew what they were looking for. And she knew they would find the knowledge soon.

She surprised the Valkyries by jerking forward, slamming her head toward the hard chest of the one in front, shoving the probe through her skull and out the back. She slumped dead in the second Valkyrie's claws. The first reeled in the probe, pulling it back through her head, blood and brain matter spilling out as it popped loose.

It turned and floated away. The second leaned over and swiped at the body with a long, razor-thin claw at the end of a finger. It sliced through the oracle's neck, severing her head from her body. It reached down and picked up the head, cradling it in both clawed hands. Exerting tremendous pressure, it crushed the skull, brains and blood bursting out between fingers.

It followed the other Valkyrie and disappeared into the dark.

CHAPTER TWELVE

THE PRESENT

Dane looked through the binoculars, ignoring Chelsea's uneasy whine. The Devil's Sea gate was a black wall to the north, extending ten miles across and a mile into the air. Radar also indicated it went a mile deep into the ocean. He was on board the USS *Salvor,* classified by the Navy as an auxiliary rescue and salvage class vessel. Two hundred twenty-five feet long and fifty-one feet wide, it was smaller than the destroyer that lurked on the horizon, providing them with a modicum of security.

Towed behind the *Salvor* was the FLIP, lying low in the water. All except the most essential electromagnetic equipment was turned off on both vessels, reducing their EM signature to a minimum. Dane echoed Chelsea's unease at being this close to a gate. He could sense the presence of the Shadow, an alien evilness, biding its time, waiting to strike again. He was on the starboard side of the *Salvor*'s bridge, feeling the cool ocean breeze on his skin.

Dane had always been different from others, and Sin Fen had been the first person he'd met like himself, with the unique ability to sense things others couldn't and to hear voices and have visions of things. She had explained it to him as best she could, and as best she knew, but given the fact that she had held back her own secrets, he wasn't sure how much of what she had imparted to him could be counted on.

She had told him that they were different because their brains were abnormal. That the speech center on the right side of their brains, which was underdeveloped and not used by most humans, was the source of most of their difference from the rest of the humans race. Sin Fen had told him that early humans had had a basic telepathic ability before they were able to communicate with language, and it was centered on the right side of the brain in the speech center. Once a spoken language developed, that ability became dormant and eventually disappeared from most of the population with the exception of throwbacks like Dane and Sin Fen.

Dane had never known his parents, growing up in orphanages and foster homes until he was seventeen and joined the army. Sin Fen had also claimed to be an orphan. As he stared at the darkness of the gate, Dane had to wonder where she – and he – truly came from.

He sensed someone coming and turned as Colonel Loomis came out of the bridge. "A *Deepflight* submersible is on site above the Challenger Deep."

"What happened to Shashenka's brother?" Dane asked. "The one who went into the Chernobyl gate?"

"We don't know. He disappeared. He took a fatal dose of radiation the minute he went into the reactor, so we assume he's dead."

"Did he go through the portal there?"

"The video cameras blanked out when he went in," Loomis said. "When they got power back, there was no sign of his body."

Dane could see the patches on Loomis' camouflage fatigue shirt, and he noted the combat infantry badge on his chest and the Special Forces patch on his right shoulder indicating combat service with the unit.

Dane had been a member of Recon Team Kansas and had accompanied the other three members along with a CIA operative from Foreman on a cross-border mission deep into Cambodia in 1968, which was his first encounter with a gate. During that mission, three of the four men were killed, and the team leader, Sergeant Ed Flaherty, was snatched away. Dane had been the only one to come out alive, and he'd sworn never again to be in such a situation.

But he'd gone back into the Angkor gate on a rescue mission for Ariana Michelet, again being manipulated by Foreman. Actually, the real reason he had gone was the copy of a radio broadcast from Flaherty. At Angkor Kol Ker, the ancient and abandoned capital of the Khmer Empire, he had met Flaherty once more, a Flaherty who had not apparently aged a day since disappearing over forty years previously.

Flaherty had warned him of the Shadow and told him of the Ones Before. He'd also said he could never come back. But the *Scorpion* had come back, although they now knew that had been a trap sent by the Shadow. It appeared that only the Shadow had control of the gates, and the Ones Before could do little inside them. Too many unknowns. For Dane, who had always been able to anticipate what others would do, this was a very unnerving situation.

"Are you ready to leave?" Loomis indicated the helicopter, which was warming up on the back deck. The colonel was uncomfortable with silence, a trait Dane didn't understand or respect. He'd always believed that as much could be learned by what wasn't said as by what was. "The *Salvor* will stay here and await the arrival of the *Grayback*."

"What about Chelsea?" Dane asked.

"I'll have someone in the crew take care of her until we get back."

Reluctantly, Dane rubbed Chelsea's head and said good-bye, then followed Loomis to the helicopter.

*****

Rain was falling, something Ariana recollected to be standard for England. A helicopter from one of her father's subsidiary companies was waiting for her as the Learjet rolled to a stop. Her dash across the Atlantic in the middle of the night after leaving New York had brought her to London early in the morning, just after sunrise.

She hurried across the tarmac, not bothering to open the umbrella that had been thrust in her hand. The skulls she had gathered remained on board the Learjet, and she had ordered the pilots to refuel and await her return. When they'd complained about mandatory crew rest, she'd gotten on the phone and ordered up two new pilots. There was to be no rest on this mission, as the incoming date from Mounts Wrangell and Erebus indicated.

The chopper was in the air within a minute, and it headed from Heathrow on the very western edge of the city toward downtown London. It was only about a dozen miles to the London Natural History Museum, and the helicopter landed in Hyde Park, three blocks from the museum, startling some early-morning walkers and joggers. A car waited. Ariana ran past the man who was waiting with an umbrella and jumped in the open door. The man climbed in after her and offered his somewhat damp hand.

"Professor Atkins, at your service." He was an old man with thick white hair and a long beard. "I am the collection leader for the mineral collection."

"Ariana Michelet."

"Your father has a long reach," Atkins noted as the car began moving. "I've never met a helicopter before for a research request. Especially such a strange request."

"You do have a crystal skull?" Ariana asked.

"Yes. Quite an odd duck. We've never displayed it. Doesn't quite fit in, you know."

"What do you mean?"

They were passing Royal Albertson Hall and then turning onto Exhibition Road. Ariana had been here before, and London was one of her favorite towns, but she knew there would be no time to savor the trip.

Atkins laughed, a deep, mellow sound. "My colleagues are not fond of displaying things they can't explain. You don't want some school-age child asking, "What's that?" and not being able to tell them. Would be quite embarrassing, don't you think?"

The car came to a halt at the Earth Science entrance to the museum, and Ariana was out the door before Atkins could move. She waited impatiently as he slowly got out and opened the umbrella every English person seemed to have permanently attached to one of their hands. They went up the stairs and into the museum, a guard opening the door for them.

"We have over three hundred fifty thousand specimens," Atkins said as he closed the umbrella and shook it. "We actually have twelve meteorites that we believe are Martian in origin. Quite unique."

Ariana had to wonder about a career that was based on the number of rocks one had and the uniqueness of them. "The skull?" she prompted.

Atkins led her through a room full of cases exhibiting various gemstones. "Yes, yes. As I said, it's not on display."

He unlocked a door and led her into an office crammed with professional journals and crates of all sizes. There was a desk in the corner, under the lone window, a narrow, barred affair ten feet over their heads. Atkins took off his coat and settled back in a deep leather chair and regarded her through rimless glasses as he reached behind himself and pulled a piece of cloth off an item on a shelf revealing a crystal skull. It was an ancient, just like the other six.

"Quite odd," Atkins said as she came around the desk and ran her fingers lightly over the skull.

"What do you mean?"

"I know this sounds strange, but it makes people feel... hmm... I'm not sure what the words would be. Weird? Uneasy? Queer?"

"Where was it found?"

"Most fascinating history, most fascinating," he said. He had a file folder that was open, but he didn't need to refer to it. "It came to us from the estate of Lord Withingham. He was a rather eccentric member of the archaeological society, and his widow gave us quite a few strange and wonderful objects.

"Withingham bought this skull in Ireland from a retired naval officer who had fallen on hard times. The officer, who was in his late nineties and in ill health, said he had found it in a burial heath at Callanish, on the Irish coast. Last year, during holiday, I was visiting friends in Ireland, and I went to check this area. Quite amazing, to be frank."

"Why?" Ariana asked.

"Why, the stones, of course."

"Stones?"

"Yes, Megaliths. Do you know anything about them?"

"I've been to Stonehenge. That's about it."

"Stonehenge is the most well-known of the megaliths, but there are hundreds of megalithic sites all over Europe. This," – he pointed at the skull—"was found inside the Callanish ring near the Great Menhir. The Menhir is a standing stone over sixteen feet high, while the ring has dozens and dozens of smaller standing stones, arrayed about it. The burial mound where the skull was found was right next to the Great Menhir."

"As I said, we have many megalithic sites throughout Europe, and Callanish is one of the most intriguing. The outer stones are aligned in patterns. Many have tried to orient these patterns on various astronomical alignments. Hard to do, though, because you have to regress the sky to the time when the stones were placed, and it's difficult to date that. After all, we can't carbon date stone, now can we? Even Stonehenge, which has been studied as deeply as any of the megalithic sites, has just rough approximations for dating various phases of its construction."

Ariana didn't see the connection between the crystal skull and standing stones. "Could ancient people have found the crystal skull and set up the standing stones around it as some form of worship?"

Atkins ran a hand through his thick beard as he considered her question. "Possibly. But Callanish is the only place where a skull has been found, as far as I know. And these sites have been thoroughly combed; Stonehenge, Averbury, Carnac, and the like. Doubt they would have missed that."

"What other theories are there about the megaliths?" Ariana asked.

"The most popular here in England is that Druids built Stonehenge and the like, but that's poppycock, as Stonehenge predates the Druids. Others say the sites were a form of astronomical observatory. Some of the sites do orient on certain stars when we regress the star field. At Callanish, most of the small outer stones are oriented on the cardinal directions. A tremendous amount of effort went into moving and setting these stones, some of which are quite heavy, and we don't quite know why the ancient people did it. Seems like they would have had more important things to do, like gathering food and such."

"Any theories, no matter how strange, would be helpful," Ariana said.

Atkins sighed. "There are those who see a grander scheme to all this, but it's quite a leap to take that in."

"What do you mean?"

"There are some who believe that there is a worldwide pattern to the megaliths and other similar structures, which, of course, is ridiculous, given the time at which they were built."

"Maybe not," Ariana said. "We very much believe now that there was an Atlantis and it was destroyed and the survivors scattered about the world. What if they were responsible for the megaliths?"

"Ah, yes," Atkins said. "I've been following the news. Most terrible what happened in Iceland. Damn shame."

Ariana had always been fascinated by the English ability to view disaster with a certain dispassion.

"We know these gates are connected," Ariana said. "So there *are* strange forces at work within the Earth."

"Hmm. Yes, I suppose. You know, there's a fellow near Oxford who's done some rather interesting work," Atkins said. "Conducting a thing he calls the Dragon Project. He's run tests on some of the stones and picked up strange energy readings emanating from them, which confirms local legends of the power of the stones. They also found slightly higher levels of radiation around megalithic sites. He did some checking and found that megalithic sites around the world are also tied to uranium-rich areas, which is quite strange, if you think about it."

Ariana felt her jet lag fade as she listened to Atkins. There was more to all this than just the skulls, she was beginning to believe.

"The most interesting readings, though," Atkins continued, "involve electromagnetism around the megalithic sites. Project Dragon picked up rapid and extreme electromagnetic fluxes around the various sites they tested. They checked this because they heard many reports that megalithic sites were almost always locally rumored to have healing properties. In ancient days, people brought the sick and would leave them inside standing circles. In some cases, I suppose, there was some recovery, but most likely due to a placebo effect rather than any magical properties."

"It has been documented that certain frequencies of the electromagnetic spectrum have healing properties," Ariana noted.

"Well, I don't know much about that," Atkins admitted. "Of course, the man running Project Dragon, a chap named Davon, couldn't stick with just the facts he picked up, and that's what caused him trouble among the more literal of our scientific community. He also reported that he and other members of his team *saw* things inside some of the circles. Strange creatures, strange people, different places. Most bizarre, and of course they had no proof of these sightings. This tainted the proof he did have."

Could the megalithic sites be some sort of alternate gates? Ariana wondered. *Or maybe just a weak point in the field between Earth and whatever was on the other side?*

"And well, some of these visions…" Atkins fell silent.

"What about them?"

"They showed people from other times, if one is to believe those who say they saw something."

"What happened to Project Dragon?" Ariana asked.

"As far as I know, they're still plugging away," Atkins said.

"Where can I get hold of Davon?" she asked.

Atkins leafed through the file folder. "Here's the address for the Dragon organization. I imagine you'll find him there, unless he's out gallivanting about. I've heard he's expanded his work overseas."

Ariana took the address, then pulled a cloth bag out of the pocket of her raincoat. "The skull, please."

Atkins reluctantly slid it into the bag. "Your father does have quite a bit of pull with the museum board of directors."

"This is much more important than my father," Ariana said. She paused at the door. "Do you know where there are any more skulls like this?"

"There's a woman named Van Liten who—"

"I've already met her," Ariana cut him off.

"Ah, well." Atkins steepled his fingers, and Ariana realized he was exercising the power of knowledge over her in a subconscious way. She waited, forcing herself to be patient.

"Our field reps get approached every so often by what you might call shady characters dealing so-called antiquities or objects they think we would think would be of value. They seem to believe we have an unlimited amount of funds, which, of course, couldn't be further from the truth, and offer us rare pieces for exorbitant amounts of money.

"About two years ago, one of our people was escorting an exhibit that we loaned to the Darwin Museum of Natural History in Moscow with whom we have a working relationship. He was approached by a fellow who claimed to have a crystal skull. Of course the price he was asking – fifty thousand in U.S. dollars – was ridiculous, so nothing came of it."

"Did the person give any contact information?" Ariana asked.

Atkins opened a drawer and pulled out a piece of paper. He slid it across his desk, and Ariana went forward to retrieve it. "You weren't going to give this to me?" she asked as she took it.

"A good researcher has to ask the right questions," Atkins said.

"This isn't a game." Ariana had had enough with PhD's and intellectuals. She snatched the piece of paper out of his hands. "The safety of our planet is at stake."

"Well…" Atkins began, but then he stopped, at a loss for a moment. "I don't see what crystal skulls have to do with what is happening with these gates."

"I don't have time to explain it to you." Ariana left the room, the skull held in one hand, the piece of paper in the other.

*****

A Shadow flitted past so quickly that Pytor Shashenka wasn't sure his eyes had actually seen something or if he was in a delusional state. But then a second went by, and he was certain. Not the white creatures but something or someone else. He also heard voices, hoarse whispers. He forced his mind to come out of the shell it had retreated to and focus.

There were people in the cavern. Free people! He saw a man, dressed in a strange outfit, some kind of armor, holding a straight, thin sword in his hand. The man was in front of a board that held one of the captives. Pytor was stunned as the man drew back the sword and with one smooth stroke cut through the neck of the body, severing it. The head remained pinned to the board by the metal ring around it, but blood pumped out of the neck, flowing down over the clear coating covering the flayed body.

The man turned and approached Pytor, blood-covered sword in his hand. Pytor could see his face now: Oriental. The man said something in a language Pytor didn't understand. He drew the sword back, and Pytor waited, eager to be done with this horror he was in.

But then the man turned as there was a noise, a clank of metal, surprised yells. Another man similarly dressed and carrying a sword came running by, yelling something in the same strange language.

The man in front ignored his partner and brought the sword up once more. As he began to swing, a slash of gold hit him. Pytor blinked as the man's skin changed color to gray, hardening until the man was nothing more than a statue.

Then a woman, tall, with short brown hair, also dressed strangely, ran by. She seemed to be in charge, shouting commands. She held a long slightly curved sword in her hand.

She glanced at Pytor, and he saw the compassion in her eyes, but she was too far away to do anything, and the body of her comrade was between them. Another flash of gold barely missed her. She turned and ran with the others. Last, a large man dressed in leather, carrying a huge ax, brought up the rear. He paused, swinging the weapon in a mighty arc as a Valkyrie came screeching toward him. The heavy blade bounced off the white armor with a loud clang, but the creature was knocked back several feet and apparently dazed.

Two more Valkyries appeared, flanking the warrior who gave a mighty shout as he swung the ax back and forth, keeping his enemies at bay. Pytor could appreciate the bravery he was seeing, knowing this man was giving the others time to escape, but in the process, his own escape route was cut off as the three Valkyries surrounded him.

Despite his own pain, Pytor was drawn into the spectacle in front of him as the man held the creatures at bay with his ax. Sweat poured down the man's body, staining the already dirty tunic. His dark hair flopped about as he twisted and turned. A savage scar lined the left side of his face from temple to jaw.

He was yelling at the Valkyries in a language Pytor didn't understand, but the gist was clear: The man was taunting and cursing them. Minutes passed, and the creatures made no serious attempt to attack the man, but they kept him constantly on the defensive with quick probes. Pytor could tell the man's strength was being sapped, the ax growing heavy in his hands.

Finally, what the Valkyries were waiting for occurred. The man slipped, slamming the head of the ax into the rock floor to keep his balance. All three leapt forward at the same time. But it was a ruse, as the man rolled on the floor and came to his feet right in front of one of the Valkyries, the ax reversed, the metal tip on the end of the handle facing forward. He jabbed, and the blow struck true, right into one of the red eyes, shattering it.

The creature let loose a wicked scream.

It was a Pyrrhic victory for the man, though, as the other two were on him, ripping the ax from his hands, pinning his arms behind his back. Pytor felt useless, worse than useless, and the pain came back into him, overwhelming his mind. The sound of the battle faded, and Pytor once more slipped into blessed unconsciousness.

CHAPTER THIRTEEN

THE PAST
79 A.D.

As soon as she saw Thera appear on the horizon, Kaia felt a surge in her chest. The oracle had been correct; this was where her ancestors had lived for a long time. She had a vision of the island as a whole, before the destruction, of a magnificent white city with a pyramid in the center. Ships sailing from the port to all points of the Mediterranean.

"What is it?" Falco was at her side.

"Do you feel it?" Kaia asked.

"I feel power, subdued power," Falco said. "This was a great place once."

"It is where my people lived for a while after they came from Atlantis," Kaia said.

"Atlantis?" General Cassius had joined them in the bow of the imperial galley. "That is a story you Greeks made up."

"It was a real place," Kaia said. "The Shadow destroyed it."

"A very powerful Shadow then." Cassius said. "What can we do against such a force?"

"That remains to be seen," Kaia said. She pointed toward the island where they could see the shattered cliff walls surrounding the place where the sea had intruded into the center of the island. "That was also done by the Shadow."

"Why does this Shadow seek to destroy people and cities?" Falco asked.

"I don't know that," Kaia answered. "I hope to get some answers here."

As they got closer, it was apparent that there were several islands making up Thera. The land, as was usual in this part of the world, was rugged and rocky. A group of white buildings clung to the cliff side that faced the sea, and the ship docked below them. The land that remained was the caldera, or lip of the ancient volcano, a long, curving, steep ridge.

"This way," Kaia led the way off the ship, Cassius and Falco following. The few fisherman who were on the dock stared at them curiously as they went up a set of stairs cut into the rock itself. They said nothing, stepping back at Kaia's approach.

A nervous Captain Fabatus immediately cast off and pulled out a safe distance from the land. Like any sailor, he felt safer on the water.

Kaia didn't stop in the small town but kept going right through it and continuing upward. Falco was sweating heavily, and despite his training, he was slightly winded as they approached the top of the high cliff. He could see the general was struggling even more, but he knew that to offer help would be an insult. He was impressed with the woman's conditioning as she hopped from step to step. He was grateful when they reached the top. They could look back and see their ship far below, like a toy floating in the water. But it was the view in front of them that had their focus.

The high land curved around left and right, surrounding the inner sea, broken in two places to touch the outer sea. In the center, two small islands poked above the water, a thin line of smoke drifting up from the larger of them.

"This was once all an island, and that" – Kaia pointed at the smoking island—"was a mountain in the center. It was called Palaia Kameni, or Old Burnt Island in your language. The other is Nea Kameni, New Burnt Island. That is where we must go."

Falco felt uneasy. He looked over his shoulder toward the ocean. It was late afternoon, and the sun was going down. "We need to do whatever it is you want to do quickly," he said.

Kaia also looked over her shoulder and nodded. "I feel it, too. Danger. But it's a distance off."

"But coming closer," Falco said.

Without another word, Kaia began scrambling down the interior of the island toward the inner sea, following a narrow track that switched back and forth across the steep, rocky slope. Falco saw where she was headed: a small dock where a narrow boat was tied up. An old man was seated in the shadow of a large boulder, watching them approach.

Kaia raised her hand in greeting as they reached the dock. "I seek passage to Nea Kameni," she said.

The old man peered at her with eyes cloudy with cataracts. He placed his hand on her forehead and remained still for several moments, then he nodded. He held out his hand, and Kaia slipped several gold pieces into it. The old man gave a toothless smile and pointed at the boat, still without saying a word. Kaia climbed into it, Falco and Cassius following.

"It seems as if we've paid for the service of the boat and not the man," Cassius noted.

"He would take forever," Falco said as he grabbed one of the oars, Kaia the other, and they began pulling.

"Talkative fellow," Cassius noted, looking back as the old man went back to his place in the shadow of the boulder.

"He has no tongue," Kai said. "He is the gatekeeper for the Akrotirian Oracle I was told of him. He brings the oracle food and water every morning, but he can never speak of what she tells him."

"I have never heard of this oracle," Cassius said. Falco could tell the general was uncomfortable sitting in the back of the boat and having a woman row.

"Few have," Kaia granted. "She has a special power, as each oracle does. Hers does not involve the future but rather the past. Most people don't care about the past, as it is over with, and they feel they cannot change it. Of course, many are fools to think the future is changeable also."

"Are we fools then?" Falco asked.

"We might indeed be," Kaia said, "but I do not think so. Fate is not all-powerful."

"It has been in my life so far," Falco argued.

"Perhaps," Kaia allowed. "But many times, we make our own fate without knowing we do so."

Falco thought of his inability to allow himself to die in the arena. He had always attributed that to his desire to remain alive to see his children, but they were dead now, and here he was on this strange quest. He could have easily refused the emperor and ended his misery with his head on the pike on the Imperial Palace wall.

Shrugging off these thoughts, Falco peered ahead and could make out a small, pebbled beach on the smaller island, with a cave right behind the beach. "If you cannot change the past, and you cannot change the future, what is the point of anything?" he asked.

"Because it is our fate?" Kaia said with a smile. "And there are some who say both can indeed be changed."

General Cassius laughed. "A philosopher. They will argue you in circles so that you end with the same question you started with, but it will take you a week to get there."

Falco wasn't amused. "I do not care for fate. It has not been kind to me or those close to me."

"Perhaps that will change," Kaia said as she pulled her oar as they approached the beach."

"I doubt it," Falco said as the boat hit the pebbles. He jumped overboard and pulled the boat onto the beach.

Kaia immediately went toward the cave. The opening was fifteen feet wide by six feet high, and Falco bowed his head as they entered. There was a dim glow ahead and they all paused to allow their eyes to adjust.

A worn pathway went down the center of the cave and curved to the right toward the glow. Falco wondered how many generations of feet had shuffled along the path. As they went around the curve, they could see the glow came from a blue rock set in the center of the cavern about thirty feet in diameter. Falco had never seen such a stone. Across the stone from them was a figure wrapped in dark red robes, seated in a chair made of black stone.

"Welcome, travelers." The voice was surprising, holding the vibrancy of youth, yet Falco could see the woman was very old as she pushed back her hood and revealed her lined face. "Have you come far?"

"From Delphi, Mother," Kaia said.

A darkness crossed the old woman's face. "My sister there is dead."

"Ah!" Kaia staggered, and Falco helped her to the ground, where she sat, dazed. Then he stood by awkwardly and waited.

"There is not time to grieve," The Akrotirian Oracle said.

"I did not feel it," Kaia said in a low voice, "but I feel it now."

"There are some things it is best not to feel," the Akrotirian Oracle said. "The emissaries of the Shadow found her and killed her. But it was you they were really searching for. My sister protected you from them and from feeling her death."

Kaia looked up. "I thought the Shadow could not come out of the darkness."

"You forget what you were told. Those who killed her were Valkyries. They had hard white skin that your blades" – she flicked a withered hand toward Cassius and Falco—"cannot penetrate. They always come in a fog that drifts over sea or land."

Falco shifted his feet uneasily. If his steel would not work against things the old woman spoke of, then what hope was there?

"My oracle sent me here." Kaia was gathering herself.

"I know. It is time."

"Why am I here?" Kaia asked.

"This was once one of the havens our ancestors sought after our home in Atlantis was destroyed by the Shadow. But almost two millennia ago, the Shadow reappeared off the coast. It was stopped at the last minute, but the island was destroyed. A few survived and hid in other lands. You and I, we come from the same line, from Pri Lo, the only surviving priestess. Many, many years ago, our line split, and mine came back here to this island while yours went to Delphi. There are others of us, here and there around the world, although in many places the line has died out or been so diluted that a true Defender or oracle is born only rarely."

"Why did you come here?" Kaia asked. "It is a dead place."

"I was charged with remembering and examining the past." the oracle said simply. "And as all oracles, to wait."

"And now the time has come," Kaia said. "The Shadow has already caused much destruction among the Romans, and a gate grows to the north."

The oracle nodded. "I have felt it."

"What am I here for?" Kaia asked once more.

"To go into the Earth," the oracle said. She stood and gestured for them to follow. They exited the cave and stood on the rough beach. "All was not lost when Thera was destroyed." With a finger that wavered, the oracle pointed at Palaia Kameni, which lay not far away. "There is where you must go. There is an opening that you will go into. Then you must follow your instincts."

"What am I looking for?" Kaia asked.

"You will know it when you see it."

"Which means you don't really know," Falco spoke for the first time, tired of oracles and priestesses and their vague words.

The old woman looked at him. "You have a dark soul."

Falco shrugged. "I've been told that many times."

The oracle's eyes shifted from Falco and Kaia. "Interesting," was all she finally said.

"What is interesting?" Falco asked.

"The balance between the two of you," the oracle said.

Falco laughed. "She is light to my darkness?" he asked, indicating Kaia.

"No. She is the light that will illuminate your shadow side," the oracle said.

"Do you sense the darkness that is close by?" Falco asked, changing the topic from himself.

She nodded. "Yes, It is closing. Valkyries are coming. There is not much time."

"Then stop playing word games," Falco said, "and tell us what we need to know."

"There is a way to stop the Shadow," the oracle said. "You" – she pointed at Kaia—"are part of it. You also need a staff with one end a seven-headed snake. On the other end is a blade. It is called a Naga staff. It must be wielded by a warrior."

"My oracle told me that." Kaia said.

"That blade will work against the Valkyries. And you will find it where I send you. That you did not know. But what I do not know is if there is a place for all this to come together near this new Shadow."

"What kinds of place?" Falco asked.

"You will see when you go there," she pointed once more to Palaia Kameni.

"Then let us go." Falco headed toward the boat.

Kaia reached out and took the old woman's hands in hers. "Thank you."

"I wish you well on your journey," the oracle said. "I am the last of my line here."

"I suggest you leave," Kaia said.

"And go where? And do what?" The old woman shook her head. "This is where I belong. Go now. Your killer is right. There is not much time."

Kaia and General Cassius joined Falco who was waist deep in the water, ready to pull the boat offshore. With a heave, he had them afloat, and he jumped aboard, grabbing an oar. Falco concentrated on rowing, his muscles enjoying the feel of the wood in his hands, the strain of exertion. He looked up and saw the oracle was still standing on the shore, watching them. Then he glanced over his shoulder and saw another small section of beach, a dark hole just above it. He adjusted his stroke so the nose of the boat was headed toward it. Within minutes, they were ashore.

As Kaia scrambled up the slope toward the opening, Falco paused. He could see the smoke coming out of the top of the cone that made up most of the island they were on. Then he looked around. There was a hint of darkness in one of the openings that led to the outer sea. He turned and ran after Cassius and Kaia.

"We have no light," Cassius noted as they stood just outside the opening. A tunnel dove steeply into the side of the cone, the sides of it smooth. They could feel heat coming out of it, washing over their skin.

"I can find our way in the darkness," Kaia said. She pulled two short pieces of rope out of her pack. She handed both to Cassius. Then she took the end of one and signaled for Falco to take the end of the other. "I'll lead." She stepped into the opening and began descending, the two Romans following, like sheep on a tether.

The light from the opening faded as they went down, and soon they were moving in complete darkness. Falco wasn't worried, though, because he could sense what Kaia did, the path of the tunnel as it made slight turns left or right, but always descending. The temperature was rising, and sweat poured down Falco's skin, irritating underneath his armor.

Kaia suddenly halted, Cassius bumping into her. "What is it?" the general asked.

"There is a branch here; two tunnels," she answered.

"Left," Falco said from the rear.

"Yes, left," Kaia agreed after a moment, and they continued on their way.

Falco could sense something ahead and below, something of considerable power but not active. It wasn't the dormant volcano, although he was picking up the power in the Earth, but something different. He stumbled as a vision of a stepped pyramid, a woman lying on a platform on top, came to him unbidden. Then it was gone, as quickly as it had come. He continued on, but then he paused when the others did, as the Earth shook under his feet.

* * *

On the small beach of Nea Kameni, the Akrotirian Oracle had watched the three disappear into the opening. She had never set foot on the other island, even though it was so close. She had always known it would not be her fate to go there. She was just a signpost.

Despite the darkness she sensed coming, her heart was joyful. When she had produced no heir to her post, she had worried that her line would die without fulfilling its destiny. But now she could die in peace, knowing that what had been slotted to her line had been accomplished. It would be up to others to take the battle further.

She startled as the ground shook. The quake lasted for almost ten seconds, then stopped. She turned toward the main island, where her gatekeeper was looking out at her, his hand covering his eyes. She waved, indicating for him to leave, but she knew he couldn't see well anymore. She yelled as he got into a second boat that he kept at the small dock and began rowing toward her.

"Go away, old fool!" she called.

He didn't stop rowing.

"Nectarous, go away. Save yourself!" she called out, but he kept coming. She sat down wearily on a stone. Then her eyes were transfixed by the site of a brownish gray fog boiling in over the water, coming through the southern gap.

"Hurry," Falco was whispering, although why, he didn't know.

"I'm going as fast as I can," Kaia replied. "What if there is a sudden drop-off or a chasm?"

"Then you die," Falco said. "But if you don't hurry, you'll die anyway."

"Hold!" Kaia called out, and Falco felt it at the same time. The air was much hotter and the walls had disappeared. They were in an open area, deep underground, how large he didn't know. Then he blinked as there was a very faint light ahead and above them.

"What is that?" Cassius asked.

"Where we are going." Kaia began moving. The others didn't need to hold the rope now as their eyes, so used to the dark, locked onto the light like a beacon. As they got closer, Falco could make out a pyramid enclosed inside the large chamber, the light coming from the top of it. It was the same as the one that had been in his vision. They reached the base and began going up the wide steps toward the top.

"What is this place?" Cassius's voice sounded unnaturally loud, echoing off the walls of the chamber.

"This defeated the Shadow long ago," Kaia said. "It was buried here when the volcano exploded."

"But why is it in a chamber?" Cassius asked.

"Even after stopping the Shadow, there was enough power to keep it from being swallowed up." Kaia was almost at the top, the others close behind. "In the old days this was in the center of a great city."

"Who build it?" Cassius asked.

"The Ones Before," Kaia said. "Those who helped my ancestors and who also fight the Shadow." She stopped as she reached the platform at the very top. "But not enough to save those who served here," she said as she saw what was before her.

Falco climbed the last step and stood behind her. There were skeletons littered all over the flat platform. The glow was coming from something next to the raised table in the center of the platform, something underneath a skeleton covered in armor

Falco went past Kaia and knelt. He recognized the armor of a warrior, but the working was very old and of bronze. The bones were large, indicating a powerful man. Carefully, he pulled the skeleton back from whatever it was covering. He blinked as his eyes were temporarily blinded by what he unveiled: a clear skull, glowing from an inner blaze of white light that now lit up the entire cavern and pyramid.

"Ah!" Kaia exclaimed as she joined Falco and reached for the skull.

"Careful!" Falco warned. "It might burn."

"It won't hurt me." Kaia tenderly picked the skull up. "This is my ancestor."

The fog was approaching rapidly, spreading in an unnatural manner, going against the wind. The Akortian Oracle could see that Nectarios would not arrive at her location before the fog.

"You foolish man," she murmured as the fog enveloped him. Her heart was heavy as he disappeared, because she saw not the old man, but the young, strapping warrior Nectarios had been when she first met him. He'd been her lover for many years, but they had never had a child, a fact she had taken as an omen that the end of her line was near, as she knew it was not Nectario's fault, but rather that her womb was barren. She had spent many a long day pondering what that fate meant. Now she knew.

She staggered as she sensed Nectarios dying, a feeling that cut through to the bone, and then was gone, just as quickly. She stood, facing the approaching fog. It swept over the beach, and her skin crawled from the feel of it.

Something came out of the fog and came to a halt just in front of her, two feet above the pebbles. She saw the hard white skin and stared into the unblinking red eyes.

"You are too late, demon," she said bravely. "They have been here and are gone."

She was uncertain whether it had heard her as a second, similar creature floated out of the fog and joined the first. This one held up it's claws, and blood dripped from them. She knew that was Nectarios' blood. At least he had died swiftly, she thought.

She could sense the creatures, and it wasn't specifically evil that she picked up but rather something so alien that evil wasn't even a concept to them. She realized suddenly that she was as much a thing to them as they were to her.

She saw a claw come up, holding a thin spear. As the probe shot forward toward her, she blocked it with her right hand, the metal punching entirely through, the tip sticking out of the other side.

"They're gone!" she screamed as she curled her fingers around the probe, trying to hold on to it, as the Valkryie reeled it back to the launching tube. She staggered as she was pulled toward the creature. Her fingers were sliced to the bone as the probe was pulled out, despite her best efforts, and reloaded.

The second Valkryie was behind her, claws grabbing her shoulders, cutting the skin as it tried to hold her still as the first aimed the tube at her head once more.

"They will kill you," the oracle said, then spat at the creature.

The probe hit her in the forehead, slicing into her brain and lodging there.

Falco stood and looked about. There was a depression in the table, human-sized. Nearby, he could see a shaft stuck into a slot, the top consisting of seven snake heads, intricately carved, as the old oracle had told them. He reached for it and pulled, but it didn't move. He closed his eyes for a second, then opened them. He twisted and then pulled up, and the staff came free, revealing a fine blade on the other end. He hefted it. Light, very light. In the gladiator school he had been trained on all weapons, including the javelin and the thrusting spear along with bow, net, trident—every device used in the arena or in war. For the first time since Vesuvius had erupted, he smiled as his hands curled around the haft of the weapon. He intuitively knew this was the most powerful killing tool he had ever wielded.

"Ah!" Kaia spun about, the skull cradled against her chest. "They are above. They have the oracle."

"Who?" Falco asked.

"The Valkyries. Two of them. She cannot stop them. They will know we are here."

"Then let us go and confront them." Falco began going down the pyramid stairs, taking them two at a time. He paused halfway down. A river of red was pouring into the chamber, boiling up through a crack at the base of the pyramid below him. Kaia and Cassius joined him, and they continued down, feeling the heat, watching the river widen from a foot to two feet.

They reached the last step. The river of lava was five feet wide and still growing. The heat was almost unbearable. Falco turned and grabbed the general and without a word threw him through the air, clearing the lava and falling in tumble on the far side. Falco looked at Kaia.

"Ready?"

She nodded. He held out the staff, and she grabbed the haft near the Naga heads he had it near the blade. "Go!" he yelled and they both jumped. He landed, rolling and coming to his feet, Kaia at his side.

"Hurry!" General Cassius was waving at them from the tunnel entrance.

The oracle's last thought was that she had failed as she looked up at her body still being held by one of the Valkyries as the blood drained from her severed head lying on the beach. She blinked once, twice, then the eyes clouded over.

The first Valkyrie reached down and picked up the now lifeless head and crushed it, tossing the mangled remains into the water. Then they floated into the fog, heading toward Palaia Kameni.

The glow from the skull being carried by Kaia silhouetted Falco as he moved up the tunnel. His shadow was long, bouncing off the walls in front of him. He was focused on what lay ahead, all his senses alert. He probed with his mind, but there was nothing.

The light changed, and Falco risked a glance behind him. Red filled the tunnel behind them, the lava coming after them, channeled into the narrow space, accelerating.

He tucked the staff under one arm as he wiped the sweat off his hands on the tail of his tunic that stuck out from underneath his breastplate. It was as hot as Hades in the tunnel, and he staggered as the ground shook once more. He spared another glance over his shoulder and saw that Kaia was right behind him, the general behind her, his sword drawn and in his good hand. The red glow was closer.

Falco tried to remember how far they had gone down, but it was difficult to estimate, given they had traveled slowly in the dark. Sweat stung his eyes, and he swung his head back and forth like a wild beast, spraying persipiration from his face.

There was a light ahead, not daylight nor starlight, but something diffuse and obscene to Falco's eyes. He tightened his grip on the staff and probed ahead with his mind. It was as if he could see two blocks of ice just outside the entrance to the tunnel. Cold, that was the aura of whatever waited; cold and uncaring.

He paused. "General."

"Yes, Centurion?"

"Guard her."

"I do not—" Kaia began, but Falco shushed her.

"There is nothing you can do against these things that wait for us." He held up the Naga staff. "This is the only weapon we have against them, and I am the best trained to handle it. Wait here until I call."

Cassius looked back at the red glow. "We do not have much time."

Falco edged forward, feet spread in the fighting stance he'd been taught as a child. He could see out of the entrance now and noted the fog that covered the area. He could still sense the two cold spots, definitely not like anything he had ever faced before, and he had killed not only humans but every manner of beast in the arena. This was something completely new. They flanked the entrance, about ten feet back on either side. Always the pincer; it was the classic maneuver of a larger force. Falco had encountered it numerous times before.

He knew there was only one way to face this threat, and that was to attack. It was a lesson that had been pounded into him by his various *lanistas* over the years. When in doubt, attack. When surprised, attack. When desperate, attack. In the arena there was only one inevitable end to the defense: death.

He gathered himself, then dashed out of the tunnel onto the hillside, and spun to the right. But there was nothing there. As he tried to adjust, he realized his opponent was *above* the hillside, floating in the air, coming in for a strike. He could also sense the danger closing from behind, He had a brief glimpse of a figure covered in white armor, red eyes, then he jabbed, missed, and rolled downslope, taking the impact of the rocks and ground and letting his body absorb the blows.

He hit the beach and rolled to his feet at the ready. The two Valkyries were coming toward him, ten feet between them, hands glittering with sharp extensions on each of the fingers. Falco tucked the haft of the staff under his left arm, blade forward, and drew his sword from across his body with his left. He knew from the words of the oracle that it could not hurt these creatures, but he needed it to protect himself.

They attacked. He jabbed at the one on the left and backed the one-handed slash of the one on the right with his sword, feeling the impact through the blade, up his arm. He staggered back. The metal was chipped where it had been hit. Falco growled and turned as they circled him. He could not sense their intentions as he could in the arena with more earthly opponents, only their cold presence. That, combined with their ability to hover and the sloping ground, put him at a distinct disadvantage. His military training had taught him that the army that controlled the high ground had the advantage, so he rushed upslope at the Valkryie closest to him.

He thrust with the staff, and the Valkyrie parried it with a slap of a clawed hand. Then it emitted a noise such as he had never heard, a scream that cut through his brain, the pain doubled as the other one added its own inhuman yell.

Falco jabbed again, and as the Valkryie slapped, he pulled back on the haft of the staff and pivoted with all his strength, directing the edge of the blade at the hand. The edge caught right at the wrist and sliced neatly through, the clawed hand falling to the ground.

Instead of blood, black steam issued from the stump, and the Valkryie screamed once more, but there was different timbre to this, one that gave Falco confidence, as it echoed of disbelief and pain. Falco's feeling was short lived as he sensed the other creature right behind him. He spun, ducking down, just in time as the tips of razor-sharp claws, sliced along his armor in the back, then cut his shoulder, splitting skin.

He stopped his slide with the Naga end of the staff, jamming it between two rocks on the slope, hands wrapped around the haft tightly, blade pointing up. The second Valkryie halted just short of splitting itself on the point.

"Come on!" Falco yelled at it.

The wounded Valkyrie joined the other, black still issuing out of the stump. As they came closer, Falco got to his feet, pulling on the staff. To his dismay, it didn't move, the snakeheads jammed tight between the two rocks. He twisted and yanked to no avail. His sword was ten feet away where he had dropped it and the staff was useless.

Falco let go of the staff and stood, hands raised, ready to fight the creatures bare-fisted. They closed on him, then paused and turned slightly. Falco saw what had caught their attention. Kaia and Cassius were in the mouth of the tunnel, silhouetted in red. The priestess had a long dagger in one hand, the skull covered in her robe in the other, while Cassius had his sword in his one good hand. They were yelling to attract the attention of the Valkyries. It worked. Both floated up the hill toward the two, leaving Falco. He cursed and rushed after them, scrambling up the slope, picking up his sword as he went.

As the Valkyries closed on the tunnel opening, Kaia pulled aside the cloak, revealing the skull. It lit up the fog around it, and Falco could swear it was pushing the foul air away from it. The Valkyries stopped abruptly. With a chorus of screams, they rose up and retreated, moving back out to sea as the fog rapidly retreated also.

Falco stopped his charge, watching the creatures disappear with the strange fog. Kaia and Cassius came down to his location. Behind them, lava began flowing out of the entrance of the tunnel.

"You're wounded," Kaia said.

Falco glanced at the cuts on his shoulder. "It's nothing."

"It could be diseased from the creatures," Kaia said. "We need to clean it."

"We need to get out of here," Falco said, pointing at the lava now flowing down toward them. He turned and went down to the Naga staff, freeing it from between the rocks. As he passed, he also picked up the severed claw of the Valkryie, sticking it in his belt.

He led the way to the boat, and they clambered aboard, Kaia covering the skull with her cloak once more. As Falco pushed off, he felt the ground shake again. Looking up, he could see that the smoke coming out of the top of Palaia Kameni was much greater than before, a thick, dark plume rising to the heavens. He grabbed one oar while Kaia took the other. They pulled, rumbling in the air giving them urgency.

"Head for the opening," Cassius ordered. "I ordered Captain Fabatus to put to sea near there if there was any trouble, and it will be quicker than going over that ridge."

Falco adjusted the course of the boat, leaning into the oar.

"What about the oracle?" Cassius asked as they passed the smaller island.

"She's dead," Falco said. He glanced up and met Kaia's eyes. He knew she had felt the old woman's death deeper than he had. "Why are these things killing the oracles?"

"They want to wipe us out," Kaia send. "End the line of priestesses."

Falco gave up the conversation and concentrated on rowing. There was the sharp crack of an explosion behind them, and he looked back. A section of Palaia Kameni had collapsed, spewing dust into the air. Lava was flowing out of the tunnel and the destroyed area, heading down toward the water. Where it touched, there was an explosion of steam as heat fought liquid. Falco and Kaia strained hard at the oars, and even Cassius tried to help with his one good arm, splashing at the water.

There was another explosion behind them, and they didn't even bother to look. The boat lifted as a five-foot-high swell passed under them and headed out to sea. The wave gave them some momentum, and Falco risked a glace back, feeling a tremendous pressure in the back of his head. At that moment, the top of Palaia Kameni blew with a thunderous explosion. Rocks and dirt flew high into the air, and a fiery cloud came racing outward.

"Over the side!" Falco screamed, emphasizing his point by tossing Kaia into the water with one thrust of his arm. He spun around and dove at Cassius, wrapping the general in his arms, and flying overboard. They hit the water, and the combined weight of Falco's and Cassius's armor took them under.

Even as he sank, Falco looked up. He saw the bright sky disappear as the ash cloud swept overhead. Then he felt Cassius struggling in his arms, and he let go of the general as they both fought to get their breastplates off as they slowly sank. Both men had worn their amour almost every day of their life, so the routine was something that was ingrained. Falco's fingers unbuckled and loosened, and in seconds his breastplate was off, plummeting to the bottom, He reached out and grabbed Cassius as the general got his off. Boulders hit water all around, racing by on their way to the bottom.

Looking up, he could see the sky was not as dark. Falco kicked for the surface, feeling the air in his lungs turning bad. He surfaced and gagged, as he sucked in huge lungfuls of ash-filled air. Cassius surfaced next to him and began coughing. Falco saw Kaia's head pop up near the side of the boat, and he swam over. He could see that the wood was singed. The sky was filled with the ash that was steadily spewing out of the volcano, but the superheated death cloud had passed.

"How did you know to do that?" Kaia got out between coughs.

"It just came to me," Falco said as he climbed into the boat and reached down to give her a hand.

Kaia got on board, and then they both helped Cassius. Kaia ripped strips of cloth from her cloak and gave them to the men. They tied these around their heads, covering their mouths, and then they resumed rowing. Behind them, the volcano was spewing a towering cloud of ash into the air, while lava flowed freely, hitting the water and turning it into steam.

As they made it into the gap, they could see the galley off to the left, protected from the direct force of the volcano by the old caldera.

CHAPTER FOURTEEN

THE PRESENT

A destroyer circled the perimeter below, the submersible on one side of the flight deck, already rigged to a crane, ready to be lowered. With a slight bounce, the helicopter landed, and Dane slid open the cargo bay door and got out, joined by Loomis. Foreman was waiting for them, wearing a one-piece black jumpsuit.

"I'm going with you," Foreman said to Dane.

"But, sir—" Loomis began, but Foreman cut him off.

"Mr. Dane thinks I always send others in harm's way," Foreman said. "I thought I'd show him differently."

Dane knew that wasn't quite true. Foreman wanted to go to the graveyard and search for his brother's plane. Still, he felt no need to mention that in front of Loomis. Dane quickly changed into a similar black suit and rejoined Foreman on the deck. The hatches were open on the two spheres that made up the crew compartments of *Deepflight*, and the pilot and navigator were already on board. Dane followed Foreman up a small ladder and then down into the small sphere. The hatch was closed behind them and screwed shut.

Dane lay down on the padded bottom of the sphere, ignoring Foreman, who was checking screens and gauges as if he had a clue how the thing operated. Dane closed his eyes and allowed his mind to roam, sensing the ocean around them as the submersible was lifted off the deck and lowered into the water. There was a jolt as the crane hook was released by divers. The nose of the submersible titled forward, and they were on their way.

Dane picked up no threat in the immediate area. He closed his eyes and within a minute was asleep as *Deepflight* continued its long descent to the bottom of the world.

He woke with a nudge of Foreman's foot in his chest. "We're at the door."

Dane looked over the CIA man's shoulder at one of the video displays. The flat, black metal extended in all directions.

"Any sign of activity in the gate?" Dane asked.

"Nagoya is monitoring from the FLIP, and he's picked up nothing."

Dane could see they were moving down along the wall. "How deep are we?"

"Ten thousand, five hundred meters," Foreman said. He tapped the screen and spoke into the headset he wore. "That's it. Go in there."

A dark circle was in the center of the metal, exactly as it had been in the Milwaukee Deep in the Atlantic Ocean. It grew closer as the pilot directed them toward it. Dane felt the same strange sensation of disorientation as they passed through; then they were in.

The submersible surfaced inside the huge chamber, exactly in the center. Dane waited calmly, Foreman not so relaxed, as the pilot prepared the craft to allow them to exit. Finally, the green light came on next to the hatch above their heads, and Foreman spun the handle, slowly unscrewing the hatch.

Dane followed him out, balancing on the grid that surrounded the rear sphere. For security purposes, they'd agreed that the pilot and copilot would remain secure in the forward sphere for the mission.

"My God!"

It was the most emotion Dane had ever seen Foreman express. The black beach was littered with hundreds -- thousands—of planes and ships. The spectacle was overwhelming both in number and variety. A clipper ship sat next to an oil tanker, next to a cluster of Polynesian rafts, next to a rowboat, next to the Chinese junk; all in just two hundred yards of beach. What was most disconcerting was the absolute stillness of everything. There was no sign of life in the graveyard, just as there hadn't been in the Atlantic one.

"There!" Foreman clutched Dane's arm, his fingers digging in painfully. A cluster of planes was just above the waterline. "That's my flight. The tail numbers match. And the nose painting. That's my brother's plane."

Foreman was already giving orders over the intercom for the pilot to head that way. Dane was looking about, not certain what he was searching for – something out of place, like the etching on the sail of the *Scorpion* or the Atlantean ship he had found in the other graveyard.

Deepflight slowly moved through the water toward the shore where the planes were. Dane saw a Russian submarine in mint condition except where the power plant had been; the deck plates had been sliced off, and the reactor was gone. A modern Japanese destroyer rested on the black beach, slightly canted because of its keel. Numerous dried blood trails were all over the side of it, ending abruptly where the waterline must have been.

There were several Flying Fortresses, lined up wingtip to wingtip, their silver skin gleaming. Dane startled when he read the name scripted on the nose of one of the planes: *Enola Gay*.

"Foreman," Dane tapped the other man.

"What?"

Dane simply pointed at the plane.

Foreman shrugged. "Yeah. I knew about that. It's in the files, classified top secret, Q-clearance. The first *Enola Gay* disappeared on the initial mission to drop the bomb. Lucky they had three bombs, not two, like history books have recorded. You can bet there were some scared people in the White House when they got that report. They covered it up pretty well, don't you think?"

It was almost as if Foreman was telling him the sky was blue.

"And still, even after that," Foreman's voice took on an edge now, "they didn't want to believe the gates were a threat. Lost in flight, cause unknown was the official determination for the first *Enola Gay*. You know how many lost in flights, or lost at sea, cause unknowns are on file?"

Foreman didn't wait for an answer. "Over sixty years I've tried to convince them. No one wanted to listen to me. No one wanted to know the truth. But they know now, don't they?"

"What truth?" Dane asked. "We know where those planes and ships are now, but we still have no clue *why* they're here."

Foreman pointed at the eviscerated Russian submarine. "For our technology, our power."

"The power maybe," Dane allowed, "but I doubt they need our technology. Did it ever occur to you that maybe they want the people, too? The craft are here, but where are the people?"

The submersible came to a halt, forestalling any answer by Foreman as he carefully lowered himself overboard and swam the short distance until he could touch bottom. Dane followed.

Foreman went directly to his brother's plane, clambering up on the wing. The cockpit glass was pulled back, and Foreman leaned inside. Dane climbed up on the other side.

"Just like the day he got in it," Foreman said. "It hasn't aged a bit."

There was a photo tucked next to one of the instrument panels. Two young men in flight suits standing on a beach smiling. Foreman noted Dane looking at it.

"Our last shore leave together in Hawaii."

It was hard for Dane to connect the smiling young man in it with the hard old man on the other side of the plane. Even in the midst of World War II, Foreman had looked happier than he did now.

"Do you think your brother could still be alive?" Dane asked.

Foreman took the picture, sliding it into a plastic bag and putting it in his pocket. "When I saw the movie *Close Encounters* – have you seen it?"

Dane nodded, and Foreman continued.

"And all those people got off the mother ship at Devil's Tower, all I could think about was my brother and all the others. I was a member of Flight Nineteen, the only one who didn't go on that last fight into the Bermuda Triangle."

"You have a knack for staying out of trouble," Dane noted.

"Sometimes I wish I had been with my brother at the end."

For one of the few times in their history, Dane believed him.

Foreman climbed off the wing onto the strange black beach. He looked about. "See anything interesting?"

Dane joined Foreman and scanned the beach. "Besides the *Enola Gay*?" He pointed. "How about the *Indianapolis*?"

The cruiser was resting on its side about a half mile away, a gaping hole where a Japanese torpedo had punched a fatal hole in the ship that had delivered the first atomic bomb to Tinian.

"That means the Shadow scavenges the bottom," Foreman noted, seeing the damage.

"There's the *Reveille*," Dane had just spotted the research ship between a World War II-era Japanese aircraft carrier and a battered steamer. He started walking in that direction, Foreman next to him.

As expected, there was no sign of life on the ship when they got to it. They climbed up a gangway onto the ship and went to the bridge. The video camera that the captain had held was lying on the floor of the wing. Dane picked it up. "Should we see if he continued recording after we lost contact?"

In response, Foreman took the camera from his hands and popped the tape out. He went into the bridge, to the rear where the captain's cabin was. A small TV with a built-in VCR was bolted to the bookcase. Foreman slid the tape in and rewound it. The he hit Play. Dane sat on the captain's bunk while Foreman sat in the chair, remote in hand. The screen came alive, showing the sea. Foreman hit fast-forward, and they saw the scene where the black sphere came up.

The opening irises shut, and they could hear the yells of alarm from the crew members. Then there was complete darkness as the top shut.

A voice—the captain's, Dane recognized—came out of the TV's small speaker. "I can hear water being pumped. The air is strange. We have no power, not even emergency backup."

A tiny shaft of light appeared.

"A flashlight. The camera is still working. So batteries work but no other power."

There was a loud metal-on-metal noise.

"We're grounded. Like a dry dock. Something's happening. A golden glow on the starboard side."

They could see the glow he was referring to on the screen now.

"Just like Ariana reported in the Angkor gate," Dane said.

"There's something coming out of the gold," the captain reported. "Several objects."

They could see about a dozen white dots silhouetted against the gold glow and growing larger.

"What the hell are those?" Foreman muttered.

The captain was yelling orders, and then he dropped the camera, and all they could see was gray metal. They heard shots and screams, and then the picture went dead. Foreman rewound it and then paused at the last useful frame, the dozen white objects against the gold glow.

"I think we might have had our first view of those who live in the Shadow," Dane said, tapping the TV screen.

Instead of heading back to Heathrow, Ariana had ordered the helicopter pilot to head northwest toward Oxford. She'd called the number for Davon that she'd been given and arranged to meet him at a site he described to the north of the town.

As the chopper banked toward the field, Ariana could see a set of headlights cutting across the grass from the stationary car. The chopper touched down, and she instructed the pilot to shut down and wait for her. She felt a bit conspicuous as she walked across the field to the car, wondering why Davon hadn't bothered to get out to greet her. As she reached the road, the passenger door swung open on the BMW.

"Get in," a voice called out.

Ariana hesitated, then slid in the seat. Before she had the door shut, the car was moving. In the dim glow from the instrument panel she could barely make out the driver's profile. A large hook nose dominated a hatchet face.

"Are you Davon?" She asked.

"Who the hell else you think would be waiting for you?" he replied.

"Where are we going?"

"Away from there," he nodded his head over his shoulder at the field. He took a turn in the road a little to fast and over corrected with a jerk of the wheel and the squeal of the tires.

"Listen," Ariana said, "I just—"

"Are you with the government?" he cut her off.

"Which government?"

"Well, you're an American by your accent," he said. "So let's try that one first."

"No, I don't work for the U.S. government."

"Any government?" he pressed.

"I don't work for any government," she assured him.

"And I'm supposed to believe you just 'cause you say so, right, missy?"

"What are you afraid of?" Ariana demanded. She was thrown against the door as he took another turn at high speed. "And would you slow this thing down?"

"They've tried to get me before," he said.

"First," Ariana spoke slowly and deliberately, "are you Davon?"

"Yes.

"Ok. Who is the *they* you're afraid of?"

"You know. They. Them. The people with the power. The people afraid of the truth."

"What truth?"

Davon gave a manic smile. "Well, if I told you that, that would mean they'd be after you, too, wouldn't it?"

Ariana was beginning to believe she had hooked up with a paranoid crackpot. She grabbed the dash as he turned off the hard road onto a thin dirt tract between two rows of thick hedges.

"Where are we going?"

"You wanted to know about the stones. About the leys of power, right?"

"The what?"

"Leys of power. A ley. It comes from the Saxon word for cleared strip of land. The lines! They are what is important." He smacked a hand against the steering wheel. "The stones are just the signs. It's the power in the Earth that is the key. And it's all over the world. Here and there." He slammed on the brakes and they came to a halt. "Do you understand?"

"No, I don't" Ariana said. She was certain Atkins had set her up for taking the crystal skull. She felt a surge of anger over the petty squabbles of academic intellectuals interfering with a mission that involved the fate of the world. She pulled out her cell phone. "I'm calling for my helicopter to pick me up." She could see another field in front of them and knew she could bring the chopper in. She had a beacon in her pocket that would give the pilot her location.

"Just take a look," Davon said. He opened his door and got out.

The pilot answered the call on the first ring. Ariana could see Davon walking toward a bit of high ground. "Hold on," she told the pilot. She turned off the phone and got out of the car. She followed Davon up the slight rise and joined him. Below them was a strangely shaped standing stone. Peering in the dark she could see two other groups of stones.

"The Rollright Stones," Davon said. "This is where it happened."

"What happened?" Ariana asked, but he ignored her as he began pointing and speaking.

"That's the King Stone." He then indicated a group. "Those are the Whispering Knights. They got that name from the way the stones all lean toward each other as if plotting against the king here." He then pointed at the second group. "Those are the King's Men. They form a perfect circle one hundred and four feet across."

Ariana was amazed at the change that had come over the man at her side. His voice was perfectly normal, and he recited the information as if he were presenting a lecture at the university. She realized she was most likely dealing with a paranoid schizophrenic, and at the moment she was seeing his lucid side.

"Scientists have come here and run their tests. They've found electromagnetic fluctuations and even traces of radioactivity. Locals have long claimed that going inside the circle of King's Men and spending the night has a healing effect." He gave a strange laugh. "No one does that anymore. Not since I did. Not after what happened."

Ariana waited, knowing that to ask questions or interrupt might bring forth another paranoid phase.

"What they don't understand," Davon said, "is that the stones themselves are not the key. Even at Stonehenge, which everyone traipses to and slobbers over, it is not the stones." He cut his hand back and forth in front of him. "It's the lines. The power of the lines."

"Geoffrey of Monmouth's *History of Kings of England*, was the first document to mention the stones and the power of the lines," Davon said. "That was in the twelfth century. At least here in England it was the first mention. The Chinese recorded it much, much earlier. They called them *lung mei*, which translates as dragon paths, thus the name for my project."

He turned to her. "You've heard of *feng shui*, haven't you?" he asked. "It's been revived lately and is actually quite popular."

Ariana nodded. "The harmony of things, their placement."

"Actually *feng shui* stands for wind and water. Most people only think of *feng shui* on a small scale," Davon said. "*Lung mei* is *feng shui* on a planetary scale and supersedes *feng shui*. The first thing a *feng* master must do is orient on the dragon lines, the *lung mei*. Then the master must determine whether they are *yin*, which is the white tiger, the negative force, or *yang*, the blue dragon, the positive force.

"The Chinese believed there was tremendous power in the planet, and of course, there is. Earthquakes, volcanoes, the movement of the tectonic plates, even the tides; all are on a scale not able to be imitated by man even with our most powerful weapons. In a most basic and primitive way, the practitioners of *feng shui* are tapping into the power."

Davon trust his hand back and forth again, a gesture that made Ariana take a half step back. "There was a group called the Straight Tracker's Club that tried to line up the various megaliths and places of worship in England. Find the pattern. They found that the Rollright Stones are on line with the Long Compton Church, the Chipping Norton Church, and a tumulus near Charlbury." He gave the edgy laugh again. "Their vision was so limited. The lines of power are much, much bigger than that. And they are all over the world, not just here in England and not just tied to the megaliths.

"In ancient China, straight lines on the landscape were considered evil. Spirits were said to travel along those lines. *Feng shui* actually started as the practice of placing tombs so they would not fall along one of the evil lines."

He turned away from the Rollright Stones and looked off to the southwest as if he could see something in the dark. "South America. Have you heard of the Nazca Lines?"

"Small stones aligned in the high desert?"

"Stones in the high desert lined up for miles and miles." Davon corrected. "Some perfectly straight, going over ridges and through gullies. Others arranged in various intricate designs. By who? And why?"

He fell silent, and Ariana felt a need to get him back on track. "What happened to you inside the circle?" she finally asked.

Davon turned back toward the stones. "In 1936, at Loe Bar on the Cornish coast, where two leys form a node, a man reported seeing a medieval army appear out of nothing and then disappear. He went back thirty-eight years later and reported seeing the same thing as if not a day had passed. As did his wife, who accompanied him.

"In 1974, at the Chanctonbury Ring, a man I've talked to, walked into the center of the ring, and an invisible force lifted him off the ground over five feet and held him up there for a minute. Three other chaps who were with him saw this. Chanctonbury is a node for five local ley lines and is the side of an ancient fort."

"In 1976, at the node of two ley lines near Cilicom, a man and a woman claimed their car engine suddenly died and they were approached by an alien, a creature with white skin and unblinking red eyes that disappeared as suddenly as it appeared.

"Last year—"Davon began but then halted.

"Last year what happened?" Ariana pushed.

"Last year, I spent a night inside the King's Men. I brought my air mattress and my sleeping bag, and I set up exactly dead center. Nothing happened for hours, and I finally fell asleep. Then, at three in the morning, something woke me. I sat up. At first I saw or heard nothing and thought maybe I'd had a bad dream. A fog had come in, and I could barely see the stones all around me.

"Then I heard the voices. Calling out for help. Asking for mercy. Dozens, hundreds, of voices. I've never heard such pain. It was terrible. Like souls in hell begging for release. And they were speaking in a strange language, but somehow I understood what they were saying. Then they came for me."

"The people crying for mercy?"

"No. The aliens. Two of them. They appeared in front of me. Smooth, white skin. Large, red eyes. With long, black cloaks. And they hung in the air over me, looking down. Their hands… they had claws on them, sharp ones, like that fellow in the American horror movie. I knew they were the reason the voices were calling for mercy, and I knew they were coming for me. I ran. Left my gear behind and ran. Didn't use my camera or recorder. I just ran."

Ariana waited, but he said nothing more. After a while, she took out her cell phone and called for the helicopter. Megaliths, lines of power, crystal skulls; she knew there was a connection with the Shadow, but she had no clue what it was or even how they connected with each other.

While she waited for the helicopter to arrive, she walked down the slope toward the circle Davon had called the Whispering Knights.

"What are you doing?" Davon asked, but she ignored him.

Ariana passed between two of the standing stones. She felt the slightest of tingles on her skin. There was power in this place. She went to the center and slowly turned about. Davon was standing outside the circle, looking worried.

Ariana cocked her head. At the very edge of her hearing she could almost pick up something. Then the sound of helicopter blades overwhelmed all other sound, and she quickly left the circle.

Pytor Shashenka's entire world was split between pain and unconsciousness. He preferred the latter, but he had no control over either.

Reluctantly, Pytor opened his eyes. The table across from him was occupied by the warrior. He was strapped down, muscles bulging against the straps as he futilely attempted to free himself. Tangled black hair cascaded over the man's face. His clothes were at his feet. His skin was pale white except the arms. He had not been worked on by the Valkyries yet.

"Who are you?" Pytor called out in Russian, not really expecting an answer.

The man looked across at him, eyes raging with fury. He seemed to understand the question because he replied with one word. "Ragnarok."

"Pytor."

Ragnarok blinked, indicating he understood. He said something in his native tongue.

"I do not understand," Pytor said. He was about to try English, when something appeared in his peripheral vision. A white form glided to a halt in front of Ragnarok. Pytor recognized it because one of the red crystal eyes was smashed.

It fired a probe into Ragnarok's head and then consulted a small device attached to the wires. After several moments, it removed the probe and tossed the machine aside. Then it lifted one arm, a razor-sharp claw extended. With a savage slice, it cut through Ragnarok's right wrist, severing the hand from the arm. The warrior didn't' even cry out, although the muscles in his jaw worked hard to keep his mouth shut.

The movement was repeated, and the left hand fell the floor, the fingers balled in a fist.

With its other arm, the Valkyrie extended a red, glowing tube. It tapped both stumps briefly, and there was the sound and smell of burning flesh as it cauterized the wounds. At that, Ragnarok passed out.

Pytor yelled curses at the creature to no avail until his own pain overwhelmed him, and he joined the warrior in blessed unconsciousness.

CHAPTER FIFTEEN

THE PAST
79 A.D.

The galley arrived at the entrance to the Hellesponte at nightfall. Captain Fabatus didn't want to try the passage in the dark, but a forceful order from General Cassius changed his mind.

The Hellesponte has a long and rich history. Forty miles long and a mile and a half to four miles wide, the Hellesponte is the dividing line between Europe and Asia, a strategic waterway, the rights to which had been the true cause of the Trojan War hundreds of years earlier. It connected the Aegean with the Sea of Mamara, which led to the Bosporus Strait into the Black Sea. In 480 B.C. Xerxes I, king of Persia, had crossed the strait on a bridge built of boats during his campaign against the Greeks.

"It is said that Helle drowned here when she fell from the back of the ram Chrysomallus," Kaia said as they entered the channel. "The legend of Hero and Leander also surrounds this area. It is legend that Leander drowned in these very waters on his way to visit his beloved Hero."

"Do you believe legends?" Falco asked. They were in the prow of the gallery watching the land slip by on either side. General Cassius had retired for the evening, Falco could tell the trip was a strain on the old man, who had not completely recovered from their ordeal at Thera.

"There is truth in all legends," Kaia said.

A voice called out in the darkness from somewhere ahead. Fabatus hurried forward, a lantern in his hand, and returned the hail. In a minute, a small boat carrying four men appeared in the glow of the lantern, just below them.

Falco could see that they were dressed in armor, and squinting, he could make out the insignia on their helmets: VII. Formed by Claudius over thirty years previously, he knew the legion was stationed in Macedonia, with responsibility for control of the straight.

"Greetings!" Fabatus called out.

A man stood in the bow of the small boat, looking up, the crest of a centurion on his helmet. "Greetings, ship bearing the imperial banner. Where do you travel?"

"To Upper Thrace to join with the XXV Legion," Falco replied, thinking the man's way of phrasing his greeting was quite odd. The farther one traveled from Rome, the less strong the hand of the emperor.

"Why are you passaging the strait at night?" the man asked.

"I am Falco, Centurion of General Cassius. And you are?"

"Attius, Centurion Primus Pilus of the VII."

Primus Pilus indicated that Attius was in charge of the first century of the first cohort of his legion, meaning he was senior centurion. Fabatus had one of his crew throw a rope ladder over the side, and Attius climbed up and joined them on deck.

"Your reason for passing at night?" Attius asked again as he looked about the ship, noting Kaia's presence.

"We are in need of haste," Falco said.

Attius shook his head. "No one passes through at night. We saw your light many miles away and kept waiting for you to drop anchor, but when I saw you enter, I thought it best to come out and warn you."

"Warn us of what?"

Attius rubbed the stubble of his beard. "There is trouble to the north. Strange stories. Ships have long been known to disappear on Pontus Euxinus, but lately this trouble has been coming south, into the strait."

"What kind of trouble?" Falco asked.

"As I said: Ships and their crews simply disappear. No sign of wreckage, and the weather is fine. But strange fogs suddenly appear when none should. Some say there are demons about, others that the gods are angry and punishing us." He indicated a light on the western shore. "You can spend the night in our fort and continue on your journey in the morning."

Kaia spoke for the first time. "There *is* danger ahead, but I do not think it will make any difference whether we try the Hellesponte at night or during the day; the danger will be there."

"There's more—" but Attius hesitated.

"Go ahead," Falco said.

"I told you I have heard strange stories told in whispers in the taverns. Traders coming from Bospora say there is a darkness upon the land that any who enter never come out of."

"Where is this darkness?" Falco asked.

"Near the Dnieper River, about four hundred stadia from the sea. And —" Attius looked about. "Where is the general?"

"Resting," Falco said.

"Are you the Centurion Falco who served with Cassius in the X? And then fought in the arena?"

Falco nodded.

Attius took a step closer and lowered his voice. "Can I have a word with you privately?"

Falco wondered what could be worse than what the centurion had already told them, but he indicated for Fabatus and Kaia to move back.

"What is it?" Falco asked.

"You said you were going to join the XXV?"

"Yes."

"Will Cassius become legatus?" Attius asked, wanting to know if Cassius was going to take command of the legion.

"For the duration of our task, he will."

A look of relief came over Attius's face. "My legatus will be glad to hear that, and he will hope your task lasts a very long time. The XXV is on our right, between us and the barbarians in Bospora, and we would be as well off if we had a wall of reeds standing there."

"Ill trained?"

Attius laughed bitterly. "No, they're trained. But they're provincials. And they don't care about Rome. The original XXV was exiled to Bospora by Vespasian because of their doubtful loyalty. And since then, they've filled their ranks with locals. They own no loyalty to the emperor, either the old or the new."

Falco considered the order that Cassius carried. What was to follow the mission with Kaia?

"I appreciate your words," he told Attius. "What of the barbarians to the north? Are they a danger?"

Attius scratched his chin. "We've had little trouble as long as we leave them alone. But any patrol going north, well, it's like in the old days when we crossed the Rhine. Sticking one's hand into a nest of hornets."

Falco knew what Attius was referring to, having served a few years on the frontier of the Rhine. Every so often it would be the emperor's whim to cross the river to try to subdue the fierce tribes living in those dark forests. Even though it was over seventy years ago, every Roman soldier remembered what had happened to Quinctilius Varus and the three legions, the XVII, XVIII and XIX which he had led across the river. The Germans had banded together and ambushed the legions strung out on the march, wiping them out and causing one of the greatest defeats in the history of Rome.

"Are you going over the border?" Attius asked as the import of Falco's question struck home.

"I do not know the wishes of the emperor," Falco lied. "It's my job to be prepared for whatever may happen. And we must pass tonight and do our duty."

Attius reluctantly nodded. "I wish you well then." He climbed over the side into his boat. Fabatus gave the order for the rowing to resume, and they plunged forward into the darkness of the Hellesponte. The boat with Attius faded into the darkness, and cliffs closed in on each side.

Falco and Kaia stood perfectly still.

"Do you sense it?" Falco asked.

Kaia nodded. "Danger ahead."

"How can these things – the Valkyries—travel far from the gate?" Falco asked, something that had been bothering him ever since Thera.

"I do not know," Kaia said. "I was told they are the only emissaries of the Shadow that can do so."

Falco was looking ahead, where the land on either side closed in, making the narrowest channel in the Hellesponte. There was a mist waiting for them, one that was not formed naturally.

"I will wake the general," Falco said. He went back to where Cassius was slumbering on the hard wooden deck, a thin blanket around his frail shoulders.

"General," Falco whispered.

Cassius's eyes were open in a flash. "What is it?"

"A fog ahead. I sense danger in it."

Cassius was on his feet, heading forward, Falco at his side. The only sound was the rhythmic splash of the oars hitting the water. The fog was now only half a mile ahead of the ship. On either side, the land was rocky and high, not suitable for landing.

"We could turn back," Falco said.

"There is no time," Kaia said. "We may well be late to the gate at this rate anyway."

"The slaves are rowing against the current coming out of Marmara," Cassius added. "They have enough energy for one try. If we turn and try again, it will take more than twice as long."

"Then we must fight." Falco had the Naga staff in his hand.

Cassius called for the leader of the small contingent. The soldiers deployed along the forward edge of the galley, shields and pilum – medium-length throwing spears—ready, as the fog grew closer. Falco stood at the very front, Cassius to the shield side, Kaia just behind the general.

There was a strange noise in the air, and Falco strained to discern it. As they came within a hundred meters of the fog, all on board could hear a keening sound, as if a pack of women were grieving over the loss of their children. It chilled the blood of all on board the ship, and the slaves lost a beat in their rowing before the drum and a few well-placed lashes brought them back on the mark.

"The sirens," Cassius said.

"It does not draw me in," Falco said. "Isn't the siren call supposed to beckon?" Even as he said that, though, the cry changed, women crying for help, for mercy.

They entered the fog. The cries were coming from the right side of the ship and slightly ahead.

"I say we steer away from that side," Kaia advised, noting that the ship's helmsman had edged slightly closer to the right where they could faintly make out a cliff.

"Ah," Falco hissed as he pointed.

A human figure was on the side of the cliff, arms splayed wide, crucified on the rock with metal spikes through her wrists and ankles. Then there was another and another. The sound was coming from them. Woman crying out for mercy, a perverted song of the sirens.

"They need help," Fabatus said.

"They're beyond our help." Falco could feel the despair of the women on the cliff. He looked at a legionnaire. "Do you have a bow?"

The man scurried to the small armory and came back with a bow and quiver. Falco handed the Naga staff to Kaia and notched an arrow. The first figure had almost disappeared behind them when he fired. The arrow flew straight and true, hitting the woman in the chest. Her body slumped back lifeless against the rock. Falco's hands moved automatically as he had been trained, pulling an arrow out of the quiver, notching it, raising up, aiming, firing. The cries grew fainter as there were less voices to make them.

The legionnaires and Fabatus watched Falco work, aghast at his mercilessness, but he could sense that Cassius and Kaia approved. Cassius had served in Germany, where captives were often used as bait to draw in the unwary, ending in the death not only of the captives but of the would-be rescuers. He knew this was the only thing they could do for the women.

There were only three arrows left in the quiver when Falco struck the last target he could see, and there were no more cries for help. The fog was as thick as ever, the right cliff barely visible, the left masked. Looking up, Falco could make out movement on the top of the right cliff, something white following their progress.

"The staff is keeping them away for now." Kaia had seen the same thing. "They wanted us close to shore for a reason."

"They must—" Falco began, but then was struck dumb as an entire section of the cliff where the last bodies were attached exploded outward, spraying the channel with rock and dirt. Several stones hit the ship, but caused only minor damage.

"If we'd been closer, we'd be on the bottom right now," Cassius said.

Falco turned and went to the small hatch leading below decks. He climbed down to the oar deck. There was an empty slot near the rear, and he made his way there, ignoring the curious and fearful glances of the slaves. Falco sat down next to a foul-smelling slave and wrapped his calloused hands around the end of the oar and began to pull in unison with the man.

CHAPTER SIXTEEN

THE PRESENT

"The *Grayback* will be surfacing any second now." Loomis pointed off the starboard side.

Dane and Foreman had returned to the surface on board the *Deepflight* without any trouble or activity from the gate. The flight back to the *Salvor* had been made in silence, each man considering what he had seen in the graveyard. Foreman had gone over to the FLIP to coordinate with Nagoya, while Dane reunited with Chelsea on board the ship to await the arrival of his next ride.

Dane watched as a periscope popped up and cut through the water, followed by a conning tower. As the sub surfaced, he immediately noted the two large metal hangars welded to the deck of the ship.

"The Crabs are inside those," Loomis said.

"How many people can each carry?" Dane asked.

"A crew of two and ten passengers."

"Weaponry?"

"Thirty-millimeter cannon. TOW missile launchers for land and MK-24 torpedoes for water. The armor can take a direct hit from large-caliber machine guns."

"How many people are going on the recon?" Dane asked.

"You, me, Colonel Shashenka, and Professor Ahana."

"Who's piloting?"

"I am," Loomis said.

"Who's handling the weapons?"

"Colonel Shashenka."

The *Grayback* circled and came alongside. Dane knew they would be leaving shortly, heading into the darkness. He reached down, rubbing the golden hair on top of Chelsea's head. He was startled when she gave a short bark. She was staring down at the sub's deck. At first, Dane thought she was looking at the two hangars, but then he noted a smaller metal box half above the waterline on the far side of the sub. A woman in a wet suit was on the deck, unlatching the end of the box. A gray dolphin slipped out of it, into the open water. It swam about as the woman watched.

"Project Rachel."

Dane had almost forgotten that Loomis was still with him. He could pick up the dolphin's happiness that it was finally free. It raced around the submarine, coming between it and the research ship, then paused, coming up out of the water on its rear fin to stare up at Dane and Chelsea before flipping over into the water once more.

"That's Dr. Martsen, Rachel's trainer and research specialist."

"Why isn't she going with us on the Crab?"

"We don't need her, just Rachel. The dolphin will swim next to us on the way in. She's trained with the Crab before. She'll have a small video camera and transmitter mounted in a pack on her back, just in front of the dorsal fin. Transmits to the Crab. So it's like having an extra set of eyes on the outside."

Dane nodded, but he was thinking that Rachel was here for a different reason that Loomis realized. What that was, he wasn't sure yet.

"Let's head on over," Loomis said.

*****

Two men were waiting for Ariana as the Learjet rolled to a stop at Central Airfield in Moscow. Both were dressed in well-tailored suits, wore dark sunglasses, and had that hard, efficient look about them that Ariana had learned to associate with security personnel.

"Ms. Michelet," one of the men stepped forward, the second facing the other way, toward the Mercedes. "I'm Jonathan Miles."

"I assume you work for my father," Ariana said.

Miles nodded. "We were alerted you were inbound." He indicated the other man. "Jim Getty." Getty didn't turn, keeping his eyes scanning his sector of responsibility. Arian noted that behind his sunglasses, Miles was looking past her most of the time.

"Do you know why I'm here?"

"That's not my business," Miles said. "My job is to keep you secure. Moscow is not a safe place."

Ariana pulled out the piece of paper that Atkins had given her. "I need to meet with this man."

Miles glanced at it, and a frown crossed his face.

"Do you know him?" she asked.

"I know of him," Miles said. "He's a black marketer associated with one of the many crime families here."

"Can you arrange a meeting?"

"How soon?"

"Immediately."

The frown was back, and Ariana figured that was the way Mile's face was most of the time as befitted a security man responsible for others' well-being.

"An immediate meeting might be hard to arrange and worse, difficult to set up in a secure place."

"I'll take the chance," Ariana said.

"Well…" Miles hesitated.

"I know you work for my father," Ariana said, "but this involves the gates that have been causing all the trouble around the world. This is more important than my father's concerns."

"Why do you want to meet with Roskov?"

"I need to purchase something from him."

"What?"

"A crystal skull. He offered it to the British Museum."

Miles didn't seem surprised at the strangeness of the item. "Is it important enough to risk your life for?"

"Yes."

"All right. Let me make some calls while we drive." He indicated for her to go to the Mercedes.

Ariana was flanked by the two men as she made her way over. She noted the thick glass and the solid thud when the door shut behind her and knew the car was armored. They sped off the tarmac and onto a road. Miles was in the forward passenger seat, talking on a cell phone while Getty drove.

Miles turned around . "One hour. Roskov says have the money with you."

"How much?"

"One hundred thousand American."

Ariana knew he had asked the museum for fifty thousand. "You have cash for your kidnap fund, right?"

Miles nodded.

"Do you have one hundred thousand?"

Mile's nod was more reluctant this time, Ariana knew her father had these security men all over the world, and each little station had a large amount of cash to buy back employees of any of his many subsidiaries who might get kidnapped. In many areas of the world, particularly South America and Russia, kidnapping was a profitable business, and there were brokers who made their living negotiating between the parties and taking a percentage of the ransom.

"Let's get it, then?"

Miles pointed past her. "We have a quarter million in the trunk."

"Good."

"I have to check with your father to disburse the fund," Miles said.

"He'll approve it," Ariana said. Her father would spend one hundred thousand on a piece of art without blinking an eye.

Regardless, Miles turned to the front and pulled out his cell phone once more. Ariana stared out the thick windows at the grimy streets of Moscow as they raced toward the center of town. She had never liked the city; it always seemed dirty, and a sense of oppression still lingered over it with a palpable air. It was just at dawn, the first rays of the sun cutting at a sharp angle across the buildings and streets.

Getty cut the wheel hard, and they entered a narrow alley, then came to a halt. There was barely enough room to open the doors on the passenger side.

"Wait inside while I break out the money," Miles said, his only indication that her father had approved the payment. Ariana knew her father would, given all the years he had worked in concert with Foreman; besides, he would probably get Foreman to reimburse him. She had recently accepted that her father cared more about his business empire than he did about her. The only reason he had been allied with Foreman was to get government contracts; she knew the main reason he was still working with the CIA man was that the Shadow, as a threat to the world, was a threat to his holdings. It was how her father had managed to become so successful: by viewing everything totally through the perspective of its effect on him.

Miles reentered the car, a metal suitcase in one hand; a long, plastic case in the other. He handed the metal one back to Ariana. "One hundred thousand. Roskov has a reputation as a legitimate dealer, which means he shouldn't try to rip us off. Not good for the business he's in, but it's not out of the realm of possibilities. I'll go forward with you to make the meet. Jim" – he indicated the driver – "will cover us with a sniper rifle. I've also got some friends in the Omon, the Moscow special police, who will be nearby."

"How much will that coverage cost?" Ariana wondered.

"Ten thousand."

"Where is the meeting?"

'Underneath the Moskvoretsky Bridge near the Kremlin. It's pretty empty this time of day."

"Let's go."

They pulled out of the alley and continued. The Kremlin appeared on the left as they drove down Alexandrovky Boulevard, then reached the Moscow River and followed the walls as they jagged left. Ariana could see the bridge ahead and the dark section of the road as it passed underneath the iron girders. A pair of headlights flashed out of that shadow.

The Mercedes stopped. Miles opened the plastic case and passed a sniper rifle to Getty. He then pulled out an MP-5 submachine gun, made sure a round was in the chamber, slid two extra magazines into his coat pocket, then looked back at Ariana. "Ready?"

"Do you have a weapon for me?"

The frown was back on his face.

"My being armed isn't going to change anything except help our situation if we run into trouble," Ariana pointed out.

Miles reached into the plastic case and retrieved a pistol. "Browning nine millimeter. Do you know how to work it?"

"Yes." She pulled back slightly on the slide and noted there was already a round in the chamber. She stuck it in her belt, underneath her jacket. He handed her a couple of extra clips, which she stuck in her coat pocket.

"All right. Are you ready now?"

In reply, she opened her door and got out. She could see a car parked on the side of the road a hundred meters ahead. It was still early in the morning, and traffic above on the bridge was light, to judge by the sound. There was no one else on this road, and she wondered if that was because of the early hour or the Russian police or a combination.

Miles joined her, the submachine gun tucked under his coat, hanging from his shoulder on a sling. They began walking forward, and someone got out of the car they were headed toward. It was a BMW, also riding low on its tires, probably as well armored as their Mercedes. A tall man with a shaved head, wearing a long leather coat, walked around and put the car between them and him.

"Is that Roskov?" Ariana asked as they got closer.

"I have no idea," Miles said. "I would assume so."

Ariana halted ten feet from the car. "Are you Roskov?" she asked, not sure if he spoke English. Miles repeated the question in fluent Russian.

The man nodded and answered in English. "Yes."

"Do you have the skull?" Ariana asked.

"Yes, I have it."

"Can I see it?"

"No."

Ariana was losing patience with people. "I'm not here to play games."

"Why are the Omon surrounding this place?" Roskov asked.

"To make sure our meeting is uninterrupted," Ariana said.

"If you have the money to pay off the Omon to guard this meeting," Roskov said, "then my asking price is much too low."

"We agreed on the price," Miles said.

"That was then; this is now" Roskov smiled.

"How much?" Ariana asked.

"Half a million."

Ariana knew they didn't have time to get that much money. "I'll double the agreed price. Two hundred thousand."

"Half a million," Roskov repeated.

She turned to Miles. "Kill him."

It was hard to tell who was more surprised, Miles or Roskov.

Roskov held up his hands. "Let's not be hasty."

"I don't have time to play games with you. Your asking price with the British Museum was fifty thousand. We doubled it, and I just doubled it again. Take it or die."

"You are not a good negotiator," Roskov said. "I did not come here alone." He nodded his head up in the darkness of the girders.

Looking up, Ariana could make out a pair of men with rifles perched on a couple of girders, aiming down at her.

"You aren't a good businessman," Ariana said. "Two hundred thousand."

Roskov smiled once more. "You may have the Omon, but I have the Mafia. They now surround your policemen and are better armed. I made some calls while I was waiting for you. You have Van Liten's skulls and one from the American Museum of Natural History and the British. They must be very important. More than just a curiosity."

Ariana looked at Miles. She realized they could stand here forever playing games. She didn't have the money here that Roskov was asking for, and she knew that leaving, getting the money, and arranging another meeting would take too much time. She smiled at Miles and the frown was there, larger than before.

"All right," Ariana said. She put the briefcase on the trunk of the car. "That's your first hundred thousand. Is that enough for me to see the skull and make sure it's what I want?"

Roskov's shoulders went down slightly in relief. "Certainly." He used a remote control to unlock the trunk. He picked up the suitcase and opened the lid. He placed the briefcase next to an item wrapped in a blanket inside a cardboard box. He opened the briefcase and checked the money, then nodded at the box.

Ariana reached in. The weight felt right as she lifted the object out. Carefully, she unwrapped it, knowing before she saw it, that it was a pure ancient from the aura. The skull glittered, even in the shadow of the bridge. She wrapped it back up and placed it back in the box.

"We have the rest of the money in our car," Ariana said.

"There is another issue," Roskov said.

"And that is?"

"You are the daughter of Paul Michelet. There are those who think that is worth much more than the skull. So I am to tell you the price is a half million for the skull and one hundred million for you. An insignificant sum for someone like your father."

Ariana didn't hesitate. She had her pistol out and shoved the muzzle into Roskov's side. Miles whipped out the MP-5 and braced it on the top of the trunk, aiming up at the two snipers, the metal lid between the two groups.

"You have one hundred thousand," Ariana said. "I meant what I said. Take it or you die now."

"You'll never get out of here alive," Roskov hissed. "This is not my idea." He nodded at the metal briefcase. "That is all I get. There is nothing more I can do. They do not care if you kill me."

"Too bad for you," Ariana said. "Where are the keys for the car?"

"In the ignition."

A pair of cars came down the street from the right and stopped twenty meters away.

"They got through the Omon or gave them a bigger bribe," Miles said, the submachine gun still steady on the top of the trunk aimed at the two snipers.

"My boss owns the city," Roskov said. "There is no way you will get out of here."

Looking the other way, Ariana could see that Getty was behind the door of the Mercedes, the sniper rifle resting on the top of the frame.

"There's only one way out of here," Ariana said.

"And that is?" Miles asked.

'Through there," Ariana pointed at the trunk.

"Go," Miles said.

Ariana shoved Roskov out of the security of the heavy trunk lid and dove into the trunk, Miles right behind her. She heard shots fired, and as Miles pulled the lid down on top of them, saw Roskov staggering back as bullets slammed into his chest. Then they were in darkness as the trunk locked shut.

There was that thud of rounds hitting the metal all around, but nothing came through the armor. A thin beam of light punctured the darkness; Miles had a small flashlight clenched between his teeth.

"Excuse me," he said, as he slithered on top of Ariana and pointed the muzzle of the sub at the seat back visible between the metal frame. He fired a quick burst, ripping through the material, then another and another and finally a fourth, stitching out a square pattern about two feet on each side. He pivoted, his hip digging into the small of Ariana's back, and brought both feet to beat at the center of the square. He kicked with no result, then kicked again, and the leather and springs gave way and sunlight flooded the trunk through the small opening.

Miles crawled through, Ariana following, cursing as a spring dug a gouge out of her shoulder. By the time she was in the backseat, Miles was already in the driver's seat and had the engine started. Bullets were smacking into the heavy glass on all sides and ricocheting off. Ariana climbed into the passenger seat as Miles threw the BMW into gear.

Ariana took a quick look around. Getty was firing while the Mercedes was also taking incoming bullets. There were men spread all across the street from the two cars that had just arrived, all with automatic weapons. The two snipers under the bridge were also firing. She could see more cars coming from both directions as Getty jumped into the temporary security of the armored Mercedes and started its engine.

Miles raced by the Mercedes only to face four white vans coming toward them. He slammed on the brakes and expertly skidded the car in a one-eighty turn. He accelerated in the other direction, Getty following. The men who had gotten out of the cars fired, bullets smacking off the bulletproof glass, leaving cracks in places. They drove out of the way as Miles continued to push down on the gas.

"Oh damn," Miles muttered. There were four more vans blocking the way under the bridge. "Better buckle up," he said as he threw the wheel counterclockwise, and the heavy car lifted slightly on two wheel before settling back down as they headed toward the up ramp for the bridge, between it and the Kremlin.

A bullet hit the glass right next to Ariana's head, and she ducked as a spider web of cracks appeared. She had just managed to buckle her seat belt when the car came to an abrupt halt and she was slammed forward, the belt keeping her from bashing her brains out on the dash. She looked up. Fifty meters in front of them, the ramp was blocked by two vans parked in a V. Behind the vans, a half-dozen men with automatic weapons and one man with a rocket-propelled grenade launcher waited. The eighty-eight millimeter wide round stuck out of the forty-millimeter tube, filled with explosives and waiting to be fired. The high-explosive warhead could penetrate over a foot of tank armor, which meant the cars were vulnerable.

Miles's hands were tight on the wheel, his foot on the brake. Getty pulled the Mercedes up next to them, Miles looked to the left and Getty nodded.

"What's he doing?" Ariana asked as the Mercedes began moving.

"His job," Miles said.

She watched in horror as the Mercedes raced toward the two vans, picking up speed. The men began firing, bullets bouncing off the car. Miles switched from brake to gas, and fell in twenty meters behind the Mercedes. The man with the RPG took careful aim and pulled the trigger. Getty swerved, but the distance was too close to make him miss but not as close as Getty had hoped. The rocket grenade needed ten meters of flight to arm. He almost made it, but impact came at twelve meters. The round hit the Mercedes just below the right headlight, punched into the engine, and exploded.

Ariana ducked as the heavy engine hood of the Mercedes came flying over the burning car and smashed into the roof and the BMW, denting it. The Mercedes was still moving, four tons of momentum smashing into the point of the V, shoving both lighter vans back and clearing the way, before the car came to a halt, fire engulfing the engine.

Miles darted them through the gap, then swerved to the driver's side of the Mercedes. "Covering fire!" he yelled at Ariana as he kicked his door open and sprayed the dazed gunmen with the MP-5.

She opened her door and fired as fast as she could pull the trigger, emptying a fifteen-round clip in four seconds. Then she looked at the driver of the Mercedes, Getty was held in place by the seat belt, but his head drooped. He was either dead or unconscious.

"Cover me," she yelled across the top of the BMW to Miles as she abandoned the safety of the door and pulled at the driver's door. It was locked. She looked over her shoulder, but Miles had already seen the problem and had his remote opener in hand. He pushed a button, and the lock clicked. She pulled the door open.

One of Getty's legs was gone from the knee down, blood pulsing out. But she took the sign of the blood flowing as a positive; it meant he was still alive. She tucked her pistol in her belt and then grabbed his arms. She turned her back to him, his arms tight over her shoulders, and dragged him.

A string of bullets whizzed by her head. "Sorry," Miles yelled as he fired another burst that narrowly missed her, giving her covering fire at whoever was behind her.

She shoved Getty into the passenger seat, then sat on top of him, pulling the door shut. Miles slid into his seat, and they were on their way. Bullets thumped on the back window as he pulled away.

As Miles raced through the streets of Moscow, darting through narrow alleys, Ariana pulled her belt off. She slid it under the stump of Getty's right leg, then pulled it as tight as she could. Then she stuck the muzzle of the Browning under the belt and twisted, tightening down the makeshift tourniquet.

"Where are you going?" she finally asked Miles, satisfied that at least there was no more blood coming out of the stump.

"The airfield."

She shook her head. "We need to get him to a hospital."

"The Mafia would have him in a heartbeat if we did that," Miles said. "We're coming with you."

*****

Dane flexed his knees, allowing his body to roll with the slight swell that the *Grayback* bobbed in. There was one Crab in each of the two hangers, and the one on the right was being prepped for the upcoming mission.

The Crab looked like a cross between a Bradley Fighting Vehicle and a miniature submarine. It had a tubular body ten meters long by three in diameter with a turret on the top center that mounted the thirty-millimeter chain gun and the TOW and torpedo launchers. At the rear were dual propellers and horizontal and vertical dive fins, while along the lower half on either side were treads, both powered by the same powerful engine, the changeover made by shifting the power train to either tread or propeller. Entry was by means of doors on either side near the rear, just in front of the power plant, that were hinged on the bottom and swung down to become ramps.

"Impressive, isn't it?" Colonel Loomis asked.

"Impressive was the B-52 bomber stuck vertically in the ground that was in the Angkor gate," Dane said. "Impressive is destroying Iceland. Impressive is sending a tsunami to wipe out a hundred miles of the coast of Puerto Rico as a by-product of doing something else. It's also destroying Atlantis so completely we thought it was simply a literary device used by Plato."

"What's your problem?" Loomis asked. "Ever since you've come here, you've been gloom and doom."

"I should be dancing with joy?" Dane asked. He faced the officer. "I've been in a gate before. I watched my team get decimated. This" – he slapped the side of the Crab, producing a dull thunk—"is not going to defeat the Shadow. It's a ride, that's all. We have no clue what we're going to find over there," Dane nodded toward the dark wall on the northern horizon. "Not in the gate and especially not once we go through the portal, if we can go through the portal."

"I know all that," Loomis said. "But we're taking the fight to the Shadow for the first time instead of reacting. I think you'd be a little more positive."

"What makes you think this is the first time man has taken the fight into a gate against the Shadow?" Dane asked.

"What do you mean?" Loomis was confused.

"Nothing." Dane said.

"We go in thirty minutes,' Loomis snapped.

"Fine." He noted Dr. Martsen near the bow of the *Grayback*, looking down into the water. He walked away, not saying anything else to Loomis, and headed forward. As he got close, he could see Rachel's dorsal fin cutting through the water and then the dolphin's head as Martsen tossed a small fish to her.

"Hello," he said as he walked up. "I'm Eric Dane."

Martsen was short and slender, with dark hair cut tight against her skull. There were deep lines around her eyes. "So this is your idea?"

"Who told you that?" Dane was taken aback at the anger in her voice.

"I was told you were the expert on that…" she pointed at the gate.

"As much as anyone is an expert," Dane said.

"So it was your idea to go in there and ask for Rachel to accompany you," she said.

"I didn't ask for her," Dane said. He could pick up the anger from Martsen and realized it mirrored the anger he had just shown toward Loomis. He glanced at the dark wall of the gate and realized being this close was affecting everyone.

The muscles on the side of Martsen's mouth were working as she tried to control her temper. "Who did then?"

"I don't know," Dane lied. "I'm not even sure why the two of you are here, but I think Rachel has an important role to play.'

"Why do you think that?"

Dane told her about what had happened on the beach in Japan. As he spoke, he could sense her relaxing slightly.

"You can read minds?" she asked when he was done.

"I can sense things."

She nodded. "Sometimes I feel like Rachel is communicating with me."

"I know Chelsea does with me," Dane said. He looked down at the water. "To be honest, I don't know much about dolphins. Aren't they supposed to be intelligent and able to talk among themselves?"

"Rachel's a *Tursiops truncates*," Martsen said. "What most people call a bottle-nosed dolphin."

"She's big," Dane noted as Rachel surfaced, then dove.

"Three meters," Martsen said proudly. "I've been with her for eight years."

"Always with the Navy?" Dane asked.

"It's the only way to get funded," Martsen replied defensively. "And our work has been related to submarine rescue and mine mapping. Nothing offensive."

"How long can she stay under?" Dane asked. He was watching where Rachel had gone under, and she still hadn't come up yet. Martsen saw him looking.

"She can stay under for fifteen minutes," she said. "And go down six hundred meters."

"Isn't she an air-breather?' Dane felt ignorant, but he had rarely been to the ocean.

"A mammal, just like you and me. Air-breathing, warm-blooded."

"How can she dive so deep and stay under so long then?"

"Her lungs are more efficient than ours. She can exchange a much higher percentage of the contents of her lungs than we can."

"And she's intelligent," Dane said.

"More intelligent than humans in some ways," Martsen said. "They don't have wars and kill each other."

"I hear that," Dane said. "One has to wonder exactly what we mean when we talk about intelligence."

"A lot of people confuse dolphins with porpoises, but porpoises have a rounded head with no beak, and their dorsal fins are smaller. And dolphins are smarter," she added.

Rachel surfaced. There was a puff of spray from her blowhole, then she began circling lazily.

"She shuts the blowhole when she dives and has to clear it when she surfaces," Martsen explained.

Dane's attention was caught by the FLIP, a quarter mile away and closer to the gate, as the bulbous bow slowly went underwater and the stern lifted. Slowly, the forward end of the ship disappeared below the waves, taking the muon generator down. In less than five minutes, the majority of the ship was underwater, the stern bobbing in the slight swell.

Martsen signed. "I know why the Navy wants her for this mission. Colonel Loomis said that they were going in blind, no electromagnetic emissions. So they're going to use Rachel as their sonar."

"What do you mean?" Dane asked.

"Rachel uses sonar, what we call echolocation, to navigate and find prey. She sends out a series of clicks that she makes with the blowhole and emits through her forehead. Then she picks up the bounce-back with her jaw. Her brain can then analyze the information and form a sort of picture of her surroundings using these sound images. There are some researchers who speculate the dolphins can even use their emitter to send high-frequency bursts that stun their prey."

"Can you communicate with her?" Dane asked.

Martsen tapped a device on her belt. "This holds recordings of sounds that I've determined the meaning of. Many researchers say now that dolphins don't communicate with each other or have a language, but my experience has been that Rachel clearly understands these noises."

She pushed a button, and a high-pitched whistle came out of the box. Rachel stopped her circling and came over, staring up at them.

Dane could sense the intelligence in Rachel's eyes, and he had the strange feeling that she was getting a reading on him also.

"That was Rachel's name," Martsen said. "Every dolphin has its own name, a specific sound that identifies it. A lot of dolphin language, such as it is, we can't hear because the frequency's too high. Rachel can hear up to one hundred fifty kilohertz, far beyond what we can. To give you an idea how far up that is, a bat can only hear up to one-twenty. So there's a whole spectrum that most researchers ignored for many years."

"So, how intelligent is she?" Dane remembered the pod of dolphins that had looked at him off the coast of Japan. He had no doubt that they were watching him and evaluating.

Martsen shrugged. "I don't know. Her world is so different from ours that it's hard to make an accurate comparison. Just because they haven't built cities doesn't mean they aren't as smart as us. Dolphins live in harmony with their environment, unlike humans. Sometimes I wonder when they made the shift from living on land to water.

"What do you mean?"

"I told you that they're mammals. They developed on land, and then some time in the course of their evolution they went into the ocean."

"That's strange," Dane said. "Why would they do that?"

'Maybe to get away from us," Martsen said.

"Why?"

"Because we're their worst enemies. It's amazing that Rachel even works with us."

"How are we their worst enemies?"

"We kill them, Mr. Dane. By the millions. Commercial fishers set out thousands of kilometers of drift nets that catch everything in their path, including dolphins. It's estimated over five million have been killed in the last ten years here in the Pacific alone. The Russians have practically wiped out the dolphin population of the Black Sea."

"That's present day," Dane said. "That doesn't explain millions of years ago."

Martsen shrugged. "There's more that we don't' know about dolphins than we do know. Sometimes I wish I could escape into the ocean."

"You don't like people much, do you?"

"I like people," Martsen said defensively. "There are some doctors who used dolphins in therapy for cancer patients. I've gone with Rachel on some of those missions."

"What?" Dane's attention was back on Rachel, the eye closest peering up at him as she swam past.

"There are doctors who think that the dolphin's echo-sounding ability can affect the brain."

Now Martsen had his complete attention. "How?"

"No one's quite sure. Some think the energy of the sound dolphins transmit can actually change cellular metabolism. There have been several documented cases of people with severe brain cancer going into remission after dolphin therapy.

"What do you think?" Dane asked.

"I think there's a lot more to Rachel than she lets me know," Martsen said. "Sometimes I think she's the one trying to train me."

Dane laughed. "When I take Chelsea for a walk back home following her with a pooper-scooper, I often think that if aliens were watching, they would think Chelsea the master and me her pet."

Dane could hear Colonel Loomis calling for him, but he didn't turn. *If dolphins could affect the brain...* Loomis called again, and a klaxon sounded, followed by a loudspeaker ordering all personnel to clear the deck in preparation for diving.

"I have to go," Dane said.

Martsen nodded. "Take care of Rachel." She took the box off her belt. She pointed at a small LED screen. "You can scroll through and see what vocabulary I've got in there."

"And what about understanding her?" Dane asked.

" I don't think you'll have a problem with that."

Dane turned. Loomis was standing on the left-side ramp of the Crab, waving at him. "You better get below," he told Martsen.

"Good luck," she said to Dane.

"This way," Loomis pointed at the Crab in the right hangar.

Dane noticed that a long, torpedo-like object had been added on the front deck. "What's that?"

"Nagoya's plug."

*****

The Learjet's medical kit wasn't designed for dealing with the type of trauma that Getty had suffered. The tourniquet had stopped the bleeding, but the man was still unconscious, slumped in one of the plush seats as the plane rolled toward takeoff position.

Miles was looking out the portholes. "I'm surprised the airfield hasn't been shut down yet."

"The Mafia is that powerful?" Ariana asked as she went through the meager contents of the kit.

"Capitalism at its worst," Miles said. He finally relaxed and sat down as the plane rocketed down the runway and was airborne.

The best Ariana could do was give Getty an injection of antibiotics and morphine. She ordered the pilot to head for Berlin and to have an ambulance waiting for them.

"And after Berlin?" Miles asked.

That was a good question, Ariana realized. She now had eight skulls, but she had no clue where others might be, although she had people in her father's employ making inquiries.

"I don't know," she finally said.

"The skull was that important?" Miles asked.

She could tell by the tone of his voice that he thought she was on some rich person's lark, something he had probably seen often enough in his business. "It's connected to the gates."

"You said that earlier. How?"

"We don't know exactly."

"Important enough for my friend to lose his leg?"

"Probably not to him," Ariana said.

"The Mafia thought you were more important than the skull."

Miles didn't' say anything, and Ariana went over to the fax machine. A small pile of paper was on the tray, and she grabbed it and brought it back to her seat.

A report from Nagoya on his latest theories on the gates and what he was proposing to do with the Crab was the first thing that caught her attention. She quickly read it through, not completely understanding the physics but grasping the concept. She had never really considered that the tectonic activity might be more than just a destructive activity but instead, a by-product of the Shadow's desire for energy. Humans had only stumbled on the theory of plate tectonics in the last thirty years, and much still wasn't understood about the forces involved.

"We're going to New York after Berlin," she told Miles.

"What's in New York?" Miles asked.

"There's something I want to see." She picked up the SATPhone to make the necessary arrangements for what she wanted.

*****

It had been christened Anak Krakatoa—Child of Krakatoa—in 1925 when its cone first peeked above the water. In 1950, a minor eruption raised the height to sixty meters above sea level. The next fifty years saw an additional thirty meters added.

The Shadow's probing undid that in less than a minute. The main lava tube underneath Anak Krakatoa was a hundred meters wide and fed by the pressure of the molten mantle below. For years it had been blocked by the weight of a quarter mile of cooled rock above it in the caldera.

The probing changed that, hitting a crack in the plug, widening it. As if sensing the weakness, the lava wormed its way into the opening, expanding it. And then the plug blew.

The explosion was heard by those who lived on the south end of Sumatra and the north tip of Java. They knew what it was immediately and hurried for high ground, just beating the tsunami that struck their shores minutes later.

*****

"How much time before the entire rim goes?" Foreman asked Nagoya as the information about Anak Krakatoa's eruption was relayed from various seismic stations to the control room in the FLIP.

"Hard to tell," Nagoya answered. "Remember that the Shadow used nuclear weapons to induce what happened in Iceland. Now it's using the power it's tapped from Chernobyl. The only thing I can do is try to match the power levels."

"And?" Foreman pressed impatiently.

"And I think we have twelve hours, with a twenty percent margin of error either way."

CHAPTER SEVENTEEN

THE PAST
79 A.D.

The Pontus Euxinus stretched ahead of the galley as far as the eye could see. Since leaving the Hellesponte, Captain Fabatus had kept the shore in sight off the port side, creeping around the sea. Falco had always found sailors a curious contradiction. They claimed to love the water, yet they feared to stray out of sight of land. It had taken a direct order from General Cassius for Fabatus to take the plunge and take a north-northeast course across the Pontus Euxinus for three straight days, out of sight of land. As soon as he had spotted land directly ahead, Fabatus, and everyone else on board, had breathed a huge sigh of relief. Then he resumed his shore-hugging navigation to the east.

Standing in the bow, Falco could see the ship cutting through the water. He sensed Kaia coming up behind him, but his attention was below, on the gray forms leaping and splashing next to them.

"Good morning, priestess."

"Good morning, soldier." Kaia glanced over the thin railing. "We seem to be making good time."

"After what happened in the Hellesponte, everyone, including the slaves, are most anxious to get us off the ship," Falco said.

"I'm anxious to get off the ship also," Kaia said.

"Do you see?" Falco pointed down at the dolphins.

"Yes."

"Do you feel them?"

Kaia nodded. "They've been sending me dreams ever since we entered the sea."

"What kind of dreams?" Falco asked.

"The past, the future, it's hard to tell. Images."

"You're lying," Falco said. "You know some of what you see, and you know what it means, buy you feel telling me will hurt me."

"No," Kaia said. "I fear telling you will change things. It is one thing the oracle taught me. She had to be very careful giving prophecies, because knowledge is a very dangerous thing."

"How do they know what awaits us?" Falco asked, indicating the dolphins. "How do they reach us?"

"I do not know," Kaia said.

"You've seen my death," Falco said it simply. "You fear to tell me because you think it will scare me. You saw me in the arena. Do you think I fear death?"

"No. You seek death."

"Then why do you not tell me what they have shown you?"

"It is not time."

Falco stared off to the north, falling silent.

"Do you know when we will arrive?" Kaia asked.

Falco pointed ahead and to the left, where a promontory of land poked into the sea. "Beyond that lies Varna where the XXV Legion is headquartered."

"Which means I can open my follow-on orders." General Cassius had come forward, dressed in his best armor, a scarlet cloak pinned to the shoulders. In his hand was a scroll with the imperial seal. Falco would have opened it the minute he was outside the gates of Rome, but he knew better than to suggest such to Cassius, a man to whom honor was paramount.

Cassius slipped his dagger under the wax seal, parting it smoothly. He unrolled the scroll and read, eyes flicking back and forth as he went down the lines.

"As we already knew. Take command of the XXV Legion. Travel under the guidance of Kaia, priestess of the Oracle of Delphi, on a reconnaissance in force north of Bospora. Upon encountering any hostile forces, engage and destroy."

"And what didn't we know, sir?" Falco asked.

"Upon completion of that mission," Cassius said slowly as he rolled the orders back up, "the XXV Legion is to continue its reconnaissance and march to the northeast until recalled by the emperor."

"That's insane," Falco said without thinking.

Cassius smiled. "My old friend, I would have thought you had been in Rome long enough to know sanity has nothing to do with decrees of the emperor."

"I don't understand," Kaia said.

Cassius peered at the land north of them as he spoke. "The legion we are meeting is not particularly loyal to the emperor. The emperor does not consider me particularly loyal, and he considers me dangerously popular with the Praetorians and legions. Falco, well, I would say he considers Falco just plain dangerous, probably the most accurate perception of the three. After we assist you, we are to march off into the unknown lands of Asia, awaiting the emperor's recall, which, of course, will never come. It's all perfectly logical if you look at it from the emperor's point of view."

"I say we—" Falco began but Cassius raised a hand.

"Hush, old friend. There are ears everywhere; ears that will return to Rome."

Falco noted that Fabatus had drifted close to them, even as the ship cleared the point and headed in toward a harbor, above which a wooden fort in the traditional Roman style was built on a hill.

"Besides," Cassius said, "we should take things one step at a time. Worrying about these orders" – he tapped the scroll—"is premature. We must first accomplish the mission assigned."

The imperial galley was a mile offshore of Herculaneum, or rather where the port city to Pompeii had once been. Now there was only mud and ash where once had been a town.

"Any survivors from Pompeii?" Titus asked Thyestes as he surveyed the damage.

"None, Emperor."

"Herculaneum?" he asked, referring to the port city that had serviced Pompeii.

"Some sailors who were offshore when the town was covered survived."

Not an auspicious start to his reign, Titus thought.

"There was a report of another similar event," Thyestes said. "Another volcano erupting."

Titus turned toward his advisor. "Where and when?"

"The island of Thera. Five days ago. And I have been told that the imperial courier ship carrying Cassius was offshore when it occurred."

"Did they survive?"

"Yes, Emperor. A galley spotted them in the Cyclades, heading toward the Hellesponte."

A week ago Titus would have preferred to hear no to that question, but seeing the destruction that had come from Vesuvius, he was relieved to hear that Cassius had survived and was continuing on his mission with the strange priestess from Delphi.

"There are reports of trembles in the Earth arriving daily from all over the empire," Thyestes continued. "From Hesperia, Gaul, even Britain. Also from our provinces in Africa. There has been some destruction in Egypt caused by the Earth moving. A temple dedicated to your father was destroyed."

Bad omens all around, Titus thought. He had never been a fervent believer in the various gods, but after seeing the way the Jews fought against his legions in Palestine, he'd realized there was a power greater than that of the sword. Even though Jerusalem had been razed, the temple destroyed, and hundreds of thousands put to death, there was still a small band clinging to a rock called Masada in the middle of the desert. Titus knew he would have to deal with that among the many other issues facing his empire.

"Thyestes, perhaps we were hasty with our orders to Cassius."

Thyestes remained quiet, waiting for his emperor's thought to be played out.

"Send a courier after Cassius. When he completes this mission, I want him to go to Palestine and take command of the X Legion once more. He will finish what we started so many years ago."

"Yes, Emperor."

A maniple was drawn up on the dock, assembled no doubt in response to the imperial guidon that flapped in the slight breeze. As the ship was tied up, Falco looked at the troops with a critical eye. Their armor wasn't polished but looked to be in good shape. The weapons were sharp and glittered in the sunlight, which was more important than bright armor. The eyes of the men were on the ship, wondering what fate was delivering them from Rome. Falco knew what thoughts were racing through their head: A recall? An expedition to be mounted against some real or imagined enemy of the empire? Simply an imperial envoy relaying normal orders? A new commander, perchance?

"They look functional," Cassius said in a low voice.

Falco had relayed to the general the words of Centurion Attius.

"Yes, sir, they do." But Falco could also see the looks in the eyes that peered back at him. No sign of fear or even respect. "However, if they get an order they don't necessarily think is a good one..." Falco didn't finish the thought, knowing that Cassius could see the same thing. Falco knew that most Roman officers would come in like a tornado, cracking the whip and using punishment to quickly take command, perhaps crucify a few men to make the point. He also knew that Cassius wasn't like most Roman officers.

The gangplank was extended to the dock. Cassius walked to the opening in the railing and paused. This was where a speech should be made, from the higher position of the ship, looking down on the troops. Cassius walked down the ramp without a word, Falco behind him.

An officer was at the head of the maniple. The tribune laticlavius, Falco knew from the accoutrements the man wore, which meant he was the senior tribune, second in command of the legion. It was also a position that more often than not went to political appointees who needed some military time to round out their records before running for the senate, rather than a career military men.

The tribune raised his arm in salute. "Hail, envoy of the emperor."

Cassius returned the salute and stopped right in front of the tribune. He extended the copy of orders that Titus had given him in Rome, ceding command of the legion to him. The tribune was a young man, his skin red from exposure to the sun, lines of sweat rolling down from underneath his highly polished helmet.

The tribune took them and unrolled the paper, quickly reading. His body stiffened, and he saluted once more. "Hail, General Cassius." He lowered his arm and his voice so the men behind him wouldn't hear. "This comes as a surprise, General. We had no word. If we had known, we would have prepared a more appropriate reception."

"We traveled as quickly as any courier might have," Cassius said, cutting him off. "You may dismiss the troops and take me to your headquarters."

"Yes, sir." He turned and issued orders to a centurion behind him, then turned back to face Cassius.

"Your name?' Cassius asked.

The officer was flustered. "Marco Liberalius, General."

"Tribune Liberalius, this is Centurion Falco."

Falco snapped a quick salute at the senior officer, who returned it.

"Where is the commander?" Cassius asked.

"Legatus Flavius is, uh, sir, he is indisposed at the moment."

"An interesting choice of words," Cassius noted. He pointed toward the wooden stockade on the top of the hill overlooking the dock. "Shall we go?"

"There will be horses here in a few minutes," Liberalius said. "My centurion is seeing to it."

"I prefer to walk," Cassius said. He headed toward the hill on which the large fort was perched, Liberalius hurrying to keep up with him, waving off his squire, who had approached with his horse. There were tents pitched outside the walls, along the low ground, something Falco found interesting. He estimated at least two-thirds of the legion was camped outside the fort, if he subtracted the usual number of patrols and outlying outposts that should be deployed about the region.

As they went up the dusty road, men came out of the tents to stare at them from a distance. Most of the soldiers were swarthy, with dark hair braided tightly against their skulls, definitely not Romans. There were also the usual camp hangers-on at the outskirts of the legion tents: whores, washerwomen, traders, gamblers. It is said wherever the Roman army camped for more than a night, a city sprang up.

Several legionnaires opened the gates to the fort, and they entered. Barracks were built along the inside of the walls, and a blockhouse was centered in the middle. The troopers who peered out of the inner barracks were predominantly Roman, Falco could tell, as if the commander was protecting himself from his own non-Roman troops, which might well be the case.

Liberalius hurried his step toward the blockhouse, getting in front of Cassius. "General, I should announce your arrival."

"I think it has already been announced," Cassius said as the door swung open and a man dressed in breeches and tunic, over which he had hastily thrown his robe fringed with red, appeared.

"Legatus Flavius," Cassius nodded a greeting.

"General Cassius," Flavius nodded in return, no love lost.

Liberalius extended the orders, and Flavius quickly read them. When done, he laughed. "You are welcome to my command, General. Or should I say Legatus Cassius? Most welcome. It's about time Rome remembered to bring me home. I see there is a new emperor," he added, indicating the scroll that Titus had signed and fixed his imperial seal to.

Knowing how Titus viewed the XXV Legion, Falco thought the legatus a bit naïve in the thought about returning home, but since Cassius said nothing, Falco stood mute.

"Your current strength?" Cassius asked. There were figures moving in the doorway behind Flavius, and several other tribunes appeared, a few of them staggering as if drunk.

"Strength?" Flavius turned and addressed one of his officers, relaying the question.

"Sixty percent," the officer answered.

"Deployed?" Cassius snapped.

"We have two patrols out," the officer said. "A century each."

Falco was amazed at that. Only two patrols and no outpost? His mind had already done the math. A legion at 60 percent was slightly over three thousand men. Two deployed centuries was about two hundred men out in the field. Being on the edge of barbarian territory that was living very dangerously.

"Ah, only fifteen percent of our strength," the officer added, "is from the original force." A not-so-subtle way of telling Cassius how many of the men were Roman.

"It appears that fifteen percent is all gathered here inside the fort," Cassius noted.

Flavius laughed once more, his face flushed. "Damn right. Can't trust these provincials."

"You may depart on the imperial courier ship that brought me," Cassius told Flavius, then he pointed at the tribunes one by one. "And the rest of you are relieved and will depart also."

Falco could see the shock on their faces as Cassius walked forward, brushing by Flavius. Falco followed closely behind. They entered the blockhouse, the interior of which was dimly lit. It stank of wine and sweat and the stale odor of sex.

"Throw open the windows," Cassius ordered, and Falco hurried to do so. He paused as he noted two figures huddled under blankets on low-lying couches: women, naked under the blankets. From their skin and hair, he knew they were locals.

"Get them some clothes, give them some money, and apologize to them on behalf of the Roman army," Cassius barked.

"Yes, General," Falco said.

"Then summon all the centurions, along with that Liberalius fellow. And bring Kaia up from the boat."

"Yes, General."

Cassius held up a hand, causing Falco to pause before carrying out the tasks. "We march at dawn tomorrow. We do not have much time."

CHAPTER EIGHTEEN

THE PRESENT

Loomis was seated in the pilot's seat, Colonel Shashenka in the copilot's with a link to the gun turret and targeting screens in front of him. Dane and Ahana were behind them, watching over their shoulders at the video monitors that showed what was outside. They were still on the deck of the *Grayback*, but it was submerging, and they could see the ocean wash over the gray metal in front of the Crab. Soon the water reached the Crab and began climbing up its side until they were submerged, going down with the submarine.

"Releasing umbilicals and locks to the *Grayback*," Loomis announced. He flipped a switch, and the Crab shuddered. "We're on our own."

With one hand, Loomis pushed forward on the throttle while with the other he turned them toward the north. "Under way," he said.

"How long until we reach the gate?" Dane asked.

"Five minutes until hold position," Loomis answered. "We're going to stand off at one kilometer and wait until Professor Nagoya opens our doorway."

Dane glanced at a monitor above and to the right. It showed the view from the camera strapped to Rachel's back. The Crab appeared briefly as Rachel turned toward them, then an empty ocean view as she turned on a parallel course, indicated by the small red symbol on the master display set in the console between Loomis and Shashenka. The Russian's hand was on the butt of the pistol in the holster attached to his belt, an unconscious gesture that Dane knew indicated the man's feelings.

Dane could feel the darkness of the gate looming ahead.

* * *

Nagoya was surprised to see that his hands were shaking. All the years he had spent theorizing and studying the gates had not prepared him for this moment, when he would actually attempt to open one. He sat in front of the computer, in what was normally Ahana's position, staring at the screen, trying to hide his trembling hands from Foreman, who was seated next to him.

"We still have a fix on both probes," Nagoya said.

"The Crab is in position." Foreman had a laptop open on his lap, the data from the Crab and Rachel being relayed to him via satellite link.

Beneath their feet, the FLIP extended over two hundred meters into the ocean, ending at the muon receiver that Nagoya had rigged to also project.

"Everything is ready," Nagoya said. He had only a hope that this theory would work, a most unsettling feeling for a scientist. He was used to proving a theory with experimentation before committing himself to it, but here he was not only putting his reputation on the line but the lives of the people in the Crab and beyond that, the fate of the planet.

"Muonic activity?" Foreman asked.

"Nothing unusual."

"Do it."

Nagoya hit the Enter key, and the program began running.

From the bulb on the bottom of the FLIP, a stream of muons began flowing in the direction of the first probe.

"We've got a path," Ahana said. Her screen showed a red line across their position and cutting into the dark triangle in front of them. "Follow it," she told Loomis as she superimposed it on his video display.

The craft began moving, following the line of muons.

Dane's hands grabbed the arms of his seat, and a line of sweat trickled down his forehead. His temples throbbed as they approached the gate. In the midst of all that pain, though, he could sense Rachel alongside, swimming less than ten feet off their starboard side. Her presence was like a light in the darkness that threatened to overwhelm him. He would have thought it would get easier, this third trip into the gate, but this was the worst.

"One hundred meters to the gate," Ahana announced. "All electromagnetic systems to minimum."

The lights inside dimmed, and only three screens glowed: the forward video, Ahana's computer, and the feed from Rachel. But Dane saw more than that. The gate was a presence, the limits of which he could feel. And he could also see the line of muons that the FLIP was projecting, punching into that darkness.

"Fifty meters," Ahana said.

"A little to the right," Dane said.

The pilot glanced over his shoulder, but Dane's eyes were closed.

"Do it," Ahana ordered. She looked at her screen. "Ten meters. Eight. Six. Four, Two. Contact."

Dane felt the entry into the gate like hitting a pool while splayed out from a high jump. His entire body jerked, spasmed, then he forced himself to focus. Rachel was in front of them now.

"We're in the gate," Ahana said. "I've lost the line to the portal!"

"I see it," Dane said, eyes still closed. "Steady as we go."

"We've got the Chernobyl probe," Nagoya said. Foreman had lost the feed from the Crab as soon as it entered the gate. Whether that was from the gate's effect or the craft's power-down, he didn't know. He was behind Nagoya now, watching.

"Linking power," Nagoya said as the program went to the next phase. The muon line that had been going from the FLIP to the first probe now made another jump to the Chernobyl probe.

"There's the portal," Nagoya tapped the screen. "I'm boosting power."

"Rachel has the portal located," Dane said. "She's on the muonic trace Nagoya is projecting." The dolphin was in front of them, swimming slowly, allowing them to keep pace.

"How far ahead?" Loomis asked.

"I can't tell distance," Dane said. "All I know is that we're closing on it."

"We need to stop just short of it," Loomis said.

From what Dane was picking up from Rachel, the portal was a sphere space in the center of the gate. The dolphin was getting echoes back from it and other objects in the water.

"There are other things out there," Dane said.

"What things?" Ahana asked.

"Living things." Dane remembered the krakens that had attacked the *Glomar*. Rachel was swimming faster, sensing the other objects. "Pick up speed," Dane told Loomis.

Something was closing on them from the right, swimming fast. Dane could sense Rachel's fear, but still the dolphin led them toward the portal.

Dane had been watching Loomis pilot the Crab. The controls were simple: a wheel that when rotated turned them left and right, when pressed in, they dove, and when pulled back, they went up. A throttle, much like an airplane's, controlled their speed.

"Move," Dane said, tapping Loomis on the shoulder.

"What do you think you're doing?" the colonel demanded.

"You're flying blind," Dane said. "I'll get us there."

Loomis reluctantly gave up his seat, and Dane took his place. He closed his eyes and saw what Rachel saw: the image of the portal directly ahead, a creature coming from the right. Rachel turned, putting herself between them and the creature, which appeared in the dark water: a kraken a hundred meters away and closing fast, tentacles trailing as it sucked in water through vents on the side of its head and expelled it.

"No," Dane whispered as he turned the wheel. "Behind us."

"Who are you talking to?" Loomis demanded.

Dane didn't even hear him. Rachel did as he asked, putting the Crab between her and the kraken.

"Brace for impact," Dane announced.

"Impact with what?" Loomis asked with alarm.

Dane reached down and shoved the throttle to maximum speed. The blunt nose of the Crab hit the kraken in the head, the collision sending a shudder through the craft. Dane spun the wheel, putting them back on course for the portal as the creature drifted, stunned by the impact. Rachel raced out in front again.

"What was that?"

Dane was getting tired of listening to Loomis. "The portal is about two hundred meters ahead," he announced as he throttled back. There were other kraken about, several coming closer to investigate. Dane estimated they had about a minute.

"I'm launching the plug," Ahana said.

"We don't' have much time," Dane said. The Crab was slowing. "The portal is a hundred fifty meters ahead."

"The plug is on its way," Ahana said.

Dane could see the torpedo moving through the water as Rachel moved out of its way. He could also see the portal now, a black circle directly ahead of them. The torpedo hit the black and stopped, prevented from going in.

"It's there." Dane said.

Ahana reached forward and threw a switch. "Let's hope this works."

The nose of the torpedo opened, and a two-inch-diameter probe appeared. The core of the probe was radioactive, emitting a weak nuclear force. It extended forward and passed into the portal.

* * *

"We've got power!" Nagoya slapped his palm on the side of his chair. "The plug is working. We're drawing power from the portal." He hit the Enter key on his computer. "Redirecting power back to the portal and opening it."

"Twenty seconds," Dane said. A half-dozen kraken were racing toward them. Rachel was close by the nose of the Crab, her fear soaking into Dane.

"If it worked, we should be able to go in," Ahana said.

"If it worked," Dane repeated, but he was already accelerating. Through Rachel, he could see the probe against the portal, but there was no apparent change.

"Brace for impact," Dane announced once more.

He throttled back just before they hit the portal, but there was no impact as the Crab, Rachel alongside, went into the portal. The Crab was suddenly jarred as one of the kraken grabbed the turret, but then the portal they had opened shut behind them, slicing the arm off.

They were in.

Ariana blocked her eyes to protect them from the debris blown up by the helicopter as it landed in Central Park. She was off as soon as they were on the ground, Miles right behind her. A man waited next to a car, and he whisked them to the Rose Center where the master programmer for the Hayden Planetarium, Professor Mike O'Shaughnessy, waited for them, just inside the large glass block that contained the projection sphere.

As soon as introductions were made, he took them inside the sphere. The interior was dimly lit by thousands of projected stars on the half dome above their head.

"Your request was most unusual," O'Shaughnessy told Ariana as he led them into the exact center where a control panel was located. "We've always projected something from the sky. No one has ever thought of projecting from inside the Earth to the surface."

"Were you able to do it? And use the data I sent you?" Ariana was too excited to sit down. Since leaving Berlin, she had pored through the data forwarded by Nagoya and set it onward to O'Shaughnessy to be programmed.

"Oh, yes," O'Shaughnessy said. "I had to contract quite a few experts over the last several hours, particularly those who know about plate tectonics. It's really most fascinating—and frightening, given the data on the Shadow's manic probing that you forwarded to me. I took into account what happened off the coast of Chile and the eruption of Anak Krakatoa." He reached down and typed on the keyboard. The enclosure went dark for a second, then lit up with a projection of the Pacific Rim.

"We're looking from the center of the Earth outward to the surface of the planet," O'Shaughnessy said. "Here are the landmasses." The outline of the continents bordering the Pacific appeared in green. "Here's the Ring of Fire." That appeared in purple, roughly following the landmass edges.

"The Antarctica plate is more interesting," O'Shaughnessy said, pointing to one edge of the projection. "It is now relatively stable but is connected with numerous plates to the north all around. Watch."

He used the computer mouse to rotate the entire image above their heads, and the world turned. Ariana could see what he meant, as the southernmost plate touched numerous others.

"Einstein had a theory called the crustal displacement, where he thought there was a good possibility that Antarctica was actually Atlantis," O'Shaughnessy said.

Ariana had heard this before, but she kept quiet and listened, knowing there was a good chance she would hear something new.

"The entire plate that now makes up Antarctica might have been located—according to Einstein—here in the middle of the North Atlantic. A traumatic event, perhaps the Shadow manipulating the plates themselves, might have broken it free from this tenuous connection to the planet below, and it literally drifted over the course of thousands of years to its current location.

"It's interesting to note that it is only very recently," O'Shaughnessy continued, "that we have an idea of the actual outline of the continent that is hidden below the ice. It is estimated that if the ice was removed from Antarctica, the removal of all that weight would allow the land below to rise over two miles. The rift around Antarctica extends for over nineteen hundred miles, comparable to the Great Rift Valley in Africa."

O'Shaughnessy moved the mouse again, and they went back to the view of the half of the planet centered on the Pacific. "In red is the current status of the muonic probing as you forwarded it to me."

The red covered the entire Ring of Fire with larger, more concentrated splotches near Mounts Wrangell and Erebus.

"When I do the stars," O'Shaughnessy continued, "there's a technique I use called progression. What I can do is show how the sky looked in the past, rotating the star fields, or even how it will look in the future. In this case, I've *progressed* the muonic probing into the future, adding power to it."

The read began to change to crimson as O'Shaughnessy had the computer work forward. Ariana could see it now, what had only been numbers on paper or flat, two-dimensional pictures. Erebus was the key, she realized not Wrangell. It would be the start point when the Shadow began whatever it had planned for the Ring of Fire. It could also be the junction point for the Shadow to extend the destruction to other plates in other parts of the world.

"Can you project what would happen if activity at Erebus is stopped?" she asked.

O'Shaughnessy nodded and sat at the keyboard, typing furiously for almost a minute. "All right. I'm going back to present levels. And projecting..." he hit the Enter key.

It fell apart. Ariana could see it. Wrangell was still affected, but the red lines all along the Ring of Fire gradually faded. She jumped to her feet.

"What are you doing?" Miles asked.

"Thank you, Professor," she said as she headed for the door, pulling her SATPhone out of her pocket.

"Where are we going?" Miles persisted as they left the planetarium.

"Antarctica. McMurdo Station." From a previous trip, she knew the research base stood in the shadow of Erebus.

"The Learjet can't land there," Miles said. "The landing strip is ice and snow."

"I'll get us a plane." She dialed Foreman's number.

CHAPTER NINETEEN

THE PAST
79 A.D.

Falco wiped sweat from his brow as Cassius signaled a halt. They were on top of a ridgeline on the west side of the Dnieper River, the XXV Legion stretched out behind them, except for a screen of scouts a half mile ahead.

They were beyond the empire's boundaries, well into the territory of the barbarians, but that wasn't the reason for the halt. They'd been outside the empire for four days now on a forced march north along the river. The XXV had done well, keeping to the normal legion pace of twenty-five miles a day.

Directly ahead, beyond several miles of swampy ground, was a dark stationary wall. It was very high, taller than any wall Falco had ever seen, and about four miles wide. Whatever it was constructed of, he had never seen. The black was featureless and seemed to absorb the sunlight completely.

There was no need to ask Kaia if that was what they sought. The priestess had taken several steps forward and was staring as intently as any of them at the blackness. Falco had sensed the darkness for two days as they marched, the sense of evil growing closer. He knew Kaia had sensed it also.

"Senior Centurion Falco," Cassius called.

"Yes, sir?"

"Make *castra* here. And I don't want any slack in the perimeter."

"Yes, sir."

Cassius looked at sky. Clear, no clouds. "No tents."

"Yes, sir."

As the men swung into the practiced movements of preparing to stop for the night, fortifying their position, making it into the traditional *castra*, Falco kept one eye on the blackness, the other on the work. Every legion *castra* was to be built the exact same way. A square wall and moat surrounded the camp. Two roads bisected the camp, one called the *via principia* and the other the *via praetorian*. The names, like the camp, were always the same. The legionnaire in a camp anyplace in the world could find his way in the pitch dark.

The sun was just over the western horizon when Falco reported all was ready for inspection. Cassius walked the entire perimeter, stopping here and there to chat with the men. Not quite X Legion standard, but the troops were getting better.

"Very good, Falco," Cassius said as they arrived back at the starting point, facing the black wall, now invisible in the dusk. Kaia was where they had left her, standing still as a rock.

"What now?' Cassius asked her.

"I'm not sure," Kaia said. "We have the staff and the skull, but it is not enough."

"What more do you need?" Falco asked.

"I don't know. I had a vision last night of a pyramid like the one we saw at Thera. But I see no pyramid here. I think I must go into the darkness."

"A reconnaissance would be a smart move," Cassius agreed. "But we will wait until morning."

"I recommend only Kaia and I enter the gate," Falco said. "I sense great danger in there."

"One does not need your special gifts to feel the danger," Cassius said. "I agree. The two of you go, but I think it best to take a third with you. I will wait nearby with a cohort."

A legionnaire approached, holding a mess tin of the same food the troops were eating. Another way Cassius was different from other officers Falco had known. On campaign, Cassius always ate the same as his troops. And he always ate next to last, Falco holding on to the right to eat last, insuring all the men had eaten; it was the way a true leader operated. Cassius accepted the tin. Another soldier approached with Falco and Kaia's food. It was one of the many ways Cassius had begun to earn the respect of the troops. Another was his refusal to ride a horse. He had walked, just as his soldiers had, moving up and down the column all day long, getting to know his men.

Just after dark, there was a commotion on the southern side of the camp, and Falco hurried there, arriving as one of the patrols they had sent out was allowed to pass. The young tribune in charge was obviously agitated.

Falco searched his memory for the man's name. "Falvius. What news do you have?"

Falvius jumped off his horse. "Barbarians. Massing to the south of us."

"Come," Falco indicated he should follow, and they went to the center, where Cassius was resting on a thin blanket. The general was up by the time they arrived. A small fire blazed nearby, and he warmed his hands over it.

Falvius snapped a salute, which Cassius calmly returned. "Report, Tribune."

"General, there is a force of barbarians to the south of us."

"The proper format for such a report," Cassius said, calm as a rock in response to the tribune's excitement, "is to be specific. How many, how far, and what are they doing?"

"At least five thousand. And we saw more heading toward the camp. It's a day's march south of here. They were camping for the night, but they were astride our trail. They're following us."

"Any cavalry?" Falco asked. He could sense Kaia's presence nearby and spotted her just outside the circle of light thrown by the fire.

"Some horses," Falvius said, "but most were on foot."

"Did you leave men to watch?"

"Yes, General. One contubernium with our swiftest horses."

Falco watched the general consider the situation. They had faced it before, especially in Germany. Every time a legion crossed the Rhine, it was usually unopposed for several days until the locals could gather their forces. Then the enemy was usually *behind* the legion, between it and the empire, meaning the Romans would have to cut their way out to return home.

Cassius nodded at Falvius. "Good job. Go get some food."

When he was gone, Kaia stepped forward into the light.

"We have company," Cassius said to her.

"I've sensed them gathering all day behind us," she said.

"And you didn't think to inform me?" Cassius asked.

"Would it have made a difference?" she asked in turn. "They are halted for the night. And they are not anxious to engage you immediately. They want to outnumber you at least two to one, and it will take a day or so for that strength to gather from the villages farther away. They think you are the vanguard for a larger Roman force to bring this land into the empire."

"You're reading their minds at a distance?" Cassius asked.

"No. It is common sense."

"I agree," Falco said. "We have at least a day."

"They'll fight us, but not that." Falco nodded his head in the direction of the gate. "It would seem they do not know their real enemy."

"They fear the darkness," Kaia said. "They think it comes from the gods. Maybe they think by killing us they will appease the gods who they believe started the darkness."

"I fear it also," Cassius said. "And we don't know what kind of enemy it is, nor do the local people, I suspect. It is easier to fight what you know than the unknown."

"*Can* we fight it?" Falco had turned to Kaia.

"I do not know," she replied.

"We best get some rest," Cassius said. "We'll need it in the morning."

CHAPTER TWENTY

THE PRESENT

Ariana woke to a gentle tap on her shoulder. In the darkened cabin of the Air Force C-130 cargo plane, Miles was leaning over her. "We're approaching McMurdo Station," he said.

It had been a long flight to New Zealand in the Learjet with several refueling stops along the way. They'd even been forced to switch out the crew to get fresh pilots halfway to their goal. Once in New Zealand, they had switched over to the Air Force cargo plane that Foreman had arranged to transport them south.

Miles was sliding up the covers on the small portals, letting bright sunlight in. Ariana pulled her seat upright and peered out. White-capped ocean was below as far as she could see. She spotted a large iceberg, at least three miles long and half that in width. She knew that recently there had been several major bergs spawned off the Ross Ice Shelf, along the edge of which lay McMurdo Station, the largest settlement in Antarctica.

Ariana went forward, opening the door to the cockpit. Directly ahead loomed Mount Erebus, towering over both the Ross Ice Shelf and McMurdo Station. A steam plume came off the summit into the cold, clear Antarctic sky. She knew the mountain was named after one of the ships in James Ross's expedition that discovered the volcano in 1841.

"We're on approach to McMurdo," the pilot informed her. "We'll be landing in ten minutes." The C-130 was equipped with skis bolted on over the wheels, allowing it to land on the forbidding terrain below them.

Ariana nodded and went back to the cargo bay. She sat down at the laptop that had a satellite link and accessed the web. She brought up the latest report from MEVO, Mount Erebus Volcano Observatory. MEVO was a joint venture run by both the New Mexico Institute of Mining and Technology and Victoria University in Wellington, New Zealand. It continuously monitored the volcano using geophones, gas emission detectors, and seismic recorders. During the short period of relatively mild weather, geologists made the dangerous climb up the mountain's slopes and checked out the crater, in which a convicting lava lake was constantly brewing.

"Better buckle up," Miles advised as the plane abruptly banked.

Ariana leaned back against the red cargo webbing that lined the wall of the plane and made up the seats. She could feel the air pressure shift in her ears, and then the plane touched down, bounced, and began sliding.

Twisting in the seat, she could see outside. A tractor with a red flag flying from a pole flashed by as the plane gradually slowed. The pilots turned the craft and headed toward the tractor.

"You can go back with the plane," she told Miles.

The security man smiled. "I don't think your father would approve. Besides, I like seeing a job through to the end."

"I don't know what the end is going to be," Ariana said.

"That's what makes this interesting," Miles said. He tossed a parka, over pants, and gloves at her. "Better put these on. It's going to get very cold very quickly," he added as the crew chief hit a lever and the back ramp of the plane began opening.

Ariana stepped into the over pants and pulled the suspenders up over her shoulders. Freezing air swirled in, and Ariana zipped up the parka. The tractor appeared behind the ramp, and men scrambled on board, off-loading supplies on a large sled that was hooked to the tractor. Two more tractors with large, enclosed cabs behind, approached the plane.

One man in a red parka came forward to Ariana.

"Dr. Michelet?" he asked, pulling back his hood and revealing a completely bald, black head.

"Yes." Ariana stood.

"I'm Professor Jordon. I'm the ranking person here with MEVO."

"How's the volcano?" Ariana asked.

"Bad," Jordon said succinctly. "More active than any time since we began recording. We estimate it'll go in seventy-two hours, but this is a rather inexact science. Add in the fact that this is being propagated by a foreign source…" He shrugged.

They walked onto the ramp and looked to the east where Mount Erebus dominated the horizon, over twelve thousand feet high. The plume of smoke seemed even thicker than just a few moments ago, when she'd seen it from the air.

Jordon jerked a thumb over his shoulder as the doors to the cabs on the two trail vehicles opened and people began piling out, carrying luggage. "First-stage evacuation of nonessential personnel. There are supposed to be two more planes en route to take the rest of us." He gestured toward the tractor. "Come on."

Ariana and Miles followed him. The cold was biting, hurting the little skin Ariana had exposed.

"It's actually a nice day," Jordan said as they climbed into the cab of the tractor, the three of them a tight fit. "We're very lucky this is happening during summer. A plane wouldn't be able to get in during winter, although we would have less people at the base. God knows what we'd do then other than bend over and kiss ourselves good-bye." He threw the tractor in gear, and with a lurch, it began moving, pulling the loaded sled.

"Why the supplies if everyone is leaving?" Ariana asked.

"Just in case," Jordan said. "If the base isn't destroyed we want to be able to get back in business quickly. Can't afford to waste a flight."

He glanced at the volcano. "I've lived in the shadow of that thing for five years. Did you know Erebus was named after one of Ross's ships? But the interesting thing is that the ship was named after a figure in Greek mythology, one who ferried the souls of the dead over the River Styx in Hades. Seems kind of appropriate now."

Ariana could see the cluster of buildings ahead that made up McMurdo.

"Are you here to observe?" Jordan asked. "We're plan to get airborne and circle in the last plane at a safe distance, or at least what we hope is a safe distance."

"No," Ariana said. "We can't let it blow. If it does, it will start a chain reaction up through the entire Ring of Fire."

"Then what are you here for?" Jordan glanced over at her, confused.

"To stop it from erupting."

The interior of the Crab was pitch-black, and Loomis's voice echoed off the metal. "We've no power at all."

That had been obvious to Dane as soon as the lights went out and the engine died. "Rachel's in front of us," he said. He let go of the dead controls.

"How do you know?" Loomis asked.

Dane didn't bother to answer. He had his eyes closed, focusing on the dolphin's aura. "The surface is just above us."

"I can drop ballast," Loomis said. "But do we want to surface if we have no power? The thirty-millimeter chain gun won't even work. It needs electricity to cycle the rounds into the chamber.

Dane sensed that Rachel wasn't scared, but she was uneasy. *Surface*, he thought, projecting it at the dolphin. He squeezed his eyes tighter shut, focusing everything on Rachel. Light. Very dim, but there was light above.

She gave a thrust of her powerful fin and went up, her nose punching up through the flat surface.

Dane could see inside his head what Rachel was seeing. Dark water, perfectly smooth. There was some light, but it was secondary, reflected, the source not visible in the haze that made visibility poor. Rachel slowly did a circle, adjusting her position with slight movement. There was a shore about three-quarters of a mile away, just barely visible through the haze. Rachel ducked back underwater and swam toward the Crab.

"There's land," Dane reported.

"What kind of land?"

"Hard to tell," Dane said. "It's very hazy outside. I can't see much. I can feel it's different, though."

"You can see what Rachel sees?" Ahana asked.

"Yes."

"Interesting."

"Different, how?" Loomis asked.

Dane ignored him and concentrated on sending another message to Rachel. Everyone except Dane was startled when there was a light thump at the back of the Crab.

"What's that?" Loomis was half out of his seat.

"Rachel," Dane said. "She's giving us a push."

With nothing from Rachel to see, Dane opened his eyes. The darkness inside the armored craft was complete. They didn't even have battery power, which meant things were different inside the portal than just being inside the gate. He could pick up the moods of the other three people. Ahana, whose intellectual curiosity kept her fear at bay. The Russian, Shashenka, who had not said a word since they entered the portal, burned with anger and a desire for revenge for his brothers; and Loomis, who was the most scared of the three, hanging on only because of his sense of duty.

Rachel's powerful tail, capable of lifting her three-hundred-pound body almost completely out of the water, was thrusting back and forth, with her forehead firmly planted against the rear of the Crab, just below the propellers and rudders. It was slow, but they were moving.

"I have a rather ignorant but important question," Shashenka broke his long silence.

"What is it?" Loomis asked,

"How do we reopen the portal to get out with no power?" the Russian inquired.

The front of the Crab bumped into something, and they came to a halt, but no one moved right away as they considered the question.

"I will figure something out," Ahana finally said. "We picked up power from the probes coming out of the portal, so there must be a way."

"Very unspecific," Shashenka said. He shrugged. "It does not matter to me, but this is a reconnaissance, and we must get information about whatever we find back so that a proper assault can be prepared."

"We'll get it back," Dane said.

"How do you know?" Shashenka asked.

"Rachel can get us out to the portal," Dane said. "If Nagoya is still transmitting, we should be able to get through, right?" he asked Ahana.

"I think so."

"I suggest we take a look," Dane pointed at the hatch.

"Are we sure the air is breathable?" Loomis asked.

Dane was getting tired of questions from the two military men. He hit the lever that unlocked the top hatch nest to the turret. It swung open on springs, and several drops of water fell in. He climbed up the ladder. The air was different, thicker, with an oily quality, just as he remembered it had been inside the Angkor gate in Cambodia.

He stuck his head up and took a look. They were grounded about five meters from the shoreline. The land was made up of a coarse, black material, and it rose to a dune about fifty meters inland, beyond, which he couldn't see. Looking up, the view faded into the haze, but he had a strong feeling there was a top up there, as if they were in a very large enclosed space. He heard a splash and turned to look as Rachel swam behind the Crab.

He leaned back in. "I'm going ashore."

"Someone should stay with the Crab," Loomis said.

Dane had expected that. For a soldier, Loomis didn't have much of a warrior's edge. "Fine. You stay. Is *anyone* interested in doing what we came here to do?"

"I'm with you," Ahana said.

Shashenka had an AK-47 in his hands. "I, too."

Dane climbed onto the top deck of the Crab. He could feel the air on his skin, almost a slimy sensation. The water didn't look very appealing, pitch-black and flat. Carefully, he edged down the slope until his feet touched the water, then he slid off the craft. He went under and kicked for a short time and in a second had something solid under his feet. Behind him, Ahana followed, while Shashenka held the AK to his shoulder, covering them.

Dane walked up onto the shore, the black material giving way slightly under his feet. It was like sand, but with larger granules. There was no indication of vegetation, and the haze still limited observation. He heard a splash and Ahana was swimming ashore. As soon as she was next to Dane, Shashenka followed, holding the AK out of the water above his head to keep it dry.

"Which way?" Shashenka asked.

Dane answered by walking inland, toward the crest of the black dune, Ahana and Shashenka following. His lungs labored for oxygen as he climbed.

Just short of the crest, he abruptly stopped.

"What is it?" Ahana asked as she came up next to him.

Dane pointed down. A set of footprints cut across their path, heading to the right.

CHAPTER TWENTY-ONE

THE PAST
79 A.D.

Falco felt the aches of old wounds aggravated by sleeping on the cold, hard ground. He slid out from under the blanket and stood. It was still dark, about a half hour before dawn, the most dangerous time for an army in the field. He stretched his arms over his head, then slipped on his gladiator's *lorica segmentata*, trying tight the laces that held the metal together in the front. He drew his sword, wiping down the metal with a cloth to make sure no moisture remained on the blade.

Putting his helmet on, he began to make a circuit of the camp along the interior of the hasty perimeter. He checked on the guards, insuring they were alert. Then he detailed a water party and made sure those in charge of breakfast were at work. By the time he made it back to the center, General Cassius and Kaia were also up, and the first hint of dawn was in the east.

"The word has spread about the barbarians behind us," Falco told Cassius. There was no such thing as a secret in a legion.

"And the mood?" Cassius asked.

"Most are more worried about the black wall than the barbarians," Falco said.

"I want a cohort ready to move in an hour," Cassius said.

"Already taken care of," Falco said.

Breakfast was eaten in silence, the men chewing on dried meat and stale bread. Falco ate nothing, his usual preparation for combat. He'd seen men with food in their gut suffer a wound in the stomach and knew the odds of survival were better with nothing inside.

He glanced over at Kaia. The priestess also was not eating. She met his gaze. Falco was startled; he caught something in her eyes, something that reminded him of Drusilla. It was gone so quickly he wasn't sure if he had really seen it.

"Let's go." Cassius was buckling his helmet. He paused, his eyes shifting between the two. "Do you—"

Falco stood. "I'm ready."

Kaia checked the knife in her belt. "I am also."

Cassius nodded. Without another word, he headed for the gap in the north side of the square camp where the cohort was drawn up. Cassius took the lead, Falco a half step behind to the right, Kaia the same distance back to the left. They moved forward, toward the wall.

They negotiated through the swampy ground, but despite their best efforts, everyone was soaked to mid-thigh and exhausted by the time they reached the quarter-mile-wide stretch of dry ground between the swamp and the black wall.

Cassius had the cohort draw up in battle formation, facing the darkness. Falco could pick up the fear among the men, but it was like the buzzing of a fly in the midst of the almost overwhelming negative aura of the gate. Even during the siege and sack of Jerusalem, he had never felt such darkness in his soul.

Cassius turned to Liberalius. "I need a volunteer to go with Centurion Falco."

Liberalius's face was pale, a line of sweat trickling down either side of it. "I would be honored to accompany the centurion."

"Very good," Cassius said. "I will have part of the cohort patrol around the perimeter of this wall."

Falco had the Naga staff. He walked toward the black wall, Cassius, Liberalius, and Kaia close behind. He could not tell what the wall was made of, and he halted less than a pace from it. He extended the staff, and the metal tip went into the black, disappearing. He quickly pulled it back out: the metal was unchanged.

"I think—" he begun, but he couldn't complete the sentence before Kaia walked past into the black and disappeared.

"I'll be right here," Cassius said. "How long should I wait?"

Falco shrugged. "That is up to you, sir, I would not recommend sending anyone in after us."

"All right."

Falco stepped forward. The moment he made contact with the darkness, his skin rebelled, almost causing him to stop, to retreat, but he pressed on. He staggered, fell to his knees, and was on his feet again immediately. There was the same ground beneath his feet, but the air was hazy, full of a thick, brownish gray mist. He could see Kaia standing still about ten feet in front of him. His sword was out of his scabbard, and he was beginning to strike at the figure that suddenly appeared to his left, when he realized it was Liberalius. Falco kept the sword in his hand as he moved up next to Kaia. They could barely see forty feet in front of them. Behind, the black wall stretched as far as they could see left and right and up.

"Where to?" Falco asked.

Kaia pointed directly ahead. "Can't you feel it?"

Falco focused his mind. The place was oppressive, but there was something even darker in front of them, a darkness so complete that Falco knew that if he went there, he would never return to the world of light.

"It matches your soul," Kaia said.

Before Falco could reply, she set off, walking briskly. Falco hurried to keep up. The land was going up. The grass and scant vegetation was brown, dying. There was no sign of anything living. The land had been swept clean of all life, or it had had enough sense to leave as soon as the gate appeared. Falco paused and kicked the dirt with his sandal. There weren't even any ants apparent. He looked over his shoulder. Liberalius was rooted in place, a stricken look on his face.

"Kaia," Falco was surprised to find he had hissed the name, as if afraid of being overheard. The priestess halted. Falco went back to the tribune.

"What is wrong?"

Liberalius shook his head. "I cannot continue. There is pain"—he tapped the side of his head—"here. Unbearable." A trickle of blood marked the tribune's face below his nose.

"Come," Falco tried to guide him forward, but the tribune fell to his knees, agony on his face.

"I cannot."

Falco glanced up the slope. Kaia was waiting impatiently. "Go back to Cassius," he told the tribune. "Tell him what you have seen."

Liberalius weakly nodded. Falco helped him to his feet and propelled him toward the black wall. He watched as Liberalius staggered downslope and then into the wall, blinking out of sight as he passed through.

Falco hurried back to Kaia. He could feel the pain that had stopped Liberalius battering at his mind, but he was able to keep it sufficiently at bay so that he could continue.

They crested the rise and halted. The ground ahead sloped down.

"It's down there," Kaia said.

"What is?"

"The way through."

"To where?"

"Where the Shadow comes from," Kaia said. She began walking, and Falco followed. They covered a half-mile, the ground continuing to go down slightly.

"Look," Kaia pointed.

A boulder was split in two where the ground continued to drop. The landscape was warped, as if a giant's fist had pounded the ground. The few trees that grew were canted outward, as if from a high wind coming out of the center of wherever they were headed.

They continued in silence, each concentrating on holding at bay the pain and darkness that beat upon their minds like an unceasing storm. Glancing over his shoulder, Falco could no longer see the top of the rise. His hands wrapped tighter around the Naga staff.

The patrol Cassius had sent riding the perimeter of the black wall returned from the opposite direction with the report that the darkness was shaped like a triangle, each side the same length.

Another patrol arrived from the camp, reporting that a scout had come from the south. The barbarian horde was on the move, less than a day's march away. Cassius looked up at the sun, noting how far it had already risen in the sky. He turned to Liberalius, who had recovered somewhat from the gate's effect but still appeared to be ill.

"Bring the rest of the legion here. Then I want an embankment built at the edge of the swamp. If they attack us, I want their formation broken by the swamp. Do you understand?"

"Yes, General." Liberalius's skin was pale, and he seemed ill, but Cassius had neither the time nor patience to be concerned about the tribune's health right now.

Hands clasped behind his back, Cassius turned back toward the gate to wait.

Kaia halted so suddenly that Falco almost bumped into her. Through the haze, they could make out a triangle of black floating a foot above the ground twenty feet ahead. Each side was about ten feet long, and it was eight feet from top to bottom.

"That is it," Kaia said.

Falco said nothing. When Kaia made to move forward, he reached out with one arm and blocked her way. When she turned to him with a question on her lips, he indicated for her to be quiet. The hair on the back of his neck was on end, his nerves tingling. He crouched, the Naga staff in the ready position, his eyes darting back and forth, searching for the cause of his unease.

A white figure flashed out of the black triangle. It spotted them as Falco sprang. The Valkyrie was raising its clawed hands when he shoved the tip of the spear into its chest. The blade cut through the white, going in half a foot.

The Valkyrie screamed, the sound shattering the eerie silence. Black gas rushed out of the hole as Falco pulled the staff back. The Valkyrie collapsed at their feet. They barely had time to register this when a second one came out of the black triangle. This one was more prepared, parrying Falco's thrust with its right-hand claw, then thrusting with the left.

Falco's instincts, honed in hundreds of fights to the death, were in top form as he ducked under the strike. He rolled, slashing down with the edge of the Naga staff, the blade cutting through the left arm, severing it from the body. Black gas issued forth, and another scream pierced their ears.

With its remaining hand, it reached down and grasped the body of its immobile comrade, lifting it into the air. It retreated as Falco struck again. The Valkyrie shoved the body between them, allowing it to take the blow. Falco growled, striking once more, piercing the first Valkyrie, but this time there was no black gas. The two disappeared into the portal. Falco took two steps back from the black triangle, Naga staff at the ready. Kaia was to his right rear, her dagger held ready.

"They'll be back," Falco said.

"No," Kaia said, and at first Falco thought, she was disagreeing with him. But her eyes were on the black triangle. She stepped forward. "We must go in. We must go to them. We cannot wait."

"Agreed," Falco said. But he paused. "Do you feel it?"

"It gives off death," Kaia said, meaning the portal.

"Yes."

"You will not return," Kaia said.

"I know." Falco shrugged. "I do not matter."

"This is your fate."

A half smile creased Falco's hard face. "A brilliant prophecy." He walked forward toward the dark triangle and stepped into it.

Liberalius had brought the legion forward in good order but then collapsed upon completing the task. Cassius stood over the young tribune as the legion surgeon examined him for several minutes. There were now red lesions on the man's face and he was vomiting.

"What is wrong?" Cassius asked when the surgeon stood and took him out of earshot.

"I have never seen anything like it," the surgeon said. "It is as if he is being destroyed from both the inside and out at the same time, but by what, I have no idea."

Cassius looked at the black wall and realized he was trapped between it and the oncoming barbarians.

CHAPTER TWENTY-TWO

THE PRESENT

Dane held up his hand, halting the other two. When he had served in Vietnam, his teammates had valued his ability to sense an ambush before they walked into the kill zone. The rolling terrain and haze combined to limit visibility considerably. Dane had once gone to Little Big Horn and walked the battlefield where Custer met his demise. He'd understood what had happened to the 7th Cavalry after seeing the land; hundreds of hostiles could have hidden in the folds of the Montana land and not been seen until the troopers literally stumbled upon them. He felt the same about this strange nether region as he stood still, trying to focus on whatever it was that had alerted him.

Dane pointed to the right, where the black terrain dropped off. Shashenka had the butt of the AK-74 tucked tightly into this shoulder, muzzle aimed in that direction. Dane held up his right hand, fist clenched, the military signal to stop. Shashenka paused, then Ahana after a moment's confusion. Dane walked forward.

Just before he reached the fold, he stopped and held his empty hands up as half a dozen men jumped up from their hiding place, as if appearing out of the ground itself. They held swords and wore black lacquered armor and ornate helmets. Their eyes were slanted, and they spread out, encircling Dane.

"Back off!" Shashenka yelled, but they ignored him.

"Don't shoot," Dane said to Shashenka. He picked up no threat from the men. One of them rattled off something to Dane in what he assumed was Japanese.

"We mean no harm," Dane said.

One of the men stepped closer. He looked up and down, as if assessing Dane, then he turned to Dane's companions. His eyes lit up when he saw Ahana. He walked up to her.

"Who are they?" Dane asked.

"Samurai," Ahana said briefly. Then she spoke with the man in her native tongue. "They want us to go with them," she translated.

"What are they doing here?" Shashenka demanded, his weapon still at the ready.

Three of the samurai circled behind, adding emphasis to the request to accompany them.

"His dialect is strange," Ahana said. "Very old. From the armor and weapons, I'd say these men are from the thirteenth century."

"That can't—" Shashenka began, but fell silent as he realized the foolishness of what he had been about to say.

"They say it is dangerous for us to stay here," Ahana said.

"Where is here?" Shashenka asked.

"No time for that," Ahana said. "They say they will take us to someone who can answer our questions."

"Let's go with them," Dane urged, feeling exposed and understanding their desire to get out of this area.

The leader of the samurai hurried off, going down into the fold in the ground where he had been hidden. Dane followed, Shashenka and Ahana right behind him, the rest of the samurai flanking them.

Dane noted that the samurai kept to low ground, keeping ridges of the black material on either side as much as possible and traveling in the draws between the ridges. It was the way soldiers in hostile territory moved.

After about five minutes, Dane noticed a change in the land. The black gave way to patches of brown soil in places, each small pocket carved out of the side of the gully. Plants struggle to grow in these spots. As they passed between the junction of two gullies, a thin trickle of water cut a path through the very bottom, in the direction they were heading.

He glanced over his shoulder at Ahana and Shashenka. They were following quietly, absorbing all they saw. When Dane returned his gaze forward, he momentarily stopped when he saw the wall directly ahead in the haze, stretching up and to either side as far as visibility would allow. Dane hurried to follow the samurai. They turned the corner of the gully, and a wall was two hundred meters in front of them, disappearing upward into the haze. Etched into the black wall were shallow caves, and in those were people. Dozens and dozens of people.

Before Dane could take in the variety of men and women who were before him, a woman came striding forward. She was tall, with curly brown hair and striking features. Dane felt as if he had met her or at least seen her before. She held up a hand, indicating for the people who were pressing forward to see the newcomers to back off.

"Do you speak English?" she asked.

Dane nodded. "Yes."

"You're American?" the woman asked.

"Yes." Dane turned as his partners came up. "I'm Eric Dane. This is Ahana, a scientist from Japan, and Colonel Felix Shashenka from the Russian Army."

The woman extended her hand. "Pleased to make your acquaintance Mr. Dane. I'm Amelia Earhart."

Ariana looked at the large monitor that displayed the computer simulation Jordan's people had developed to show Mount Erebus. It not only mapped out the exterior of the mountain but the crater and as much as they had been able to tell about the interior from their various monitors, sensors, and probes. They were inside one of the buildings that made up McMurdo Station. People were hustling about, grabbing essential material for the evacuation while Ariana, Miles, and Jordan were in the eye of the storm.

"The main force vector is here," Jordan tapped the screen with a pencil. "There's a lava tube that extends down at least four miles and is almost a quarter mile wide. It extends laterally also, underneath the sea below the Ross Ice Cap. According to the data you sent, the muonic activity from the Devil's Sea gate is also centered in that tube."

"How do you know about the tube?" Ariana asked.

"We've got two aces up our sleeves," Jordan said. He flipped a photo on the desk. "That's Dante III." The image was that of a mechanical spider with eight metal legs. In the picture, Jordan was standing next to the robot, giving an idea of its size, about three meters high, two and a half meters wide, and three and a half long. The body was a metal frame with various electronic sensing devices loaded on board. A metal arch made up the majority of the height, with an antenna bolted on top.

"We use Dante to go down into the crater itself. We've made three trips in, the latest just two days ago to update our data. That's what's prompted the evacuation. Dante analyzes the high-temperature gases on the crater floor. We also can get video images, which are helpful."

"Where's Dante now?" Ariana asked.

"On the rim. It requires someone on site to operate it as it's a tethered device." He slid another photo onto the desktop. "This is our other ace and the one that found the main tube."

It looked like a remotely operated submersible to Ariana, something she had used before.

"That's called TROV—telepresence remotely operated vehicle. It was designed by NASA, and they let us use it to test it out. We sent it under the ice cap at the base of the volcano. It located a vent line off the tube, and we fired a probe in that relayed data back to us."

"Is there any way to stop Erebus from erupting?" Arian asked. She had her own ideas that she'd been contemplating and researching on the flight down, but she wanted to get feedback from the on-site expert first.

"Stop a volcano from erupting?" Jordan shook his head. "No one's attempted that. Everything has always been in reaction *after* the volcano erupted and mostly to stop the lava flow. There are three major methods for that. One is detonating explosives to divert the flow, another is constructing barriers to also divert the flow, and lastly there has been some success using water to cool the lava at the leading edge, in effect using cooled lava as a barrier against the flow behind it."

"Stopping the lava is the least of our concerns," Ariana said. "We have to stop the detonation. It's the initiator to everything the Shadow is doing on the Pacific Rim."

"When I had Dante in the crater, it confirmed what we had long suspected," Jordan said, "The lava lake in the crater has been acting like a large plug since the last eruption, containing the power. If that plug blows, it'll take out most of the top of the mountain, which in turn will devastate everything within a five-hundred-mile radius. Most importantly, and dangerous, is the effect on the Ross Ice Shelf. My calculations estimate that eighty percent of the shelf will either be melted or broken off.

"Given the data you sent me, Erebus will start a chain reaction up the Ring of Fire," Jordan continued. "It'll make the destruction of Iceland seem minor by the time the Ring has been activated."

"You haven't answered my question," Ariana said. "I know it has never been done, but do you have any theories on how we can stop it from erupting?"

Jordan sighed. He tapped the screen. "If we can stop or divert this main channel from being forced up against the lava lake plug in the crater, we might be able to minimize the effect." He shrugged. "But I don't see how we can do that."

"I have an idea," Ariana said.

CHAPTER TWENTY-THREE

THE PAST
79 A.D.

Falco had the Naga staff at the ready as he went through the portal. He stumbled slightly, then regained his balance. Kaia was right behind him, and they both paused to take stock of the new environment. The ground was black and grainy. The air was still hazy, making visibility poor. To Falco's relief, there was no sign of the Valkyries, just rolling black hills all around as far as he could see. Behind them, the black triangle hovered in the air.

"Where did they go?" Kaia asked.

Falco shrugged. "I don't know. Is this where they live?" he asked in turn.

Kaia was slowly turning, looking about, but Falco knew she was doing more than simply looking; she was projecting her mind outward. Throughout the journey, he had picked up much from her, and he knew her powers were far greater than his, especially with regard to working over a distance.

"There are others here," Kaia finally said. "Other people."

"Where?" Falco could sense none of that. All he knew was that this place was dangerous.

Kaia pointed. "That way."

Falco didn't like the idea of leaving the portal. There was no way to tell direction in the strange place, and once it was out of their sight, it might be hard to find again.

"They are in great pain," Kaia said. "We must help them."

"That's not what we are here for," Falco argued.

Kaia said nothing more but began heading in the direction she had pointed. Reluctantly, Falco followed.

* * *

Cassius had fought from Britain to across the Rhine in Germany to Palestine. As a young tribune, he had even been on a campaign in Africa near Carthage. He had studied Julius Caesar's accounts of the Gallic Wars and then served under many fine generals before receiving his own baton of command.

One of the many lessons he had learned was that defense was the position taken by the weak, and it could rarely lead to victory. So even as the men of the XXV Legion dug into the ground with their spades at the edge of the swamp, their backs to the black wall, he gathered together every mounted man in the unit.

Falco and the priestess had been gone the entire day and night was falling. Cassius was worried at the length of time that had passed, but there was nothing he could do about that except make sure he held this side of the gate. The death of Liberalius had cast a darkness over the entire camp, increasing the effect the dark wall already had.

As the sunset, he led the cavalry through the swamp. It was dark by the time they reached the other side and continued to the south.

The barbarian camp was easy to find, despite the lack of light. Hundreds of campfires gave off a glow that touched the sky and was visible from miles away. Cassius was at the head of the column, and he rode slowly, aware that it was possible for the force in front of him to have put out a skirmish line, although he doubted it. They were in their own land, and they outnumbered his forces at least four to one, judging by the number of fires he could make out as he got closer. Overconfidence. It was what had destroyed Varus in Germany when his three legions had been overwhelmed and the eagle standards taken by the barbarians. Cassius had learned as much, if not more, from studying the defeats of Rome's generals as their victories.

When he was less than a quarter mile from the barbarian camp, Cassius halted the troop. He had already given his instructions, so the men spread out on line, lances at the ready. They moved forward at a walk, then a trot as they closed to within two hundred meters. At a hundred meters, Cassius spurred his horse to a full gallop, and the men with him did likewise.

There were no breastworks built up to protect the camp, no sentries on duty. Cassius and his men hit like a tidal wave, spitting barbarians on their spears, then drawing their swords and cutting down men as they jumped up from their sleep.

A clock was ticking inside Cassius's brain, and when he had gone forward about a hundred meters into the camp, he shouted the order to fall back. The cavalry wheeled and galloped back the way they had come, fading into the darkness, only the bloody bodies' evidence of their assault.

The sound of turmoil faded behind as Cassius led his men back north. He figured he'd gained another day with the assault, unless the barbarians were led by a particularly strong chief.

As he headed back to the rest of the legion, he prayed to the God Lupina had worshipped, asking that Falco and Kaia come back soon with a way to defeat the Shadow.

Falco put his hand on Kaia's shoulder and pushed her down to the ground just short of the crest of the ridge they were approaching. He could sense it now also; the agony of hundreds, maybe thousands, just ahead. It was worse than the most terrible games he had ever experienced, where thousands of Christians had been slaughtered by wild beasts. At least then, there had been hope, emanating from their faith as they died; but whatever was ahead, there was no hope. Only overwhelming pain and despair.

Falco crawled up to the top of the ridge and peered over. He swallowed hard as he saw hundreds of white vertical tables on which were strapped men and women. On many, the skin had been flayed away, and the body inside was covered with some sort of clear, shiny material. Their suffering was almost overwhelming, a tidal wave of pain that hammered against his mind.

"We cannot save them," Falco said.

"We need information," Kaia said. She pointed. "Him. He knows."

Falco followed the line of the finger. The man she indicated was huge, his body covered with scars as befitted a warrior. But his hands were gone, severed at the wrist.

"All right." Falco got up and ran down the slope toward the tables, his body hunched over in a crouch. He arrived at the man and quickly cut the bonds using the Naga staff. The man's eyes opened. With the stump of one arm, he indicated for Falco to slit his throat.

Falco shook his head, pointed back up the slope at Kaia. The man frowned, then nodded reluctantly. He began heading in the direction, Falco following. The gladiator paused when there was a noise to his left. The man on the table that was across from the one he had just been at was saying something, but Falco didn't understand the language. Falco hesitated, tempted to put the man out of his misery as he had done many times in the arena, but he felt it was best to disturb things as little as possible for now.

He hurried up the slope. When he arrived, the warrior was standing next to Kaia, his head bent over, her hands on either side.

"He knows where there are others here," she said. "He will lead us."

*****

General Cassius stood less than an arm's distance from the black wall. A second day had gone by with no sign of Falco or Kaia. The barbarians were on the move again, closing on the legion's position. He could pick up the unease among the men, the desire to leave this godforsaken place. But their discipline was holding, and there had been no outright signs of disrespect.

He'd tried entering the gate but had barely made it a few steps inside before the overwhelming pain in the head that Liberalius had described forced him to retreat.

Cassius blink, startled out of his thoughts. He could swear the wall was closer that it had been just a minute ago. He stared but could see nothing. He took a pebble and placed it right in front of the blackness and waited. After a minute, the black slid over the pebble. The wall *was* expanding.

Cassius looked over his shoulder. The earthen barrier his legion was arrayed behind was less than a quarter mile away. Beyond it was the swamp. And even as he watched, there were yells of alarm as the vanguard of the barbarian force appeared on the ridgeline three miles away.

It was difficult to judge, but he doubted they had a half-day before the expanding gate overtook the barrier, forcing them into the swamp and at the mercy of the barbarians.

Whatever decision he was going to make would have to be made soon.

Pytor had watched the man in armor free Ragnarok and then disappear out of sight behind him. Less than two minutes after they were gone, a Valkyrie appeared. It paused in front of the empty white slab that had held the Viking. It hovered there for several seconds, and then more Valkyries began appearing from different directions until there were over. More and more white forms came until Pytor lost count and the rows of Valkyries stretched beyond what he could see.

From his military training, Pytor could guess the reason for this unusual display of numbers. The Valkyries were preparing an attack.

CHAPTER TWENTY-FOUR

THE PRESENT AND THE PAST

"How long have you been here?" Dane asked. The shock of meeting the legendary lost explorer had been greater for Shashenka and Ahana than Dane, who had been aboard the lost *Scorpion* where the crew had not aged a day in over thirty years. He had also seen her plane in the graveyard.

It was apparent that Earhart was in charge of the community of lost souls, which numbered about eighty people. After the initial greetings and excitement, Earhart had led them to one of the narrow caves where they sat on old wooden boxes. A samurai stood guard at the entrance.

Earhart shrugged. "I don't know. There's no way of telling time here. Watches don't work, in case you haven't noticed. I would guess I've been here about a year, but it's hard to say. They" – she nodded at the group of samurai who had escorted Dane, Shashenka, and Ahana—"think they've been here about five years. But they come from thirteenth-century Japan. There are others here" – she indicated the people occupying the caves along the wall— "who come from all different times. From as early as two hundred B.C. to my future, like you. Some people from times earlier than mine arrived here *after* I did, which I don't understand, either.

"We think time is a variable here that doesn't flow in a linear fashion as we are used to," Ahana tried to explain.

"I do have to say that you're the first people who ever came here on their own," Earhart noted. "Can you get back out?"

"We're working on that," Dane said. "We have a submarine on the water, but we lost power when we entered the portal. We think we can get out to the portal, and then we hope our people are still keeping our hole in the portal open."

Earhart nodded. "Nothing works here." She pointed at Shashenka's rifle. "Go ahead. Try it. It won't fire."

Shashenka frowned and aimed into the air. He pulled the trigger and, as predicted, nothing happened other than the click of the trigger and the firing pin clicking uselessly on the cartridge in the chamber.

"That's why we use these," Earhart had a sword in her hand. "The only good thing is that the Valkyries can only use blades also. Our weapons can't penetrate their armor, but we've learned hitting them in the eyes disables them. They pretty much leave us alone as long as we aren't a nuisance. They do have another weapon that can turn people into stone, but they rarely use it."

"Where is here?" Ahana asked.

"I've been trying to figure that out since I got here," Earhart said. She described what had happened on her last flight, and Dane realized her experience was similar to what had happened to the *Reveille*.

"After the large sphere engulfed my plane," she continued, "I was in darkness. Then there was a blue glow and—"

"Blue?" Dane interrupted her. "Are you sure it was blue?"

"You don't forget something like that," Earhart said.

Dane remembered the two different color beams he had seen inside the Angkor gate. Gold seemed to be that used by the Shadow, but blue was that used by the Ones Before.

"I think the craft was automated," Earhart continued, "because I saw no one. The blue light seemed to point a direction, and I left my plane and followed it. I walked along the inside of the sphere along a flat surface until I reached the outer wall. There was a hatch. I opened it and went inside. There was another hatch in front of me, and I shut the one behind and opened the other one. I didn't' know *why* I was doing this, but felt compelled to.

"When I opened the outer hatch, I was surrounded by the blue light, which was fortunate, because water poured in. The light kept me in a small circle of air, though, and pulled me out of the craft. And then I was here," she finished simply. "On the beach, half dead. That's when they found me." She indicated the people on our side. They all had similar experiences. Entering a fog, being taken by the sphere, being rescued by the blue light.

"We've made the best we can of this place. We divert water here. And the soil was gathered before I arrived from smaller deposits into sections large enough for us to grow food. Sometimes an animal from our side comes through, sometimes it's one of the strange creatures from the other side."

"Wait a second," Dane said. "You just said the *other* side. Isn't *this* the other side?"

Earhart shook her head. "You asked me where this was, and I couldn't tell you, but if you asked me *what* this place was, I would call it the space in the wall between our world and their world. We're like rats trapped in the wall.

We can see the sphere come through every so often. Sometimes the blue light brings us people. Sometimes the sphere drops people off at the Valkyrie camp, which is about four miles that way," she pointed. "They work on the people they get there. Experiment on them."

"How many people?" Shashenka asked.

"Hundreds, maybe thousands. We raided it not long ago and put some of them out of their misery, but the Valkyries droves us off."

Dane could pick up the small flicker of hope in Shashenka that his brother might still be alive. From the agony he could sense in the direction that Earhart had pointed, he hoped that wasn't the case.

"So there is another portal inside the water?" Ahana asked. "One that leads to the Shadow's side?"

"I would assume so," Earhart said. "There are several portals here. We've tried to explore as much as we can, but it's huge and sometimes seems to even shift shape. I followed the wall that way" – she pointed in the opposite direction from the Valkyrie camp—"for a long time. Probably several days. It curves slightly, but I never completed the circle. I had to return the way I came, as I was running low on food. There might even be other free people in here."

He thought of his teammate Flaherty and wondered where he was. "Do you have contact with the Ones Before? The ones who use the blue power light?"

Earhart shook her head. "No."

"Have you tried any of the portals?" Dane asked.

"Some have, they either don't come back, or they come back with a strange sickness that kills them quickly."

Dane was tired. All this effort, and all they had done was to get halfway to where they wanted to go.

"This would be a good area to stage an assault," Shashenka said.

"It is most fascinating," Ahana said. "This area is most likely a buffer between the laws of physics and the environment on both sides."

"Can you get us out of here?" Earhart asked Dane.

'We can take about a dozen people," he said. "Then when the rest of our forces come through, they can take out the rest. But first, we have to figure out what good it would do to bring our people here. Since we can't use modern weapons, and this really isn't the other side like we had hoped..." He trailed off.

"We're one step closer to the Shadow's home," Ahana said, trying to put a positive spin on things.

"I don't think—" Dane began, but there was a commotion among the samurai. One came running up to Earhart and rattled off something quickly.

She stood, slipping the sword in its sheath. "More visitors are coming. A man in armor and a woman in robes. They have Ragnarok with them."

"Ragnarok?" The name sounded familiar to Dane.

"A Viking. He was captured by the Valkyries during our raid on their torture chambers. Come." She strode toward the gully, Dane and the others right behind.

As they turned the corner into a cross-gully, three people appeared. As Earhart had described, a man and woman were accompanied by a hulking warrior whose hand had been amputated.

"Damn them," Earhart hissed when she saw Ragnarok's condition. "They must have probed him and learned it is the greatest insult a Viking can receive before death to not be able to defend himself in Valhalla."

"How do they know that." Ahana asked.

"They have ways to getting into people's heads," Earhart answered enigmatically.

Earhart greeted the Viking in his language, and he said something to her. Dane could see the other man's armor dated and placed him to sometime in the middle of the Roman Empire. The woman was less easily placed, but he picked up the same aura from her as he had with Sin Fen. She was a priestess, of that he was certain. He noted the Naga staff in the soldier's hand.

Earhart said something to the Roman in what Dane recognized as Latin. They conversed, the priestess joining in for several minutes. The Viking had slumped down and was being attended to by one of Earhart's group.

"Centurion Falco of the XXV Legion and Priestess Kaia from Delphi," Earhart introduced them. Then she gave their names to the others. "They came through a gate in what I think is southern Russia," Earhart finally said to Dane, Shashenka, and Ahana. "It caused the eruption at Vesuvius and is threatening the Roman Empire."

Dane frowned. "But we know our history. We know that gate couldn't have—"

"No," Ahana's voice was sharp. "You cannot think like that . What we are facing may be an attack that spans time. Because we are here, and they are here" – she indicated Falco and Kaia – "there is a connection between their time and ours."

Dane held his hands up, trying to think. "All right, all right. Hold on for a minute here. They came through a portal inside a gate, right?" he asked Earhart, indicating Falco and Kaia."

"Yes."

"And they can go back out that way?"

"They think so, but it will probably take them back to their time. And things are not so good there and then, apparently the legion they came with is surrounded by barbarian forces."

"Can we stop the power that the Shadow is using to affect the Ring of Fire?" Dane asked Ahana.

"We have to find the portal the power from Chernobyl is being channeled through," Ahana answered. "It's the one that we have to destroy."

'How do you propose to do that?" Dane asked.

"I don't know yet," Ahana answered. "Perhaps Rachel can help you find it?"

Dane could still sense the dolphin's presence, even though she was a distance away. He closed his eyes.

'What is he doing?" Earhart asked. "Who is Rachel? What is Chernobyl?"

Dane tuned out Ahana as she explained. Rachel was nervous, he could tell that immediately. She sensed danger closing in all around. The Crab with Loomis was still just offshore, she also had the location of their portal still firmly in mind, and to his relief, it appeared that Nagoya's plug was still in place. He asked her to see if she could find the portal that was channeling the Shadow's power.

Dane was completely unaware of the people around him as he immersed himself in Rachel. He had never felt such an experience. It was as if he were inside her head, swimming with her as she dashed through the water, sending out clicks to echo sound.

"She's found it," Dane said, slowly opening his eyes. "Not far from our portal."

"Then we—" Ahana began but she stopped as another samurai came running up, rattling off something.

Earhart cursed. "An army of Valkyries is massing. They are moving to surround us."

"We need time," Ahana said. "We have to go back to Nagoya, figure out how to cut the power. Then come back through and do it."

Falco understood nothing of what was being said except for what the brown-haired woman called Earhart had translated for him. That the people here were from different times he found confusing but not important. He could see the darkness in the man—Dane's – soul: almost as black as his own. Their time was threatened by the same enemy as his: that was the important thing.

He turned to Kaia, who was also observing auras since she didn't understand the languages either. "Can you get my men in here?"

Kaia frowned. "What do you mean?"

"You protected us at Thera. Can you protect General Cassius and the men long enough for them to come here?"

She slowly nodded. "Yes, I have seen it. The skull can protect them long enough."

Falco knew what she meant by long enough. He turned to Earhart and got her attention, quickly explaining his plan to her in Latin. When he was done, she interrupted the others and spoke to them.

The B-1 Bomber did one pass low over the flat plain of snow and ice that served as the landing strip for McMurdo. It had made the flight from the United States at supersonic speed.

Ariana, Miles, and Professor Jordan stood off to the side and watched as the large plane did a long, curving turn and headed back toward them, losing altitude as it came.

"This will be interesting," Jordan said.

"You must have some pull with the Pentagon," Miles said as the plane came in long and slee. It was the model of aerodynamic forms, from an age of warplane construction where speed was considered more important than stealth. Two massive engines were under the body of the plane, just behind the swept wings.

"The Pentagon finally appreciates the threat," Ariana said.

The B-1 was just fifty feet above the ice, two miles away, and the landing gear had not been lowered. It crept downward toward the surface, and when it was a half-mile away, the bottom of the engines touched down, sending up spume of ice and snow. The plane bounced, was airborne, then was down again.

The sound of metal tearing echoes across the frozen space as the engine intakes scooped into the ice. The plane slowed, then the right engine gave way, and the nose of the bomber turned. Fortunately, the left engine ripped off a scant second later, and the belly of the plane grounded.

The bomber slowed and finally came to a halt a half-mile from their location. Jordan already had the tractor in gear, and they headed toward the aircraft. By the time they arrived, the crew was already outside, standing on the ice looking at their stricken plane.

Ariana jumped out of the tractor, yelling orders. "We need the bombs off-loaded immediately! Put them on the sled."

The pilot of the B-1 turned toward her. "We had orders to do this, but I don't understand why. Why couldn't we have just dropped the damn things wherever you wanted?"

Ariana pointed over the inert metal of the bomber. "Because that's going to blow any minute now, and where we need to put those bombs you can't get to from the air. Now move!"

* * *

Falco ran behind Kaia, trusting that she could get them back where they came from. He could sense the cold presence of Valkyries all about, but Kaia was weaving a path through gullies that avoided the creatures.

Amelia Earhart signaled for Dane, Ahana and Shashenka to halt as two samurai slowly crept up a ridge to peer ahead. When they turned back and gave her a sign, she indicated for Dane and his companions to follow.

They crept forward, heading toward the inner sea.

"Muonic forces are peaking at Erebus." Nagoya was looking at the feed being sent to him via satellite from the superkamiokande in Japan. "It's almost at the level we registered when Iceland was destroyed."

"The Shadow needed our nukes to destroy Iceland," Foreman noted.

Nagoya shook his head. "The Shadow needed nuclear weapons to initiate the destruction. Here they'll use the pent-up power already in Erebus."

"Let's hope Ariana is right," Foreman said.

"Even if she stops Erebus, the Shadow can shift the power elsewhere," Nagoya said.

"One thing at a time," Foreman said. "How long before Erebus goes?"

"Any minute now."

Ariana staggered as the ground shook and cracks appeared in the ice, accompanied by sharp sounds like cannons going off.

"Here!" Jordan shoved a black box in her hand that had a small video screen and several toggles. They were parked on the Ross Ice Shelf, right next to the base of Mount Erebus. There was a square hole cut in the ice, extending downward over forty feet. The TROV was attached to a crane, two of the B-1 crewmembers working quickly to attach one of the two nuclear bombs they had flown down to the craft.

"This is the remote for TROV," Jordan said. "You'll get video feedback, and the controls are easy. The map of the tube and surrounding area is already in the hard drive. I hope you're correct about placement."

"Eight years of graduate school should have taught me something," Ariana tried to joke, but Jordan didn't crack a smile as he looked up at the slope of Erebus.

The second bomb rested on a small ice sled behind a powerful snowmobile Jordan had appropriated, which had been off-loaded from the tractor's sled.

"Will you have enough time?" Ariana asked,

"We'll know soon enough," Jordan said as he sat on the snowmobile and revved the engine.

"Good luck!" Ariana yelled above the sound.

"You, too," And then Jordan was off, racing up the slope of the mountain, the bomb right behind.

General Cassius was disgusted with himself. The black wall had moved forward half the distance between its former position and the beginning of the swamp. His flank fortifications had been overrun by the wall, and his men were running out of room.

The barbarians could see what was happening and were waiting on the ridge. The swamp, which was to have been the Romans' killing ground, would soon be their dying ground.

There were shouts of alarm, and Cassius turned his attention from the barbarians to the wall. Falco and Kaia had appeared and were running toward him.

"It's been two days!" Cassius exclaimed as they came to a halt right in front of him.

"Two days?" Falco seemed dazed and shook his head as if to clear it. "Sir, we must go into the gate."

"Liberalius is dead from going into the gate," Cassius said.

"We aren't," Kaia said. "I can protect you and the men. Long enough to do what must be done."

"What must be done?" Cassius demanded. "What is in there?"

"The enemy," Falco said. "And allies who need time to help us." He swept his arm, taking in the legion. "We must give them time against the Valkyries."

Cassius stood silent for several seconds. Kaia began to say something, but Falco raised a hand, indicating for her to wait. Finally, the general nodded. "Centurion," he said to Falco, "get the men into marching order."

* * *

"Damn it," Dane cursed. His eyes confirmed what he had sensed. There was a line of white forms stretched across the shoreline and the black surface of the lake was empty. Loomis must have seen them coming and submerged by manually opening one of the tanks.

"What now?" Ahana asked. "We must get through."

"I can provide a diversion," Shashenka offered.

"One man?" Dane shook his head.

"We can go back and wait," Earhart suggested.

"There's no time," Dane said. He could pick up Rachel's projections. The dolphin was swimming around the power portal, sensing the growing level. The Shadow was making its push.

"I do not have the forces to fight that many Valkyries," Earhart said. Her people were lined up in the gully behind them, their weapons in hand. "We would be overwhelmed quickly."

"We have to—" Dane began but paused as the line of Valkyries began moving forward, approaching their position at a steady rate. "Time's up," he said.

CHAPTER TWENTY-FIVE

THE PRESENT AND THE PAST

The TROV slipped under the surface of the still, black water, descending into the icy depths after being lowered on the crane. Ariana stared at the small video screen on which was superimposed the model of Erebus's interior. Her hands were already freezing as she alternated between directing the TROV and slipping them inside her jacket to warm them.

"How long until you have it on target?" Miles asked, stamping his feet, also trying to stave off the cold.

"I don't know."

The ground shook, and a large crevice opened less than fifty feet away.

"I'd suggest sooner rather than later," Miles said, "if at all possible."

Ariana rubbed the screen, clearing off a thin layer of snow. The TROV's camera showed nothing but dark water, with the submersible's searchlight cutting through only about twenty feet. According to the computer projection, she was on course for the underwater base of Erebus where the main lava tube was.

*****

Jordan desperately turned the handlebars of the snowmobile as the sled threatened to pull him to one side, sending him tumbling down the slope. The front-runners made the correction and dug into the ice, straightening him out. Looking up, he could see the thick plume of smoke from the summit, now less than a half-mile away.

He gunned the engine.

*****

"Got a sword I can borrow?" Dane asked as the Valkyries closed on their position. His mind was being pounded on all sides by input: Rachel, circling the power portal; the approaching cold wave of Valkyries; the almost overwhelming feeling of failure that pervaded it all.

"We should pull back," Earhart said.

"And then?" Dane asked. "Get pinned in your caverns like animals being hunted down?"

"We were doing all right until you showed up," she snapped.

"What the hell is all right?" Dane shot back. "You're the one who said you were rats in the wall."

"At least we were live rats," Earhart said. She said something to one of the samurai, and he pulled a short sword out of its sheath and handed it to her. She passed it on to Dane. "I'm sorry. You're right. At least we'll make a stand here."

Dane remembered how he had compared this place to Little Big Horn when he had first entered. The allusion was becoming more and more appropriate. He noted another of the samurai with the Viking, strapping an ax to the man's arm. Ragnarok looked up at Dane and smiled, ready to go to Valhalla fighting.

*****

"Damn it," Ariana muttered as the TROV missed the tunnel opening and banged into the side of the volcano.

"Easy," Miles said. "Better to be exact than fast."

"Better to be both," Ariana said as she realigned the submersible and gunned it into the dark opening.

*****

When Jordan turned off the snowmobile, the trembling didn't stop. He realized that the entire mountain was shaking. No one had ever been this near a volcano about to explode and survived to tell about it.

Dante III stood on the rim, ten feet away, like a large metal spider, frozen in place. The control mechanism was next to it, set on a small platform, waist high. Scrambling off the snowmobile, he ran over to the robot and looked down into the crater.

"Oh, my God," he muttered. The lava bed had risen almost three hundred feet from the last time he'd been up here. It was bulging in the center, the twenty feet of hardened lava barely containing the forces below. He knew from what he was seeing that there was no time to hook the sled to Dante and walk the robot down. He keyed the FM radio connecting him with Ariana.

"Are you in place?"

*****

Ariana heard the voice through the small earplug, but she didn't reply right away. She had hardly any feeling left in her hands as she made an adjustment on the joystick, maneuvering TROV around a bend in the old lava tube.

"Give me a minute," she finally said.

"We don't have a minute."

Ariana abruptly halted the submersible as a red glow appeared on the screen directly ahead. "I'm there. Do you have Dante in place?" she asked."

"Detonate," Jordan said. "Now!

Ariana nodded at one of the Air Force men, who pressed a red button on a transmitter.

For a second, nothing happened; then the ground shook worse than it had yet, and Ariana fell to her knees. Looking out, she saw the ice shelf buckle along the side of the volcano.

Four miles away and eight hundred feet down, the nuclear bomb ripped into the main lava tube, splitting it wide open. Red-hot lava met freezing seawater and initially won the battle, pouring out into the water underneath the Ross Ice Shelf.

*****

Jordan was seated on the snowmobile, the front skids on the very edge of the crater's rim. The ground trembled fiercely, and he knew Ariana had detonated her nuke along the main tube.

He twisted the throttle, and the snowmobile edged over, into the crater, pulling the sled with it. He screamed at the top of his lungs as he plummeted down the side.

The nose of the snowmobile hit a boulder and it, and Jordan, went airborne, the sled right with him. Looking down, he could see the lava plug. In that brief glimpse, he knew it was subsiding, although there was still a lot of pressure under it that needed to be dissipated.

Jordan slammed his fist against the transmitter taped to his other arm.

The nuke went off with a flash halfway down to the lava plug.

*****

Ariana was still on her knees when she heard the explosion. Looking up, she could see the top of the volcano blast outward, relieving the pressure there. She knew there was no way Jordan had gotten clear in time.

She staggered to her feet.

"Oh, no," She murmured as the buckling of the ice continued like a slow, forty-foot-high wave toward her position.

Miles stepped between her and the approaching wall of ice and wrapped his arms around her. Then the ice below them rose up, and they fell between the blocks.

CHAPTER TWENTY-SIX

THE PAST AND THE PRESENT

Ragnarok charged past, screaming like a berserker. The line of Valkyries were less than forty feet away, and he made the distance in a few seconds. He swung the ax tied to his arm, and it smashed into the face of the closest Valkyrie, shattering both eyes. As that one screamed, the ones closest veered toward the Viking warrior, who spun about, ax extended.

Dane stood. "Let's go."

Amelia Earhart was at his side, her sword ready. "It is time."

They both began to run forward, the others behind, when they suddenly noticed a bright light to the left. They stopped abruptly as a roar from thousands of throats—human throats—rushed over them. Out of the fog, a line of armored men with red cloaks appeared, spears at the ready. They clashed into the Valkyries with a thunderous cacophony of metal on alien armor.

"Erebus hasn't erupted," Nagoya announced. "Ground monitoring station and satellite tracking picked up two nuclear explosions. Ariana was successful."

There was an explosion of applause in the FLIP control room. Foreman said nothing as the small plug in his ear had relayed reports from the National Security Agency satellite monitoring Antarctica. He also knew that Ariana was not responding to SATPhone hails.

The cheering was quickly silenced by Nagoya's next announcement. "The Shadow is shifting power north."

"How long do we have?" Foreman asked.

"We've gained an hour, maybe more. Maybe less."

An *hour,* Foreman thought. A very expensive hour, but it could turn out to be very critical if Dane was successful. "Is there any word from the Crab?"

"No, sir."

"Go for the eyes with your pilum!" Falco's yell echoed in the fog.

He was next to Kaia, who held the Thera skull in her hands above her head. The light it was projecting pierced the fog, pushing it back. It also seemed to have a negative effect on the Valkyries as the creatures gave way before the onslaught of the XXV Legion. As importantly, it had allowed the men of the XXV to enter the gate and then the portal without suffering the devastating mental effect that had crippled Liberalius. General Cassius was next to Falco, issuing orders and deploying his men.

Dane and Earhart met Falco and Kaia in the midst of the battlefield as legionnaires pushed past them, rushing the heavily outnumbered Valkyries.

"The skull," Dane said to Earhart, seeing what Kaia was carrying.

"What about it?"

"It's what I need to stop the portal." Dane was looking out over the smooth, black surface of the inner lake. He saw a dorsal fin rapidly approaching. Ahana and Felix Shashenka were behind him.

The Roman said something to Earhart and then she translated. "Without the skull, the legion will be unprotected."

"Without it," Dane replied, "this is all worthless. Tell him the Shadow's power we're trying to stop is going into his time also."

Falco knew what the strange woman would translate from the man even before she spoke. He turned to Kaia. "None of the legion will return, either, will they?" He looked at the fight that was being waged. General Cassius was in the middle of the line, yelling orders. He felt the pull of the battle.

"No," the priestess said, "they won't."

"And you?" he asked.

"He is correct about the role the skull must play but wrong about who must accomplish the task," Kaia said. "It is my destiny to be part of the last role it will play." She ran a hand over the smooth crystal. "This is *my* ancestor."

Falco understood what she meant and hefted the Naga staff. He was needed in the fight "Go with them. And then fulfill your destiny as I do mine."

With that, he sprinted toward the front lines of the battle between man and creature.

Rachel rose half out of the water, then flipped over on her back, making a splash. Earhart was listening to Kaia and put out a hand as Dane reached to take the skull from her.

"It is her destiny to finish this," Earhart said. "You must go back to your time."

"And you?" Dane asked.

"These are my people here," Earhart said. "Some may survive this battle. I imagine almost everyone I know is dead in your time."

Dane knew there was no more time for debate. "All right."

Shashenka stepped forward. "Where are those the Valkyries torture?" he asked Earhart.

She pointed. "That way."

Without another word, the Russian was sprinting over the coarse black ground.

Dane felt like it had all unraveled, everyone going in different directions, but a part of him felt comforted, as if far-flung pieces of a puzzle had suddenly come together to produce something sane in this mad place.

As the priestess headed toward the water, he followed. "Wait at the edge," he yelled over his shoulder to Ahana.

He was next to Kaia as she entered the water. She glanced at him and smiled. Then she dove forward. Rachel was at her side, and Kaia placed her left hand on the dolphin's dorsal fin, the right clutching the glowing skull. The two raced away.

Dane had to force himself to take his attention from them to searching for the Crab. He could pick up Loomis's frightened aura not far away, and he swam in that direction.

He reached the Crab, which was just under the surface. Taking a deep breath, Dane dove down. He slid along the side of the craft until he was at the bottom. He found a line of ballast and hit the manual release. The craft bobbed to the surface. Dane climbed on board and opened the hatch.

Kaia felt at peace as the dolphin pulled her through the water. The skull was a warm, solid presence in her right hand, pressed tightly against her chest. She knew this would complete the circle.

Falco had passed through the forefront of the legion and was engaged in combat. The Naga staff had already dispatched a half-dozen Valkyries. The creatures were falling back, the legion advancing, General Cassius issuing orders calmly, insuring the men kept in line. They were doing as well as the Xth Legion, even better, considering the strangeness of the environment and enemy, Falco thought.

Ragnarok was ever farther ahead of Falco, the battle rage consuming him, the ax crushing into white armor, smashing red eyes.

"Come on!" Dane bellowed to Ahana. As the Japanese scientist ran into the water, Dane slid down into the Crab.

Loomis had a pistol in his hand, pointed directly at Dane. "Get out! Get out!" the colonel screamed.

Dane ignored him and headed for the controls. When he heard the click of a firing pin hit a cartridge, he spared a moment to snap punch Loomis in the side of the head, sending the man to the deck unconscious.

"Close the hatch," Dane ordered as Ahana came in.

"Do we have power?" she asked.

"No."

"What do we do then?"

"We wait."

* * *

Falco ducked under the Valkyrie's swipe and with one smooth stroke parted the creature's head from its body. He shifted, looking for the next target, but they were withdrawing, floating back.

Yells of victory rose out of the throats of the men of the XXV Legion. Falco turned toward General Cassius, and they made eye contact.

"Hold!" Falco yelled. "Hold the line!"

But the men were caught up in the excitement of victory, having faced a dark fear and overcome it, or so they thought. They pressed forward, following the Valkyries over a long, black ridgeline.

Felix Shashenka had to stop in shock when he saw the hundreds of people strapped to tables in front of him, their bodies in different stages of torment. His eyes went right to his brother, the connection strong. Shashenka drew his bayonet as he ran toward the table.

He had seen many terrible things in his time in the Spetsnatz, but nothing had prepared him for what had been done with Pytor. His brother's skinned lips twisted upward in a smile as he recognized his sibling. The head bobbed in the slightest of nods.

Felix drew the blade across his brother's throat, feeling the warm blood flow over his arm. It was the last thing he felt as a golden glow suffused him and his skin turned gray and hard.

The crystal skull was growing hotter as Rachel pulled Kaia closer and closer to the power portal. Then Kaia realized the heat wasn't just coming from the skull in her hand but was also inside her own head.

Suddenly it was there, right in front of her in the water. A cylinder of black with red lines swirling through it coming out of the water and disappearing into the haze overhead. She let go of Rachel, and the dolphin regarded her with one eye, chattered something, and then sped off.

Kaia waited.

* * *

Falco was trying to get the men under order, stopping them from their headlong rush after the Valkyries. Cassius was also moving along the line, trying to get control. It took a few minutes, but they finally managed to get the legion drawn in ranks and in place.

Both looked up in shock as a golden glow came over the hill, rolling over the men, transforming them. Falco held the Naga staff up, a futile gesture as the golden wave hit him. He felt unbearable pain, from the marrow of his bones out as his body solidified. His last thought was of his children, even as his heart leapt at the hope of joining Drusilla.

Rows upon rows of legionnaires froze in place, solidified, their bodies encased in stone.

The Crab shuddered slightly.

"Rachel," Dane said simply in response to Ahana's questioning look. He could feel Kaia, the heat from her in the distance, and knew she was waiting as long as she could.

"Wrangell's beginning to erupt," Foreman informed Nagoya.

"The power is increasing from the gate," Nagoya said. "If it keeps up…" He fell silent.

"Directly ahead," Dane said, seeing the Devil's Sea portal they had come through. He knew Kaia wasn't far away, waiting at the power portal that was also using the Devil's Sea gate.

Amelia Earhart had been behind the legion with her samurai and other survivors. As the golden flow swept over the Romans, she turned and ran, the others following. She dove into the lake barely in time as the glow went over the water briefly, then pulled back.

When she came back on shore, there was no sign of the Romans. She signaled for the others to follow, and they headed for their caves.

Kaia knew she could wait no longer. She could sense the power level increasing in the portal next to her. She wrapped her ancestor's skull in both hands and kicked with her feet toward the power portal.

"She's going in," Dane said, his hands steady on the controls.
"How close are we?"
"Not close enough," Dane said.

As she entered the power portal, the skin on Kaia's head began to glow dark blue. The skin peeled away, and bone appeared. Her eyes were two burning orbs of blue. Her mouth was twisted in an agonized smile.

A bolt of blue shot from her head into the crystal skull in her arms, which magnified it, and then in both directions through the cylinder of power. Up and down, the blue suffused into the black, fighting it. The air crackled thunderously, and lightning bolts streaked out of the power portal.

Kaia's head had completely transformed to crystal, power pulsing out of it into the skull held between rigid fingers and slashing into the darkness. With a final surge of power, the fingers went limp.

But the surge was enough as the cylinder of dark power shattered with a massive explosion and collapsed on itself. A tidal wave roared out from the site.

Go! Leave us. Dane urged Rachel. The dolphin got the message and sped past the craft into the portal.

"Grab something," Dane advised Ahana.

The tidal wave slammed into the Crab, and both were thrown about as it pitched forward, riding the wave. The nose hit the portal, and then all was still.

CHAPTER TWENTY-SEVEN

THE PAST AND THE PRESENT
3378 B.C.

Just in from the coast, in what would later be called France, there had been a strange fog upon part of the land for days. The local people avoided it, noting that even the wind could not stir it. The nearest village was called Carnac, and the word had passed down through the generations to avoid the fog when it came. Anyone foolhardy enough to enter it never returned.

After four days, the fog was suddenly gone one morning. As the people crawled out of their huts, they were amazed to see that the fields where the fog had been were now full of rows of thousands upon thousands of stones. Aligned as if for battle, there were over three thousand stones, stretching as far as the eye could see.

Where the stones had come from, who had arranged them, were both mysteries. But as the months and years passed, it was agreed among those who dwelled close by that on very still evenings, one could faintly hear the cries of men and the sound of metal clashing as if in combat.

79 A.D.

Two months had passed since Titus had dispatched General Cassius with the gladiator Falco and the strange priestess. A courier had arrived from the XXV Legion's headquarters reporting that the entire legion had disappeared. The courier also informed the emperor that the strange black Shadow was also gone.

Titus pondered this for several days, but since there was no more information forthcoming, he moved on to other things such as the rebuilding of Pompeii and the construction of the Coliseum. He did have General Cassius's name added to the roll of honor.

The gladiator Falco was soon nothing more than a tale a few experts on the games told among themselves and, after a generation, his name was spoken no more.

In Delphi, a new priestess took the place of the oracle. She was a niece of the slain oracle. Her first duty was to add the name Kaia to the roll of the true priestesses.

PRESENT

Dane threw open the hatch, and sunlight hit his skin, a most welcome feeling. He pulled himself up the ladder onto the top of the Crab and peered about. The gate was gone, open ocean all around except for the destroyer headed toward them, the *Salvor* right behind it, and the top of the FLIP bobbing on the surface. Ahana joined him, blinking in the bright light.

"We did it," she said.

"We only stopped the Shadow temporarily," Dane said.

"We stopped it this time in between our world and its," Ahana corrected. "That's an improvement."

"We still didn't get to the other side." Dane was weary.

"We will," Ahana said. "We'll take the war to their side next time."

THE END

Next book in the Atlantis Series
Atlantis Gate

ABOUT THE AUTHOR

NY Times bestselling author **Bob Mayer** has had over 50 books published. He has sold over four million books, and is in demand as a team-building, life-changing, and leadership speaker and consultant for his *Who Dares Wins: The Green Beret Way* concept, which he translated into Write It Forward: a holistic program teaching writers how to be authors. He is also the Co-Creator of Cool Gus Publishing, which does both eBooks and Print On Demand, so he has experience in both traditional and non-traditional publishing.

His books have hit the *NY Times, Publishers Weekly, Wall Street Journal* and numerous other bestseller lists. His book *The Jefferson Allegiance,* was released independently and reached #2 overall in sales on Nook.

Bob Mayer grew up in the Bronx. After high school, he entered West Point where he learned about the history of our military and our country. During his four years at the Academy and later in the Infantry, Mayer questioned the idea of "mission over men." When he volunteered and passed selection for the Special Forces as a Green Beret, he felt more at ease where the men were more important than the mission.

Mayer's obsession with mythology and his vast knowledge of the military and Special Forces, mixed with his strong desire to learn from history, is the foundation for his science fiction series *Atlantis, Area 51* and *Psychic Warrior.* Mayer is a master at blending elements of truth into all of his thrillers, leaving the reader questioning what is real and what isn't.

He took this same passion and created thrillers based in fact and riddled with possibilities. His unique background in the Special Forces gives the reader a sense of authenticity and creates a reality that makes the reader wonder where fact ends and fiction begins.

In his historical fiction novels, Mayer blends actual events with fictional characters. He doesn't change history, but instead changes how history came into being.

Mayer's military background, coupled with his deep desire to understand the past and how it affects our future, gives his writing a rich flavor not to be missed.

Bob has presented for over a thousand organizations both in the United States and internationally, including keynote presentations, all day workshops, and multi-day seminars. He has taught organizations ranging from Maui Writers, to Whidbey Island Writers, to San Diego State University, to the University of Georgia, to the Romance Writers of America National Convention, to Boston SWAT, the CIA, Fortune-500, the Royal Danish Navy Frogman Corps, Microsoft, Rotary, IT Teams in Silicon Valley and many others. He has also served as a Visiting Writer for NILA MFA program in Creative Writing. He has done interviews for the *Wall Street Journal*, *Forbes*, *SportsIllustrated*, PBS, NPR, the Discovery Channel, the SyFy channel and local cable shows. For more information see www.bobmayer.org.

Books by Bob Mayer

Duty, Honor, Country A Novel Of West Point To The Civil War
The Jefferson Allegiance

Black Ops Series
Black Ops: The Gate
Black Ops: The Line
Black Ops: The Omega Missile
Black Ops: The Omega Sanction
Chasing The Ghost
Section 8

Cellar Series
Bodyguard Of Lies
Lost Girls

Green Beret Series
Eyes Of The Hammer
Dragon Sim-13
Cut-Out
Synbat
Z
Eternity Base
Non-Fiction Books By Bob Mayer

Who Dares Wins: The Green Beret Way To Conquer Fear And Succeed

The Novel Writer's Toolkit
Write It Forward: From Writer To Published Author
The Shelfless Book: The Complete Digital Author
102 Solutions to Common Writing Mistakes
The Writer's Conference Guide

Science Fiction Series

I, Judas The 5th Gospel

Area 51 Series
Area 51
Area 51 The Reply
Area 51 The Mission
Area 51 Sphinx
Area 51 The Grail
Area 51 Excalibur
Area 51 The Truth
Area 51 Nosferatu
Area 51 The Legend

Atlantis Series
Atlantis
Atlantis Bermuda Triangle
Atlantis: Devil's Sea
Atlantis: Gate
Atlantis: Assault
Atlantis: Battle For Atlantis

The Rock
Psychic Warrior
Psychic Warrior: Project Aura

Made in the USA
San Bernardino, CA
14 October 2013